RHYME AND PREJUDICE

By

JANE AUSTEN

(well, more or less)

EBENEZER BEAN

Copyright © MMXIII Ebenezer Bean

All rights reserved.

mail@ebenezerbean.co.uk

With the exception of events referred to which are established matters of public record, all characters, events and other material are entirely fictitious and any similarity to actual events or people, living or dead, is entirely coincidental.

ISBN: 1492131741
ISBN-13: 978-1492131748

ACKNOWLEDGMENTS

I am grateful to Miss Jane Austen who wrote the original book. Much better than this one. Enough said.

EBENEZER BEAN

PROLOGUE

There isn't one.

But there is an epilogue at the end.

Chapter 1

Everyone knows, the writer said,
A man who sleeps in a single bed,
If he's got money in his life,
He must be desperate for a wife.

And if this man should go to dwell,
Someplace where he is not known well,
The local ladies will assume,
That in his house he has got room,
No matter down or up the stairs,
For one or other girl of theirs.

Now Mrs Bennet comes on scene,
This woman knows how to be mean,
"Now have you heard, good Husband Dear,
That house not very far from here -
You know the one, it's big and dark,
They call it Netherfield Park?
It has been let at last," she swooned,
"A man will move in very soon"

"I had not heard," her husband said,
Who did regard his wife with dread.

"Oh yes it has," his wife replied,
"For Mrs Long has been inside;
News of the man she did me bring,
She has just told me everything."

Her husband now failed to reply,
So Mrs Bennet with a sigh,
Cried, "Surely you do want to know,
Who might now want our girls in tow."

"If you'll tell me I will not mind."
Bennet knew how his wife to wind.

So Mrs Bennet now began,
To tell the news of this new man,
He was so young and wealthy too,
She really was in quite a stew.

"His name is Bingley and he's rich,
And he is single, needs to hitch,
And we have daughters, don't forget,
That none of them are married yet."

"I cannot see it matters much,
About this Mr Such and Such,
So how can it affect us pray,
That he'll be moving in one day?"

RHYME AND PREJUDICE

"Oh Husband Dear, you are so slow,
Round to his house you soon must go,
To introduce us to his self,
Lest our girls get left on the shelf."

"I do not see why I should go,
It's you that wants to meet him so,
But why not send them round alone,
To have a look at his new home?

'Tis better that you not go too,
Or he may take a shine to you;
Although you're old and have five girls,
I know you can still do the twirls,
And if there is a beauty race,
You haven't such an ugly face."

"But whether it is rain or sun,
For me to go just isn't done,
This you really must now handle,
So that we avoid a scandal."

"I will give you a letter thin,
To introduce ourselves to him,
And I may write a special word,
For Lizzy, one before the third."

"You must not do that, it's not fair,
Although she has got curly hair;
Our Jane is handsome, Lydia's fun,
But you still always think the sun,
Although this next line may seem crass,
Shines always out of Lizzy's ass."

"The truth," said Bennet, "please don't rant,
Is that our girls are ignorant,
But Lizzy, when she wears a garter,
Can sometimes be just that bit smarter."

"How can you speak of them like this,
I wish you would not take the piss;
Tonight you will not eat or sup,
If like this you just wind me up.
My nerves are bad, you know the score,
They have been since the days of yore."

"Do I not know? It's been that way,
At least back since our wedding day."

"Enough of this, I hope you live,
To see fine gentlemen, not spivs,
Come for to live here, perhaps then,
You might just go and visit them."

RHYME AND PREJUDICE

"That's not my job, I've said before,
But if of men there is a score,
I will perhaps upon them call,
So I may then solicit all."

Now Mrs B was none too bright,
And when upset she got uptight,
Her husband found it quite a bind,
Surviving with her nervous mind;
Her aim in life, please do not scoff,
To get her daughters married off.

Chapter 2

Now Bennet thought he'd play a joke,
And at his wife some fun would poke,
So round to Bingley he did go
Although his wife he had told 'No';
Then after he the visit made,
Fine plans to play the trick he made.

He went into the drawing room,
Where ladies sat all filled with gloom,
Lizzy was trimming her new hat,
Her father looked and said, "What's that?"

"It is the hat for my next ball,
It's in two weeks, it's in the hall."

"I hope then that old Bingley will,
Like it if you then have it still."

"How should we know?" cried out his wife,
You could the air cut with a knife,
"For we'll not visit, that is plain,
Though doubtless Long's been round again."

"But don't forget, my mother dear,
We'll meet him at assemblies here,
And Mrs Long, God bless her soul,
May do the introduction role."

"I'm sure she'll not," her mum replied,
"She has a lot of selfish pride;
And she has nieces, there are two,
She'll push them in front of the queue."

Bennet then said, "I am not fond,
Of your once good friend Mrs Long;
'Tis well to meet this wealthy sir,
You do not need depend on her."

But mother now was getting cross,
And looked for someone else to boss;
"Kitty, will you just stop that cough!
One day your head will come right off!"

Then in as well did Bennet chime,
"She coughs her head off all the time;
The timing of her coughs is ill,
I wish that she would take a pill."

Now Kitty, who was getting sad,
Said, "My cough is not all that bad;
And even when my nose doth run,
I don't do coughing just for fun."

Then Mrs Bennet spoke again,
For always on her mind were men,
"That Mrs Long, I do recall,
Will be away until the ball;
She won't have met him I dare say,
So she'll be no good anyway."

"Perhaps you could, if I'm not wrong,
Have him meet with your Mrs Long;
Her nieces will still get their chance,
At this or at some other dance,
And so that they will not think ill,
If you won't then perhaps I will."

The girls' spirits now soon should lift,
If they could get their father's drift,
But Bennet's wife had missed the point,
Her nose was still right out of joint.

Then Bennet said that Mary ought,
To tell him now just what she thought;
She wanted to say something now,
But wasn't really sure just how,
So Bennet said, "Let's give her time,
We'll ask again at half past nine."

But Mrs Bennet opened wide,
She could, no more, emotion hide,
"Of Mr Bingley I am sick,
I think that you just take the mick."

Bennet then feigned a big surprise,
He looked his wife right in the eyes,
"I wish you'd told me this before,
Ere I had knocked on Bingley's door;
But now, alas, the deed is done,
You'll have to meet him, everyone."

His daughters giggled with delight,
While Mrs Bennet in her plight,
Pretended that she'd known his trick,
And of this Bingley was not sick.

She thanked her husband 'cos he had,
Been such a good and helpful dad,
And all the fun that he did poke,
Was just a very clever joke.

Now Bennet, so pleased with his ruse,
Said, "Kitty, cough as you may chuse;
I will retire, though not too far,
And go and smoke one more cigar."

EBENEZER BEAN

The door swung shut, the mother said,
"Your father, who wins us our bread,
Is such a good and kindly man,
You must all thank him when you can.

And when the invites all come through,
Dear Lydia he should dance with you,
Though you're the youngest of us all,
You must go see him at the ball."

Lydia said, "I am not afraid,
Although I just drink lemonade,
I'll seek him out there at the ball,
Because, though young, I am quite tall."

That was the end of all the fuss,
So they all started to discuss,
When he might come round to dinner,
And which girl might be the winner,
And little else did any say
To end a very stressful day.

Chapter 3

Day after day six voices trilled,
As Mrs and her daughters grilled
Bennet about old Bingley's life,
Until he was sick of his wife.

Her husband had seen this before,
His best defence was to ignore,
So Mrs B then would resort,
To ask her friend for a report;
That Lady Lucas, 'cross the wall –
The one she couldn't stand at all.

But Lady Lucas was not mean,
To tell her all, she was quite keen,
"Bingley is truly young and smart,
And planning to play such a part,
At the next big dance in the town."
She hoped he might then settle down.

Mrs Bennet got excited,
That she might get one girl plighted;
She then proclaimed unto her man,
"I will be happy if I can,
Just get my daughters married all,
The first one after this next ball."

EBENEZER BEAN

A few days later Bingley came,
He saw just Bennet, what a shame,
He'd hoped to meet his girls that day
But Bennet kept them far away.

The girls, however, went to hide,
And Mr Bingley they all spied,
They saw, though they were hid from view,
His jet-black horse and coat of blue.

No sooner was he out of sight,
Than Bennet sent round an invite,
"To come and dine with them and me,
And please could Sir R.S.V.P."

So Mrs Bennet lost no time,
In planning all the food and wine,
But ere she ordered the best joint,
Bingley's reply would disappoint.

He sent a note round to explain,
He had to go to town by train,
And as it would be the next day,
This time he'd have to stay away.

No-one could now his wife console,
Her catering now had no role,
She was beside herself with fear,
That Bingley might not spend time here.

RHYME AND PREJUDICE

But Lady Lucas' next report,
Left Mrs B much less distraught;
She said Bingley had gone to bring,
A large group to this party thing,
Of ladies, there would be a dozen,
And one of them would be his cousin.

The girls began to panic then,
He'd not have time to dance with them;
The girls, though, did not need to fret,
For Bingley's guests had no plans set,
The ladies he brought were quite few
And one of them was married too.

The party day at last arrived,
And all the women had contrived,
To learn as fast as they could then,
About all the attending men.

Bingley, who was not known as Stan,
Was quite the perfect gentleman,
He was so pleasant at the ball
And very handsome overall.

His brother-in-law and sisters two,
Were gentleman and ladies too,
But 'twas Darcy, man of fashion,
Who aroused the ladies' passion.

EBENEZER BEAN

He was tall and fine clothes did wear,
And rumoured ten thousand a year,
Opinions, though, turned to disgust,
When he his views on others thrust.

It seems that Darcy was quite proud,
Expressed opinions out loud,
And although Bingley danced each dance,
Darcy just would not take the chance;
To flirt or dance he did seem loth,
Except with Bingley's sisters both.

The one who liked him not at all,
The more so right after the ball,
Was Mrs Bennet, Lizzy's mum,
Who had badmouthed him and then some.

This really wasn't out of spite,
On Lizzy he had cast a slight,
For why? her mum was at a loss,
But still it made her very cross.

The problem was, Liz overheard,
What Darcy said, most every word,
It went like this, we can relate,
When Bingley said, "Come, Darcy mate,
You should now dance, the girls aren't fat,
Don't stand around just like a pratt."

RHYME AND PREJUDICE

"You know I do not like to dance,
Around the floor with one to prance,
Unless my partner is to me,
Known quite as well as well can be.

And as I look around tonight,
Your sisters are engaged all right,
And though the dance floor is quite roomy
The other girls are rather gloomy."

His friend replied, "That's total crap!
One of these girls upon my lap,
I would like to have here tonight,
Although I might just have to fight;
For all are charming, maybe witty,
And some of them are really pretty."

"But you have got the best one, Sire,
And all the rest are pretty dire."
Darcy was still not that amused,
As his friend he now disabused.

"She is, no doubt, one of the best,
But that is not to say the rest,
Are not also quite lovely too,
And one is sitting next to you.
Perhaps I might," Bingley went on,
"Arrange for your introduction."

"Which do you mean?" said Darcy then,
He turned around and looked again,
And seeing Lizzy sitting there,
Trying hard not to look or stare,
He said, "Perhaps, but I can see,
She isn't good enough for me.
Now go and dance some more awhile,
At least your girl knows how to smile!"

Lizzy, by now, was slightly sad,
The words he said of her were bad,
But as she told her friends the tale,
She never once began to wail.

But overall, the evening went,
Much as Mrs Bennet had meant;
Bingley had danced two times with Jane,
He hadn't had to catch his train,
And someone said that Mary was,
The most accomplished there because,
Although she might not have the looks,
She had a great big pile of books.
And Cath and Lyd as was their plan,
Had never been without a man.

RHYME AND PREJUDICE

So when, at last, it got quite late,
They went back to their small estate,
Found Mr Bennet reading there,
Afraid his wife her views might air;
She'd hardly got in through the door,
Than she took centre of the floor.

"Oh Mr Bennet!," then she cried,
"I'm really bursting quite with pride;
Bingley thought Jane was really nice,
He asked her hand in dancing twice,
She really is now in her prime,
No others got a second time.

And as for that poor Lucas girl,
After she had had just one twirl
Around the dance floor, that was it,
Back then down she had had to sit.
This all so pleases me no end
I need not Bingley's ear now bend."

But Mrs Bennet then went mad,
Telling Bennet whom Bingley had
Been dancing with – 'twas quite a list –
So few of them could he resist.

"That is enough," said Bennet then,
"Of his good looks and partners ten;
My ears would not now have to smart,
If he'd been injured from the start."

But Mrs B was not put off,
She carried on about this toff,
"He was good looking in his face,
His sisters had fine gowns of lace."

But Bennet now had had enough,
He raised his hand and cut her off,
But scarcely had he turned his back,
Than his wife tried a different tack.

"And that man Darcy, what a dude!
He was tonight extremely rude.
He walked about, nose in the air,
Calling people without a care.

His features they are all for nought,
You should have gone to cut him short,
I'm sure that he will be a pest –,
A person I could quite detest."

Chapter 4

Jane and Eliza sat alone,
Neither girl given much to moan,
And Jane decided to announce,
On Bingley, she could now pronounce,
That she thought he was pretty brill,
And wished that she were with him still.

"He's very smart, and lively too,
Sensible – quite as much as you,
And he knows how to do things right,
For indeed he is so polite."

Lizzy said, "He's also dishy,
But, I fear, his friend is fishy."

"I did not expect," Jane said then,
"That he'd ask me to dance again."

"Why did you not?" said Lizzy wise,
"Compliments take you by surprise;
But never me, you were the best,
Far prettier than all the rest.

But he is fine, I think you should,
Like him quite as much as you could,
And perhaps, you should thank Cupid -
You have liked men far more stupid."

"Dear Lizzy! What a thing to say!
These compliments I like to pay,
But though it sometimes makes a stink,
I always say just what I think"

"It is, to me, a great surprise,
That, though you do have open eyes,
You never can see people's faults,
Whether they're rude or drinking malts,
And do you like his sisters quite?
They are not very much polite."

"Well, not at first, but then again,
They're all right when you talk with them;
The single one who must not shirk,
Will live in and do his housework,
And judging from my first brief sight,
I think we'll find she is all right."

Now Lizzy, who was more astute,
And thought her sister quite a fruit,
Did not agree with this at all,
The girls almost did her appall.

Extremely handsome and quite fine,
They were stuck up most all the time,
They'd been to schools that cost a lot,
And didn't talk to those who'd not.

RHYME AND PREJUDICE

From the north, they were quite wealthy,
Having each a fortune healthy,
They didn't mind it had been made
Not so politely, but by trade.

Bingley, they say, was rich and rash,
A hundred thousand there in cash,
His father had bought no estate,
And then had died during the wait.

This might be Bingley's new intent,
But now he'd just got one to rent,
And those who knew he was laid back,
Believed he might not now change tack.

His sisters wanted him to buy,
And surely you can all guess why,
But though they'd like it more that way,
They both seemed quite content to stay.

Bingley liked friend Darcy a lot,
Though much like him Bingley was not,
His temper was so strong, he found,
Yet in opinion he was sound;
He was haughty, he was clever,
But his manners – pleasant? Never!

And so it was, their thoughts were true,
About the ball they'd just been to,
Bingley had liked it, all were friends,
But Darcy saw no fashion trends.

Bingley had thought Miss Bennet nice,
But Darcy acted just like ice;
He agreed Jane was pretty while,
Thinking that she too much did smile.

Like Bingley, both his sisters thought,
That Jane was pleasant, not distraught,
And so they did approve, all three,
That Bingley more of her might see.

Chapter 5

Not far from Longbourn lived a friend,
The Lucases with cash to spend;
Sir William his fortune made,
Engaging in all sorts of trade.

But after he became a knight,
He thought that trade was p'rhaps not right,
And, more than that, the town was small -
He knew that would not do at all.

So then, one day, he upped and went,
And some of his new money spent,
Buying a house called Lucas Lodge,
Where in his wellies he could splodge.

For Willy had some airs and grace,
And liked to walk about the place,
Being so friendly when he can,
Indeed he was a gentleman.

The Lady Lucas was nice too,
All sorts of things she'd do for you;
Mrs Bennet liked her all right,
Because she wasn't all that bright.

And Mrs Bennet was no fool,
Her friends, she liked them as a rule,
With brains that were just partly full,
To her that way they were useful.

The Lucases had several child,
Not one of whom was really wild,
The eldest, who was wise, not silly,
Was best friend of Bennet's Lizzy.

And so, the morn after the ball,
The Lucases had come to call,
On Bennets' household, yes that's right,
To share discussion of last night.

Now Mrs Bennet, never shy,
Began first by remarking, "Why,
Charlotte, my girl, you started well,
And Bingley liked you, I can tell;
Without him quenching out his thirst,
He picked on you to dance with first."

Charlotte said, "Well, yes but I see,
He liked his second more than me."

"Indeed," said she, now feeling bright,
"You mean Jane? I suppose you're right;
He did dance twice and so I heard,
A compliment, though not the word."

So right on cue the girl, the dear,
Filled in what Bennet had to hear,
She said, "A man called Robinson,
Remarked Jane was the pretty one."

"Upon my word!" said Mrs B,
"This man is right as one can see.
But though her beauty she can show,
We must not count our chickens so."

Charlotte then thought it well to say,
What Lizzy heard just yesterday,
When Darcy said, "She's very plain,
I hope I don't see her again."

"Please do not talk about that sod,
He struts round thinking he is God;
To think one were liked by that cad,
Would only make one sad, not glad;
And Mrs Long told me he's rude,
Sat next to her in solitude."

Jane then spoke up after an age,
"I saw them talking at one stage."

"Ah, but a question she asked then,
But he liked not her mouth open."

EBENEZER BEAN

"Miss Bingley said," now Jane did tell,
"He's OK if you know him well."

"Don't you believe it," (Mrs B),
"He is too proud, we all can see;
No doubt he heard that Mrs Long,
Who wouldn't do folk any wrong,
Came by a taxi from afar,
Because she doesn't have a car."

Miss Lucas said, "I do not mind,
That he had found it such a bind,
To talk to Mrs Long at all,
While they were both there at the ball;
But he should, 'twixt drinking Tizer®,
Have danced with Lizzy, your Eliza."

Now Mrs Bennet spoke again,
"I'd not, were he the last of men,
Dance with that Mr Darcy tall,
At this or any other ball."

Lizzy said, "No, I never will,
He really did make me feel ill."

Miss Lucas said, "Forgive his pride,
For he's got money on his side,
And so long as he is not tight,
To have his pride he has a right."

RHYME AND PREJUDICE

"That's very nice," replied then Liz,
"His pride, I s'pose, is really his;
But I don't really like this toff,
Because he went and slagged me off."

Now up popped Mary from her book,
Which everywhere with her she took,
"Now pride in humans will remain,
But this man Darcy is just vain."

Now Master Lucas, he the brother,
Brought along by his own mother,
Said, "Were I rich and well could pay,
I'd drink a flask of wine each day."

Now Mrs B thought this not nice,
A chance to offer some advice,
"If you did that you would get drunk,
You silly little foolish punk."

Chapter 6

It was not long ere Bennets went,
To Netherfield with the intent,
At least of Mrs Bennet, note,
Her daughters' fortunes to promote.

Both Hurst and Bingley, Miss and Maam,
Decided it would do no harm,
To be acquainted now with Jane,
Also her sister, Liz by name.

As for the younger Bennets three,
They did not think that they could see,
That it was worth them talking to,
Because they hadn't got a clue.

They were too frivolous, they thought,
And would not waste time on their sort;
As for their mother, she did seem,
Intolerable in extreme.

Jane was so pleased they liked her well,
But Lizzy, as I can now tell,
Did not like them, they made a fuss,
Thought they were supercilious.

RHYME AND PREJUDICE

They liked her Jane, she surely knew,
Because she on their brother grew;
Whene'er they met it was quite plain,
    He wanted to see her again.

And though Jane also loved him so,
She would not let her feelings go,
So therefore Bingley might not be,
So sure that he was loved by she.

Liz spoke to Charlotte Lucas then,
    To seek her friend's opinion,
"It may be cool," Charlotte replied,
"One's true emotions for to hide,
From all the world and Bingley too,
    But it may then the love undo.

It wouldn't help much if it meant,
That one's true lover's good intent,
    Begun with Cupid's arrow sent,
Then went as cold as wet cement.

For, mostly, lovers need to know,
Their girlfriend really loves them so,
    Or true love will develop not,
And their friendship will go to pot.

So, sister Jane, I would advise,
Not to her feelings to disguise,
She must help him to love some more,
Or else she might be out the door."

"But I am sure," said thoughtful Liz,
"She helps him but the problem is,
Her nature just will not allow,
Her to do more than take a bow;
If I can see she likes him quick,
And he does not he must be thick.

"But you know Jane," Charlotte replied,
"And know well what's her head inside"

"That may be so," said Liz Bennet,
But it is Bingley's job to get,
Acquainted better without doubt,
And her true feelings winkle out."

"Perhaps he must," Charlotte again,
"He should do so, but then again,
Although they meet quite oftentime,
As I will tell you now in rhyme,
And doubtless sometimes in his home,
They are so often not alone.

RHYME AND PREJUDICE

But on occasions when they are,
Perhaps just sitting at the bar,
She should let him know what she feels,
And not just sit there eating meals.

It really is the only way,
She can be sure of him today,
Then when his mind is free of fog,
There will be lots of time to snog."

"Your plan is good," Eliza said,
"And if I had planned to get wed,
To someone rich or even poor,
I would adopt it I am sure.

But Jane feels different, that I know,
Although she has not told me so;
She has not worked out in her mind,
Whether this piece of humankind,
Is one that she might like to wed,
Or even sleep with him in bed.

For character is important,
So that they will not rave and rant,
And she has not enough time had,
To find out if it's good or bad.

EBENEZER BEAN

She's known him just about two week,
Has danced with him in shoes that creak,
Has called on him one morning bright,
And dined four times with him at night."

"You're sort of right, but you forget,
Dining would tell her what he ate;
But also they the evenings spent,
And we don't know their true intent."

"That may be so," said Lizzy then,
"We know they played at cards 'til ten,
So she knows he prefers pontoon,
But still the guy might be a goon."

"Well, anyway, I wish her well,"
Charlotte was fed up we can tell,
"I think that she should just get wed,
Or else we'll all get ache of head,
By studying her man for years,
And marriages all end in tears.

For even if folk are the same –
I mean the man and, too, the dame –
When both of them in marriage start,
They nevertheless grow apart,
So it is best that one does not,
Know much before one ties the knot."

RHYME AND PREJUDICE

"You know you're talking utter crap,
And would not this way pick your chap."

But while observing Bingley and,
How he might want her sister's hand,
Liz failed to see that Darcy cad,
Might start to think her not so bad.

To start with, as we all know well,
He'd thought that she was not so belle,
And when they met a second time,
As I have said before in rhyme,
About her he did simply scoff,
And, in the end, he slagged her off.

But though he'd said her face was plain,
And in so doing been a pain,
He was now drawn to her dark eyes,
Which were attractive, we surmise.

And though her form was not perfect,
And several flaws he could detect,
He had to admit as a lad,
Her body wasn't all that bad.

And though not quite as posh as him,
Her manners were quite far from grim.
(He said not posh, we all can bet,
The word was not invented yet.)

Of all this Liz was unaware,
For him she really did not care,
To her he was a frightful bore,
And might just slag her off some more.

So Darcy was now keen to know,
A bit more about Liz and so,
When he saw her conversing now,
Instead of thinking her a cow,
He went across and listened in,
Which did not make Eliza grin.

"What does he mean?" she asked Charlotte,
"He seems to listen quite a lot;
He puzzles me with his intent,
For I do not know what he meant.

He can be hurtful," Liz again,
"And so I think if I don't deign,
To ask why he behaves this way,
I'll be afraid of him today."

Darcy walked up and did not budge,
Charlotte gave Lizzy quite a nudge,
"Now is your chance, while he is there,
But now I bet you wouldn't dare."

"Don't be so sure, he might think ill,
But never mind – you bet I will."

RHYME AND PREJUDICE

And so, with just a bit of dread,
Eliza turned to him and said,
"Do you not think, old Darcy mate,
That when just now I did berate
The Colonel to arrange a ball,
I expressed myself well and all?"

"Indeed you did, but then again,
Most other girls would do the same."

"You are severe, you just find fault,
Your criticisms never halt."

"Enough of this," her friend then said,
"Why don't you play and sing instead?"

"Oh, if I must, but people here,
Will have such a critical ear;
Of them I am quite nervous lest,
They do compare me with the best."

So Lizzy played, she was OK,
She'd better played another day,
But very soon, her sister plain,
Who was named Mary, not called Jane,
Took her place and performed so well,
Though it was boring I can tell.

EBENEZER BEAN

She played again but she was dull,
Played a concerto, long, in full,
And as her audience grew bored,
She realised she could afford,
To answer her young sisters' prayers,
And play some Scotch and Irish airs.

Her sisters liked this change of style,
Went off to dance which made them smile,
For officers, dressed smart in red,
Whom they might like with them in bed,
Were at the party and were spare,
So free to dance a Scottish air.

As we know, Darcy was stuck up,
Evenings were there to talk and sup;
They were not meant to dance and giggle,
And bosoms at the soldiers wiggle.

Thus Darcy was lost in these thoughts,
When Lucas took a sip of port,
"How charming, Darcy, this must be,
For all these girls and soldiers three.

For dancing really is refined,
To twirl one's chest, also behind,
And very truly it's a mark,
Of fine societies, not dark."

RHYME AND PREJUDICE

"Of course," said Darcy, tongue in cheek,
"But one more comment I must speak,
A further benefit you know,
Is savages all like it so.

I've seen this in an old cartoon,
One night when there was a full moon,
I turned around, there was a plop,
The vicar in the cooking pot,
While savages danced round and round,
All making such a dreadful sound."

Sir William made no response,
A nervous smile upon his bonce,
"Your friend, that Bingley, has much grace,
He likes to dance around the place.

And I don't really have much doubt,
If on the dance floor you go out,
At dancing you would be adept –
See Bingley there, how high he leapt."

"I think you saw me once before,
At Meryton, I am quite sure."

"Indeed I did, enjoyed it well,
But please, kind Sir, perhaps you'd tell,
If at St James's you dance oft,
With all the London girls and toffs."

"Upon my soul, I never do,
The dances I have had are few."

"But surely," Will went on to say,
"It would a great compliment pay,
To that posh part of London where,
Rich folk do dwell without a care."

"A compliment like that I'll not,
Pay any place, wet, dry or hot."

"Nevertheless," Lucas went on,
"You have a house there in London?"

Darcy did not reply out loud,
Instead of this he simply bowed.

"I had once thought," said Lucas quick,
"In London I might my home stick,
For of superiors I'm fond,
And as for shops in that Street Bond,
My wife would like there to spend cash,
And would not think it at all rash,
But then the air might just her choke,
Because it's full of soot and smoke."

RHYME AND PREJUDICE

At this point Darcy did not speak,
As Lizzy Bennet, rather sleek,
Sidled across and stood close by,
So Mr Lucas asked her why
She was not dancing – was she shy?
And he told Darcy that he should,
Dance with this creature while he could.

"You can't refuse, she's in your sight,
And she is a bit of all right."

He took her hand, quite premature,
To give to Darcy for the floor,
But Darcy, who was quite surprised,
Nevertheless had now surmised,
That dancing with this girl might be,
Enjoyable and nice for he.

But Lizzy said, without a pause,
"I will not dance with him because,
I did not sidle o'er this way,
To seek a dancing partner – nay!"

But now, for sake of etiquette,
Darcy requested that she get,
Her dancing shoes on right away,
Then on the floor they could foray.

But Lizzy's mind was quite made up,
Her resistance she'd not give up,
And though she said he was polite,
She would not dance with him tonight.

She turned away, he lost in thought,
Perhaps now thinking that he ought,
Not to despise her quite so much,
When he could dance and maybe touch.

Miss Bingley now pokes in her nose,
"I know what your thoughts are," she goes.

"I'm sure you don't," said Darcy tall,
I bet you cannot guess at all."

Undaunted, she continued on,
"You're thinking it's dreadful for one,
To socialise with all these folk,
Who're not that wealthy – in fact broke –
For all they do is rave and rant,
They're dim and quite self important."

"You are quite wrong, I do declare,
I was just thinking that the stare,
Of a fine woman with nice eyes,
Can well cheer up a lot of guys."

RHYME AND PREJUDICE

Miss Bingley, now, was quite intrigued,
Which girl around was in this league?
"Do tell me now and do not snitch,
Who is this pretty handsome bitch?"

Darcy said quick, without a care,
"Miss Bennet, see – she's over there."

"Well goodness me, I am amazed,
I think that she must have you fazed;
So let me ask, it must be said,
When are you planning to get wed?"

"I knew as much, all girls assume,
That if you dance around the room,
With any girl, it will be said,
One day they're certain to be wed."

"I wish you well and good luck for,
You'll have a nice mother-in-law;
She's charming and does not drink gin,
And doubtless will want to live in."

But Darcy did not give a toss,
At tittle tattle she was boss,
He let her ramble on some more,
'Til he could escape out the door.

Chapter Seven

Now Bennet was not all that rich,
His father had once queered the pitch,
By specifying in his will,
That if his son had no sons still,
Then when he died, unfair or not,
A distant male would get the lot.

This totalled then two thousand pound,
Each year this cash would come around,
And Mrs Bennet's fortune small,
Was really not much help at all.

It was OK, about four grand,
But once her husband's cash was canned,
It would not make up for the loss,
A fact which made her rather cross.

She had a sister, this is true,
Married to Mr Philips who,
Had once been a good clerk and mate,
To her father, attorney, late,
And, too, a brother, not called Stan,
Who was a London trading man.

RHYME AND PREJUDICE

Now Longbourn lay one mile, no more,
From Meryton where daughters four,
And maybe, too, the fifth so sleek,
Would venture three times every week.

To see their aunt was their excuse,
But really, this was just a ruse,
To get the gossip of the day,
And find where officers might stay.

The youngest two, Lydia and Kate,
Whose minds were really not that great,
Were more keen that the other three,
To go and see what they could see.

This way they'd while away the hours,
Hoping for sun instead of showers,
And they would get ideas too,
For evening chit-chat after stew.

At present they were rather glad,
Because a regiment just had,
Arrived in town, would stay for weeks,
With officers all smart and sleek.

Their visits now were much improved,
They found to where the men had moved,
And pretty soon they found that they,
Had some more info every day.

It wasn't long, you may surmise,
Before the girls grew far more wise,
About the men and got to know,
Who they were for they were not slow,
In things pertaining to the heart -
In fact at this they were quite smart.

And notwithstanding mother's wish,
That Bingley with his piles of cash,
Should be the favourite suitor for,
One girl but not the other four,
The girls all thought a better plan,
Was try to get themselves a man,
With coat of red and ensign bright,
With whom they'd like to sleep at night.

'Twas thus one day at breakfast time,
That they were talking one more time,
About the officers in red,
When Mr Bennet coolly said,
"From all that I now see and hear,
To me it is extremely clear,
That you two, Lydia and Cate,
The pair of you must really rate,
As two of the most silly girls,
In this county if not the world.

RHYME AND PREJUDICE

I've thought this for some little time,
As I'm expressing now in rhyme;
It seems your brains have been removed,
For now my theory is proved."

At this Catherine got quite perturbed,
When she her father's words thus heard;
But Lydia could not care less,
Ignored her sister's slight distress,
And said, "That Captain Carter seems,
To be the man of all my dreams.
I hope to meet him on this day,
For after that he goes away."

Hit wife put down her china cup,
Said, "Really, I don't know what's up!
When father thinks his kids are daft,
It's not a matter to be laughed.

If I decided that I should,
Think that some kids were not so good,
I'd find some others, not too wise,
That I could scorn and criticise."

"But if my girls are none too wise,
This fact I ought to recognise."

"I really don't know what you mean,
All five are bright in the extreme!"

"My Darling Wife, most oftentimes,
When sober or if drunk on wines,
On most things we do both agree,
Except that all our girls save three,
Are foolish to a large degree,
On which you don't concur with me."

"My Dearest Husband, don't expect,
Girls to have the same intellect,
As you or I for we are old,
And as I might before have told,
When I was closer to their age,
And possibly a bit less sage,
I fancied just a brief romance,
With redcoats I met at a dance.

And if a smart colonel might chuse,
A girl of mine 'twould be good news,
As long as he just didn't smell,
And preferably had cash as well."

"Mama," cried Lydia, "I've been told,
That two officers, not so old,
Have been seen if I'm not mistook,
In Miss Clark's library with a book."

RHYME AND PREJUDICE

The footman, maybe Fred by name,
Came in, said, "I've a note for Jane.
So here it is, it's rather small,
In fact it weighs not much at all."

Jane took the note, began to read,
While Mrs Bennet, in great need
Of knowing what was this news new,
Was getting into quite a stew.

"Well, spit it out, Jane, what's it say?
And who has sent this note today?
Suspense is almost killing me,
So quickly read those words to me."

"It's from Miss Bingley," Jane said quick,
"I'll read it out in just a tick,
So you won't have a swift decease,
And all of us might get some peace."

So Jane read out the note that day,
And this is what it had to say.

"My Dearest Friend, please come to dine,
We will provide the food and wine,
If you'll provide good company,
For my sister Louise and me.

We're here all day just on our own,
And, as you know, sisters can moan,
So if you don't come here by eight,
   It's likely I'll her strangulate.

My brother and the other men,
Will all have left the house by then,
For dining elsewhere's their intent,
   With people from the regiment."

"With officers!? That is not fair!"
   Said Lydia, "I wonder where."
   While Mrs Bennet, in a stew,
   Said, "Dining out's unlucky too."

"I'd like the carriage," Jane said then,
"To get me there by who knows when."
   But mother, missing not a trick,
   Said, "Jane, you really are so thick!
Instead on horseback you must go,
   It looks like it will rain and so,
   When dinner's done and it is late,
You'll likely have to stay the night."

"That might just work," Eliza said,
"Then she could sleep in Bingley's bed*,
But they might still just send her home,
Inside a carriage that they own."
* presumably a bed owned, but not occupied, by
Bingley – this is the early nineteenth century after all

"I've thought of that," she gave a stare,
"But Bingley's one will be elsewhere,
And the Hursts' coach lacks things it needs,
Because it hasn't any steeds."

But Jane would not to mum defer,
"It is the coach I would prefer."

Now Mrs Bennet had plan B,
"Unfortunately, I can see,
Our steeds are likely needed though,
Upon the farm to plough and hoe."

She turned to Mr Bennet who,
Was waiting for the tea to brew,
"That is quite true but I should say,
Quite oftentimes before today,
When I've required them on the farm,
I've realized to my alarm,
That social pleasures seem to take,
Precedence over plough and rake."

So Jane set off later that day,
Her mother pleased with skies of grey,
And soon after she'd left the door,
She got what she'd been praying for,
For it went dark, began to pour,
And there were puddles on the floor.

He mother rubbed her hands with glee,
Her plan was working well, you see;
But after breakfast the next day,
Her plan seemed to have gone astray.

A note arrived for Liz from Jane,
Which said, "I got soaked in the rain.
So I'm in bed, the doc's been called –
His name is Jones and he is bald –
So I'm stuck here with poorly throat,
Which is why I've sent you this note."

"Well Dear," old Bennet said at last,
"If Jane's life should be in the past,
We will know it was all your fault –
Now be a dear and pass the salt."

"I'm not concerned that she might die,
Because the flu of things that fly,
Has not been seen just round here yet,
And really, she's just soaking wet.

RHYME AND PREJUDICE

They will look after her no doubt,
And if she does not venture out,
She'll be all right, will soon get well,
So we'll not need to toll the bell.

In fact, you know, my Husband Dear,
If we had got the carriage here,
I'd go and see her right away,
And maybe stay throughout the day."

Elizabeth now spoke up loud,
She said, "I really am avowed,
To go and see her, I'll walk tall,
'Cos I can't ride a horse at all."

"Don't be a fool!" her mum exclaimed,
"Remember that it's rained and rained;
When you arrive you'll not be clean,
And therefore not fit to be seen."

"It matters not," the girl replied,
"Because, for sure, when I'm inside,
I will be fit to see poor Jane,
In spite of all your mud and rain."

Then up spoke Bennet, "Dearest Liz,
I'm wondering if this discourse is,
A hint to me with all this grime,
To send for the transport equine."

"Why, thank you, but in fact, it's not,
It's three miles so I'll walk or trot,
And I'll be back by dinner time,
So please save me a gin and lime."

Now up spoke Mary, boring still,
Said, "I know that our Jane is ill,
But exertion should not exceed,
What one may reasonably need."

This thought, wise and also profound,
Was left around the room to bound,
Since it was by them all ignored,
Because, most likely, they were bored.

So Kate and Lydia volunteered,
To walk with her 'til Meryton neared,
"And if," said Lydia, "we make haste,
Our efforts might not go to waste,
Because Captain Carter we might,
Just see before he leaves tonight."

So presently, Lizzy arrived,
Not quite what mother had contrived,
She'd walked through fields, jumped over stiles,
Her face bright red with healthy smiles.

RHYME AND PREJUDICE

And though her shoes were caked in mud,
They showed her in just as they should,
Into the breakfast parlour where,
The Bingley women had to stare,
In disbelief at what she'd done,
Which they thought wasn't that much fun.

And Lizzy, who was rather wise,
Believed that in the women's eyes,
They held her in contempt that day,
And maybe liked her not to stay.

But nonetheless they were polite,
Although perhaps a bit uptight,
Whereas their brother was most kind,
And genuinely didn't mind,
That she was looking down at heel,
And, by the way, "How did she feel?"

Another there, Darcy not Hurst,
Thought that her cheeks looked fit to burst,
And put a sparkle in her eyes,
Though he, too, thought the walk not wise.

And Mr Hurst said nought at all,
As he spread butter on his roll,
His appetite was seldom small –
He didn't have a view at all.

EBENEZER BEAN

Elizabeth spoke up at last,
"So how was Jane, this night that's passed?
I hope she's better, no more ill,
So that she doesn't need a pill."

"Alas, she's not," came the reply,
"Although she's up she's not so spry.
She's got a fever, can't go out,
Not even with a stick that's stout."

So Lizzy went up to her room,
Anxious about impending gloom,
But Jane was pleased to see her though,
Her conversation was quite slow.

The breakfast done, the sisters came,
To see the patient once again,
And then the chemist said she had,
A dreadful cold which was too bad.

He said that she should stay inside,
Take potions that he had supplied,
And then for the rest of the day,
The best thing she could do was pray.

When he had left by means of door,
These ladies, now in total four,
Stayed with the victim of the flu,
For they had not much else to do.

RHYME AND PREJUDICE

The clock struck three, Liz said, "I'll go,
But I don't want to leave you though;
I will accept Miss Bingley's kind
Mode of transport for roads that wind,
That's a carriage with horses four*,
Which will convey me door to door."
* probably one or two actually. JA does not say.

"That is too bad, a dreadful blow,
I worry that you leave me so."
Again speaking was sister Jane –
The one who got soaked in the rain.

She might not have meant it all right,
Perhaps was being just polite,
But Miss Bingley then spoke again,
Said, "I've been thinking, it is plain
That maybe you should just stay here,
For Jane's still feeling rather queer."

We'll send a servant back instead,
To tell your mum you are not dead,
That you'll stay here because you care,
And bring back some clean underwear."

Chapter Eight

At half past six Liz heard a 'Bong',
Which meant dinner would not be long,
So down she went to join the Hursts,
Who'd dressed so they'd not look their worst.

She had to say to their enquires,
That Jane would likely still require,
Potions and rest, perhaps a spell,
To help to make her fully well.

The Hurst sisters expressed dismay,
And added in that both of they,
Detested colds and things like that,
Which could just lay the victim flat.

But Lizzy noticed after this,
They didn't talk about her sis,
And this seemed to confirm to her,
That really these two didn't care.

But Bingley, as Liz now observed,
From care and concern never swerved,
And made her now feel quite at home,
For he had not a heart of stone.

RHYME AND PREJUDICE

The Bingley sisters just had eyes,
For Darcy, handsome, also wise,
But as for Hurst whose aim in life,
Was eating, drinking, cards with wife,
When he found Liz preferred food plain,
He didn't speak to her again.

The meal all done, Liz went to Jane,
To check the status of her pain,
And after she had left the room,
The Bingley sisters very soon,
Began poor Liz to criticise,
Which did seem more foolish than wise.

"She has no manners and no style,
She's far too proud most all the while,
And doesn't converse well at all –
Her lack of beauty does appall."

"I quite agree," the other sis,
"In fact her only merit is,
That she can walk in rain and hail,
And comes here looking flushed, not pale."

"I really could not agree more,
For when she walked in through the door,
She was untidy, caked in mud,
Or even what had been the cud."

Then Bingley spoke, as well he might,
To try to end his sisters' spite,
"You are observant Lou," he said,
"But after I'd got out of bed,
And watched her enter as she should,
I didn't notice any mud."

So she tried Darcy with her view,
To see if he would concur too,
"I'm sure," she said, "you wouldn't like,
Your sister to go on a hike
Like that and then to embarrass
Herself which really is so crass."

"Indeed I'd not," he replied quick,
Which made the Bingley woman stick
To her tirade against this girl,
Who, once again, she called a fool.

Then Bingley spoke in her defence,
Said, "She has got a lot of sense,
And clear affection for her sis,
Which we should not too quick dismiss."

Miss Bingley then, in soft whisper,
Said, "Mr Darcy, I infer,
That now her eyes which you admired,
Must now be seeming rather tired?"

"Why, not at all, the exercise,
Had brightened them so please surmise,
I liked them maybe even more,
Once she had come in through the door."

But Bingley's sister gave not up,
Determined to her chances scup,
"I do regard Jane rather well,
Wish she could find a husband swell,
But with her dreadful parents though,
And connections which are so low,
Although she can sing well and dance,
Of marriage she has little chance."

"I think," said Darcy, "that you said,
Their uncle, who is not yet dead,
In Meryton a lawyer is,
And doubtless there conducts his biz."

"And there's another in Cheapside,
To live there he must have no pride,
For that place is so very low,
And somewhere I'd not dare to go."

"If they had uncles," Bingley cried,
"To fill up the whole of Cheapside,
It would not make them any worse,
As I'm now telling you in verse."

"But surely," Darcy went on then,
"Their finding eligible men,
Must be diminished by this fact,
For all odds are against them stacked."

Bingley, the nice one, replied not,
But both his sisters laughed a lot,
At the expense of Bennet's kin,
Whom they derided with a grin.

The laughing over, a disgrace,
The two put on their other face,
And went to sit with Jane some more,
Until the butler at the door,
Announced that coffee had been made,
For those who had to dinner stayed.

Jane was still ill I can relate,
So Lizzy stayed with her 'til late,
Until Jane fell asleep and then,
She ventured down to see the men,
And ladies seated downstairs who,
Were all engaged in playing loo.

RHYME AND PREJUDICE

"Do come and join us," they all cried,
But Lizzy looked and then espied,
That they were playing for high stakes,
And so she did an excuse make,
And saying that she'd read a book,
A volume from the shelf then took.

"Well, bless my soul! I do infer,
You must these books to cards prefer;
That is quite singular I'd say,
For most people prefer to play.

Oh Brother Dear, you ought to know,
That Lizzy, the one with the glow,
Despises cards but reads a lot,
And for pleasure it's all she's got."

Up Lizzy spoke on hearing this,
She said, "I have a life of bliss,
From many different things I do,
Including reading – not like you!"

"I'm sure," said Bingley, "you must get,
Much pleasure from your nursing yet;
And I hope you will get more still,
From seeing Jane no longer ill."

"Why thanks," said Liz, "you are so kind,
I'll read these books if you don't mind."

"Why, not at all, please help yourself,
There are a few more on the shelf;
I wish I had more, I can say,
So you could have more choice today,
But I am idle, just have few,
Though more than I do look into."

"No, these are fine, enough to read,
And they will suit me well indeed."

Miss Bingley, then, romance in mind,
Spoke up again, words less than kind,
"I am amazed that my papa,
Left no more books that here there are,
But Darcy, Sir, at Pemberley,
Your library's used so many trees!"

"It should be good," Darcy replied,
"My ancestors built it with pride,
And I think it's my duty to,
Add more books every week or two.

For to neglect a library fine,
Perhaps while gambling, drinking wine,
Would be a sin, there is no doubt,
And I would seem a dreadful lout."

Chapter Nine

Liz spent the night in Jane's bedroom,
Which was not quite so filled with gloom,
For sister Jane, Liz could reveal,
A modicum did better feel.

But, nonetheless, a note was sent,
To Longbourn for 'twas her intent,
To ask her mum's opinion for,
To see if she was at death's door.

This course of action was quite rash,
To ask her mum round quick to dash,
Because, as you know from before,
She has opinions by the score.

So Mrs Bennet with her plan,
To find for Jane a wealthy man,
Although Jane needed not a pill,
She said she was extremely ill.

"We cannot move her," she exclaimed,
As Lizzy shared expression pained,
"And the apothecary too,
Says she will have to stay with you."

EBENEZER BEAN

"Why, yes of course," Bingley replied,
"She must not venture yet outside;
She shall stay here quite calm and still,
Until she is no longer ill."

Now mother, having made a start,
Thought she could recommend her tart,
So she exclaimed in words profuse,
How Jane was better than the deuce
Of daughters she had brought with her -
That's Kitty and young Lydia.

"She is so sweet, and patient too,
And this house occupied by you,
Is very pleasing, isn't naff,
And has a charming gravel path.

I hope you do decide to stay,
And do not think to go away,
It is our pleasure that you're here,
Because we live so very near."

"I do not plan to leave this place,
Which I do think is really ace,
But if I do decide to go,
I'm sure you'll be the first to know."

Liz said, "That's what I would expect."
Bingley replied, "Do I detect,
That you can comprehend me now?
Come, spill the beans, you silly cow."

"I did see through you right away,
Politeness means I should not say,
But you are shallow, more than deep –
Quite different from that other creep."

"Just mind your tongue," her mother said,
"Don't act like you're back home instead."
But Bingley really was quite nice,
And so again he spoke up twice.

"To study character," said he,
"Must really quite amazing be."

"It is indeed," fair Liz replied,
"Especially folk deep inside."

"Then you've a problem," Darcy said,
"For in the country things are dead.
There isn't much of that in store,
For everybody's such a bore."

EBENEZER BEAN

Now this got Mrs Bennet's rag,
And she was dying for a fag,
So she told him where he could stick,
Opinions which just made her sick.

"I can assure," she told the brat,
"That wife-swapping and things like that,
Are just as common in the shires,
As in the town with smoke and fires.

In fact I think it's just the shops,
That sell all things from clothes to mops,
In cities large and towns quite small,
That anyone could like at all."

She prayed that Bingley would agree,
But wishy-washy then was he,
"I will opine now like I should,
But I think both are pretty good."

"Glad you agree," she said quite quick,
"But your friend Darcy makes me sick.
He's got me in a real flap,
By saying we're a load of crap.

RHYME AND PREJUDICE

We dine with people all the time,
On mutton, leek, New Zealand wine,
And when, in turn, we have them back,
Our cook gets a pat on the back,
'Cos all the food back at our place,
Is thought to be extremely ace."

Now Lizzy, seeing things were fraught,
Decided that perhaps she ought,
To get her mum to shut her gob,
Instead of all these insults lob.

So, changing subject, she enquired,
If Chalotte Lucas had aspired,
To come to Longbourn while she'd been,
Away and so by them unseen.

But mum could never take the hint,
And finish her insulting stint,
So as I'll now relate in verse.
It all continued to get worse.

"Why, yes she has," her mum went on,
"And with her father – he's the one
Who's always trendy, so refined,
And though rich really doesn't mind,
With whom it is that he might speak –
It was the parson just last week.

Contrast Sir Lucas, if you would,
With someone who thinks he's so good,
And though important he might be,
Will never deign to speak to thee."

As if that wasn't quite enough,
She carried on with all this guff,
And started now to criticise,
The poor old Lucases beside.

"Poor Charlotte couldn't stay to eat,
Which would have been a lovely treat,
Because she had to go and bake,
Her mother's tea – most likely cake.

My daughters do not have to cook,
And if you'd care to take a look,
You must agree the one called Jane,
Is really anything but plain.

She very near was wed before,
Of suitors there has been a score,
One in particular did write,
A sonnet one December night,
But that was it, they split apart,
'Cos he was just a stupid fart."

RHYME AND PREJUDICE

"I thought it likely could have been,
The poem which by her was seen,
Which put the kibosh on their plans,
And thus removed the need for banns."

Thus spake Elizabeth but then,
Young Darcy spoke up, said, "Ahem.
But poems of love are the food,
As long as they are not too rude."

"That may be so, but anyway,
What I just want to say today,
Is in this case with little doubt,
His sonnet likely snuffed it out."

The conversation at a pause,
Liz crossed her fingers now because,
She hoped that her old mum's intent,
Was silence, not embarrassment.

Her mother silent did remain,
But then her sister - what a pain -
Piped up and asked young Bingley to,
Arrange a ball or other do.

But Mr Bingley was polite,
Said he would hold one any night,
That she might chuse but they should wait,
'Til Jane was well to set the date.

The Bennet party left at last,
A really rather tragic cast,
And Lizzy went upstairs again,
To tend her poorly sister Jane.

Chapter Ten

Next day the whole group sat at ease,
Doing whatever they might please,
As Liz watched, Mr Darcy wrote,
While Bingley's sister, she did note,
Was such a pain, though rather bright,
Remarking on what he did write.

Liz thought she really took the piss,
The conversation went like this:

"By crikey! You write bloody quick.
You will be finished in a tick."

"You're wrong, I really write quite slow,
So I still have some way to go."

"I s'pose in business that you must,
To make sure that you don't go bust,
Be writing letters all the time –
I'm glad that's not a chore of mine."

"Then you are lucky, don't you think,
That they come from *my* pen and ink."

"Pray tell your sister if you would,
I'd long to see her if I could."

"Don't pester me, you silly pratt,
I have already told her that!
And don't forget, you little pest,
The comment was at your behest."

"Your pen looks like it might be broke,
Which could affect your flair and stroke,
So let me mend it if you will,
Then you'll write better with your quill."

At this point he made no reply,
And though she probably knew why,
She acted like he had not heard,
And carried on quite unperturbed.

"Pray tell her that I think she's ace,
There on the harp with endless grace,
And as for joinery she's great –
Her table would withstand a plate."

"I haven't room as you can see,
My letter's long as long can be,
So your words to this sis of mine,
Will have to wait another time."

RHYME AND PREJUDICE

"Oh never mind, I'll see her soon,
Then p'rhaps she will play me a tune,
But tell me, Mr Darcy please,
These letters that you write with ease,
Are they all long and charming too,
If so, that's really good of you."

"They're always long, but charming? Hey!
That is for someone else to say."

"One would find if one did a test,
Your letters are by far the best."

At this point Bingley deigned to speak,
"But Darcy's hand is not so sleek;
He ponders far too much each word,
So saying that is quite absurd."

"At least," said Darcy, "how I write,
Is different from the dreadful sh*te,
That you compose from time to time,
And seldom does it ever rhyme."

"Quite right," his sister said with glee,
"A careless writer sure is he;
He certainly would fail the test,
Leaves out some words and blots the rest."

EBENEZER BEAN

"I really couldn't give a toss,
My carelessness is not much loss;
I think much faster than I write,
And that's why it is mostly sh*te."

Elizabeth then intervened,
She'd been observing so it seemed,
"Your modesty is plain to see,
So nobody should censure thee."

"That is just crap," Darcy again,
"It is deceitful and a pain;
When folk act like Uriah Heap,
They're really boasting on the cheap."

"That's quire unfair," Bingley replied,
"For what I say is said with pride;
I always mean it as I say –
Or for the most part anyway."

"You're just a scatterbrain, I think,
And change your mind each time you blink;
That's not commendable or good,
To try improve yourself you should,
But now this bickering should stop,
Or our friendship will be a flop."

Elizabeth spoke then and bid
Him finish writing, so he did.

RHYME AND PREJUDICE

When pen and ink was put away,
The girls were entreated to play,
The pianoforte in the room,
In order to dispel the gloom.

It was now while the music flowed,
Including singing of an ode,
That Lizzy saw, for she was wise,
That Darcy could not keep his eyes
Off her and she just could not say,
Why he was acting in this way.

He liked her not, that was for sure,
But then he should give glances fewer,
So he must think, as told in verse,
Of those there she was quite the worst.
But, anyway, she liked him not,
And so just could not care a jot.

The music now moved on to Scotch,
And he who continued to watch,
Said, "How about a dance or two?
This Scottish reel might be a cue."

But Liz replied, "Get on your bike!
For your intentions I don't like;
I'm sure you will at me just scoff,
So you can go and bugger off!"

To her surprise, he was polite,
For now he fancied her all right,
And she whom we Miss Bingley call,
Did not like this affair at all.

So she sought to upset the plan,
Of Darcy whom she thought her man,
And the next day while walking out,
Quite subtlely with no need to shout,
She told him what would be in store,
With his imagined mother-in-law.

In midst of this, 'Lizbeth turned up,
Which put the bitch on the wrong foot;
She worried she'd been overheard,
And Liz might know her every word.

Soon Liz departed on her own,
She was relieved and did not moan,
But what was now clear as can be -
Darcy was now polite to she.

Chapter Eleven

When all had eaten then their fill,
The eldest, Jane, who was still ill,
Came down into the dining room,
Where there was not now any gloom.

The girls, not men, were only there,
So they could talk without a care,
And all four chatted and conversed,
A skill in which they were well versed.

An hour went by, and then returned,
The men who had tobacco burned,
And as Mr Darcy came in,
Miss Bingley's eyes were fixed on him,
For she was, if you didn't know,
The one with whom she'd like to go.

Darcy and Hurst both gave a bow,
To Jane, she feeling better now,
But Bingley, Mr, not the girl,
Whose heart was now in quite a whirl,
And who of Jane would often dream,
Was attentive in the extreme.

EBENEZER BEAN

He bid her sit close by the fire,
Jane, the object of his desire,
He almost on his knees did fall,
And spoke to no-one else at all.

Now Mr Hurst was keen to play,
At cards which he did every day,
But Bingley, Miss, who hatched a plot,
Knew very well Darcy was not.

She said, "Nobody wants to play,
A boring game upon this day;
I'm pretty certain that I'm right,
So why not go to sleep tonight."

"Perhaps I will," then Hurst replied,
To play with one's not good – I've tried;
One cannot play just on one's tod,
So I'm off to the land of nod."

By now Darcy'd picked up a book,
He opened it to have a look,
But as he read, Miss Bingley there,
Quite often at his page would stare.

She tried to engage him in speech,
Was sticking to him like a leech,
But Darcy, firm but still polite,
Would not engage with her that night.

RHYME AND PREJUDICE

Rebuffed, she gave a great big yawn,
Said, "Reading, now or at the dawn,
In fact, throughout the day and night,
For one is always good and right."

The others, though, ignored all this,
The thoughts of Carol Bingley, Miss,
So she turned to her brother tall,
Who planned soon to arrange a ball.

"I think," said she, "you ought to ask,
Us 'ere you carry out this task,
For some of us to dance detest,
And might like conversation best."

"If you mean Darcy," he replied,
"Who could dance if he really tried,
He needn't come, he can just sleep,
In bed or a disheveled heap.

The ball is settled, 'twill be here,
And as the day and date come near,
My cook will make white soup for all –
We don't want starving at the ball."

Rebuffed again, Miss Bingley stood,
She knew that standing she looked good,
She hoped Darcy would have a look,
And put away his sodding book.

At her request our Liz stood too,
They promenaded, just the two,
But Darcy still would not join in,
Though he was not the worse for gin.

"I think," he said, "that probably,
There are two reasons I can see,
Why you should chuse to walk about,
Within this room, that's not without.

The first, if I may be so bold,
Is that one has the other told,
Some secret I could never guess,
Am I not right – well, more or less?

Alternatively, it might be,
You realise that when I see,
You standing there in dress and gown,
Appealing more than when sat down.

So if the first, I would intrude,
And so to do would be quite rude,
The second, though, doth suit me best,
Because I can admire your chest."

"Oh, shocking! These words I have heard."
Miss Bingley thought she might have erred.
"How shall we punish him for this,
And teach him not to take the piss?"

"Just laugh at him," Eliz Proposed,
But Carol was not thus disposed,
"I like to laugh," Liz said again,
"But Darcy's not one of those men,
At whose actions one may fun poke,
And make him subject of a joke."

"I do have faults," Darcy said quick,
"You might spot some in just a tick,
But I'm superior to most,
So justifiably can boast."

"Enough of this!" Miss Bingley said,
Let's have some music before bed;
My playing is not quite the worst,
Though it might waken Mr Hurst."

Chapter Twelve

Elizabeth wrote home next day,
To tell her mother, by the way,
That to return was their intent,
And could she have the carriage sent?

Her mum replied, "No, not at all.
Jane's coming back will me appall;
You must stay and don't moan or bitch,
I want her there to get her hitched."

Their minds made up, the girls then asked,
To be allowed to leave at last,
But they were pressed, I have to say,
To stay on for just one more day.

Bingley was quite upset to know,
His girlfriend, Jane, was soon to go,
But Darcy really was relieved,
Because he truly now believed,
He liked Liz more than he had dared,
And didn't want to be ensnared.

The next day came, he barely spoke,
And she at him no fun did poke,
Although he did at her make eyes,
She really must not realise.

RHYME AND PREJUDICE

On Sunday, then, soon after church,
They went home in a cart of birch,
But Mrs B was none too pleased,
The visit had her mind not eased,
About whom her two girls might wed,
Prerequisite, back then, for bed.

But Mr B, laid back as he,
Was pretty much inclined to be,
Said, "I'm quite pleased that you're both back,
In evenings, conversation's slack,
For where you sit there is a gap,
And all the rest talk total crap."

Chapter Thirteen

"I hope," said Bennet to his wife,
"Today's meals will create no strife,
For we've a visitor tonight,
And he might really get uptight,
If we don't offer him some food,
And I don't want him in a mood."

"What do you mean?" his wife replied,
"Is one to come our house inside?
I really don't know who you mean,
Will want to dine in our canteen."

"A gentleman, he is polite,
And will arrive before tonight,
But ..." "Ah, I know who it must be –
That Mr Bingley, known to me.

Why, Jane, you really should have said,
Not up the garden path me led,
So I'd have more time to prepare,
To keep it quiet is not fair."

"It is not he," Bennet replied,
as wife and daughters all then tried,
To guess just who this man could be –
They hoped one they would like to see.

RHYME AND PREJUDICE

"A month ago, let me explain,
I read a letter with my brain,
From Mr Collins, cousin mine,
And replied at a later time.

This Mr C, you all will know,
Will get this house when I must go,
To meet my maker in the sky,
What I mean is when I shall die.

And since he might just turf you out,
Because he'll have a lot of clout,
We should hear what he has to say,
'Cos that is your best chance to stay.

He sent this letter, by the way,
Which I will read to you today;
The paper is quite good, not cheap,
But he writes like Uriah Heap."

"My Dearest Sir, you must recall,
My father liked you not at all,
But on this let no more be said,
Because the old git is now dead.

But now I'm a man of the cloth,
For Lady Catherine – she's a toff -,
Has made me now the parson where,
There was a parish going spare.

And since I'm now a holy man,
I bring good tidings when I can,
And hope that when I take your place,
I'll do it with the utmost grace,
So your girls will, long as they live,
For this just try to me forgive.

I do intend to make amends,
But as for what my mind intends,
You'll have to wait to hear my plan,
So please be patient there, my man.

But now I will come to the point,
I do not want to disappoint,
So though things may seem rather bleak,
I'd like to come and stay a week."

"So there we are," said Mr B,
"Today he's coming for his tea;
He says he wants to make amends,
So let him say what he intends,
And if I give him lots of gin,
It might just be our luck is in."

Then Jane spoke up, "I cannot see,
What he might plan to do for me,
But I suppose that his intent,
Does quite deserve a compliment."

Elizabeth thought he was odd,
Though seeming quite a kindly sod,
While Mary, often so depressed,
Said his letter was quite the best.

As for the youngest sisters there,
About him they just did not care,
For what they both preferred instead,
Were soldiers in their coats of red.

The clock ticked on, a knock was heard,
Collins it was upon my word;
He was quite tall, thickset as well,
Quite grave and stately I can tell.

He complimented Mrs B,
On her fine daughters, two plus three,
And said though he'd heard people tell,
The five were really far more swell.

"There is no doubt," he said quite quick,
"They'll all be married in a tick;
All five of them are really cute,
So they'll not end up destitute."

"It grieves me," this is Mrs B,
"That you, our guest, that's come for tea,
Who's so polite, if rather stout,
May one day have to kick them out."

"They're so delightful," Collins said,
"That though I have no coat of red,
I really do them want to please,
And so perhaps your anguish ease."

The dinner gong rang out at last,
They ate their food, though not too fast,
And then old Collins dropped a blob,
By pointing to the kitchen hob,
And asking which girl made the tea,
So he could congratulate she.

"I must point out," Collins, My Dear,
It wasn't any of us here,
For we can quite afford to pay,
A cook to work here every day!"

Chapter Fourteen

While dinner passed, old Bennet thought,
In their own interests that he ought,
To let young Collins have his say,
On any subject that he may.

To help achieve this happy state,
He did invite him to relate,
About his wealthy patroness,
One Catherine de Bourgh, no less.

Collins was pleased then to relate,
His tales of this lady's estate,
And how she'd always favoured him,
And he would satisfy her whim.

"Though she is really stinking rich,
She is polite and doesn't bitch;
She does approve my sermons when,
I take them round to her and then,
If she's short of folk for quadrille,
She'll let me play if I'm not ill.

She doesn't mind me going down,
The Dog and Duck with half a crown,
As long as I'm not drunk all day,
So that I can kneel down and pray."

EBENEZER BEAN

"That's very nice," Bennet replied,
"The lady should not be decried.
But tell me, has she children too,
And are they p'rhaps well-known to you?"

"She has a girl, she thinks she's swell,
But, sadly, she is non too well,
And though her mother thinks she's ace,
Just wait 'til you have seen her face!

It matters not, I know just how,
To keep her happy – and the cow -
I compliment them all the time,
So they'll keep me in ale and wine."

"It's pretty clear," Bennet again,
"That all your crawling's not in vain;
But tell me, these points that you air,
Do you in advance them prepare?"

"I do sometimes but I pretend,
That though the comments do not end,
I try to hide this small deceit –
You must admit it's rather neat."

Now of the six who listened there,
The youngest two just did not care,
While, of the others, Dad and Liz,
Both just thought how absurd he is.

RHYME AND PREJUDICE

The dinner done, Bennet now planned,
To chuse a book with his own hand,
And ask his guest if he would please,
Read and perhaps the boredom ease.

"Why, yes I will," Collins replied,
"But when I look this book inside,
I see it is a novel new,
And so not suitable for you.

They can be racy, that's the rub,
More suitable for down the pub,
To read from this just isn't done,
So have you got another one?

And what do I see over there?
Books from which we can chuse with care,
Fordyce's Sermons, that will do,
And I will read it now to you."

Well, as you can imagine well,
The youngest girls thought this was hell,
And Lydia interrupted so,
With words so trivial although,
The other girls made no protest,
At least it did shut up the pest.

Rebuffed like this, he took the hint,
Abandoned now his reading stint,
And said to Bennet, "Since I stay,
Perhaps we could backgammon play."

So that was it, the reading done,
It hadn't been all that much fun,
So now they could discuss once more,
Just fashion and the clothes they wore.

Chapter Fifteen

Now Collins not sensible was,
And this was probably because,
His father, whom we know was dead,
Would often beat him round the head.

This made him humble, we surmise,
But since then came a nice surprise,
When Lady Catherine, head of clan,
Appointed him a clergyman.

He was important now, you see,
Invited often round to tea,
And he would preach to folk his views,
While they, some snoring, sat in pews.

So now that he had house and cash,
Which was just adequate, not flash,
He'd come to Longbourn on this day,
To get a wife to take away.

With their good looks he was well-pleased,
They all were nice, his choice was eased,
And so he told the girls' old mum,
He wanted Jane, he liked her bum.

"How wonderful," Ms B replied,
"But she's a bit now on the side;
And, sad to say, for you at least,
We soon must plan her wedding feast.

But worry not, I have some more,
Just chuse one from the other four,
And when you've done, just let me know,
Which one you'd like us to let go;
They're all quite good, I think you'll find,
And Bennet really will not mind."

"Why, thanks so much, I will take Liz,
Because I'm certain that she is,
Quite beautiful with gorgeous legs,
And certainly is not the dregs."

This really suited Mrs B,
Who was beside herself with glee;
She'd hoped to get one daughter wed,
And now it might be two instead.

Now later on and just as planned,
Four girls plus Collins, hand in hand,
Set off to Meryton to walk,
And probably to also talk.

Bennet was pleased with what they did,
Of Collins he had now got rid,
And had his library back for now,
No hangers on to scrape and bow.

As they arrived the girls ignored,
The parson with whom they were bored,
And two at least were keen to see,
Some officers, just two or three.

Then all at once, across they saw,
More than they had been hoping for;
A young man there across the street,
And, goodness me, he was so neat.

They rushed across, he said, "Good day.
I'd like to you respects to pay.
My name is Wickham and I think,
I really could do with a drink;
But there is none so I should say,
I'll join the army here today."

Just then two more came on the scene,
Bingley and Darcy, they I mean;
And when old Darcy's eyes met his,
As witnessed there and then by Liz,
One man went red, the other pale,
Though neither had been drinking ale.

EBENEZER BEAN

What could it mean? She had no clue,
They couldn't like each other, true,
But it must be much more than that,
They really must have had a spat.

The two gents both departed then,
So leaving Liz to wonder when,
She might find out about these two,
Which she determined now to do.

They moved to the Phillips' abode,
As I will tell you in this ode,
And Reverend Collins did in fact,
Put on his best Uriah act.

It seemed to work, they asked him back,
Along with all the Bennet pack,
To play some games, perhaps to eat –
A social gathering compete.

And to improve this gathering,
Old Mr Phillips said he'd ring,
And ask Wickham to come as well,
Which Kate and Lydia thought was swell.

As they walked home, Liz said to Jane,
"Did you see Wickham's look of pain?
And not just him but Darcy too,
He looked like he could run him through."

"I did not see," then Jane replied,
"And can't imagine, though I've tried,
What it may be between them both,
For neither looks much like an oaf.

It was a shame, though, that today,
They didn't want some more to stay,
And though nobody had a cough,
They just got up and buggered off."

When they got back, nobody swacked,
The Rev did his Uriah act,
The second or third time that day,
That he had acted in this way.

He said how nice Ms Phillips was,
He knew she was like this because,
She'd asked him back another day,
And it was free, he need not pay.

This rather pleased old Mrs B,
Who had all day of him been free,
For, know one thing, if not the rest,
That she likes compliments the best.

Chapter Sixteen

Next day Collins and cousins five,
Set off as planned upon their drive,
To Meryton, Phillips' to see,
For card games and a bit of tea.

Upon arrival they were thrilled,
To find that Wickham whom they'd willed,
To be there also was indeed
There though he'd travelled not by steed.

You will not be surprised to find,
That Mr Collins turned his mind,
To commenting on what he saw,
Of which he mostly was in awe.

"I do declare," said he at last,
"That judging from experience past,
Your house is not too bad at all,
Just like one Rosings room that's small."

At first this went down non too well,
His hostess thought, "Why, what the hell,
Does he think that he's playing at,
Comparing with a room like that!"

RHYME AND PREJUDICE

But as her guest explained some more,
That Rosings' owner was not poor,
And was, in fact, owned by a bitch,
Who really was quite stinking rich,
She changed her mind, thought, "It's not bad,
Being compared to one who had,
A huge estate and loads of dosh,
And was, for sure, extremely posh."

So Mrs P was then content,
To take in all that Collins meant,
But all the girls, both dim and smart,
Thought he was just a boring fart.

Eventually, the men came in,
Old Phillips quite the worse for gin,
And when, again, Liz Wickham saw,
She really wanted to say "Cor!
Compared to others he is ace,
And I do not just mean his face."

Well, as you can imagine then,
Wickham was the one of the men,
That all the girls fussed round, that is,
Until he sat down next to Liz.

EBENEZER BEAN

So Collins was left on his own,
He was much too polite to moan,
So really disappointed, he
Had to make do with Mrs P.

The game that night was to be whist,
An early start so none was pissed,
And Collins, who was not much good,
Told Mrs P he really should,
Improve himself in this regard,
So, should he have to play at cards,
With Lady Cath, his patroness,
He could join in – well, more or less.

Now Wickham did not play much whist,
And so at cards he did desist,
And sat twixt Lydia and Liz,
Both desperate to learn his biz.

At first Lydia would not shut up,
Not even for her drink to sup,
But by and by she stilled her words,
And went to watch the game of cards.

So Liz could Wickham's ear now bend,
And really she did now intend,
To find out why Darcy did not,
Seem to like Wickham such a lot.

RHYME AND PREJUDICE

The problem was, she couldn't ask,
Was scared to undertake this task,
But luckily, Wickham spoke first,
About the man whom he had cursed.

He started with a simple Q,
"How long has he been close to you?"

"About a month," Eliz replied,
And he's got a big house beside;
It's up near Derby, I hear tell,
And people say it's awful swell."

"It is indeed," said Wickham then,
"Income's near one thousand times ten,
And I've known him since we were kids,
When we would get in scrapes and skids."

"Well bless my soul, I never guessed,
You had for so long known the pest;
I have just lived with him four days,
And can't abide his awful ways."

"I would advise you," Wickham said,
"Not to say that, for you're well-bred,
Where it might just be overheard,
And folk might retail every word."

EBENEZER BEAN

"I'll say it when and where I chuse,
There isn't all that much to lose,
For he is hated just round here,
Consequence of his pride, I fear."

"It serves him right, he's really bad,
And is a really dreadful cad;
The wealth he has makes people blind,
So they can't analyse his mind,
And so he gets away with it,
It is too bad, the little sh*t."

"I do agree, that's what he is,
Though Caroline's still in a tizz;
She clearly is his favourite fan,
And quite besotted with the man."

Wickham then whispered in her ear,
"How long d'you think he'll stay round here?"

"I do not know, he might be stuck,
I wish he'd go and sling his hook!
But will this stop you staying here?
You may not want him very near."

"Oh no! He will not drive me out,
Although he has a lot of clout;
If he wants not his cap to doff,
He can just go and bugger off!

His father, Lizzy, was quite nice,
You'd really want to meet him twice;
He was my godfather, you know,
And promised me he would bestow,
A cleric's living on my head,
Including after he was dead.

But after he had gone to hell –
Or maybe heaven – who can tell? –
Another got the vicar's job,
Who I think was an idle slob."

"That is too bad," 'Lizbeth again,
"That you were left out in the rain;
This really would stick in my craw,
Did you not think to go to law?"

"No chance of that, the will was vague,
So once he'd died, not from the plague,
One couldn't challenge what was done,
Specifically by his own son."

"That is quite shocking," Liz exclaimed,
"He really, truly should be brained;
But that's against the law, it's true,
So public exposé would do."

"It's bound to be eventually,
But it will not be done by me,
For I'm attached still to his dad,
And so will not do down the lad."

At this point Lizzy went quite woozy,
In terms of men she was quite chusy,
And this man Wickham was quite nice,
She might just like to kiss him twice.

"But why," she said, "was he so bad,
And acting so much like a cad?"

"I really, truly do not know,
Why he must really hate me so;
All I can think is that his dad,
Preferred me to his only lad,
And so, perhaps, the envy will,
Inside his head be raging still."

"Darcy is one I do not like,
Although he really did not strike
Me as malevolent like that,
Who would go round and kick the cat.

But wait, I do recall one day,
When he boasted about the way,
That he, so elegant and tall,
Would not forgive a man at all.

But still it makes me really cross,
Although I s'pose he was the boss,
That he would treat his dad's godson,
In this way, really, it's not done."

"Well, when I was a little child,
The time with him away I whiled,
While my dear dad, who is now late,
Ran all of Darcy's huge estate.

That's Darcy senior, also dead,
And who, when on his own death bed,
Had promised to provide for me,
In gratitude to him, you see."

"How strange," said Liz, "I would have thought,
That really, Darcy's great pride ought,
To have made him honest with you,
For that is what proud people do."

"I am afraid and sad to say,
He always acts in such a way,
For pride is really his best friend,
And from which he will seldom bend."

"But do you think – do eat your pud -
His pride has done him any good?"

"It often has, but he is rich,
And really doesn't have to snitch,
At giving cash for things quite good,
As wealthy people always should.

And he looks after very well,
His sister who, as I can tell,
Although quite proud and proud as he,
Accomplished pretty well is she."

Liz had been thinking all this time,
And could not make reason nor rhyme,
Why Bingley, who was awful nice,
Would speak to Darcy more than twice.

"I think that Bingley cannot know,
That Darcy is conceited so."

"Most likely not," Wickham replied,
"For Darcy shows his other side;
He is quite clever doing this,
So people his real self do miss."

By now the whist was almost o'er,
And Collins, every bit the bore,
Had lost all of his money but,
When Mrs Phillips said, "Tut-tut,
It is quite sad that you have lost,
It seems to be a tidy cost."

"I can assure you, though," said he,
"My patroness gives generously,
And so it is a matter small,
That I should lose a crown at all."

Now Wickham, in a voice quite low,
Asked Liz should she happen to know,
If Collins knew his patroness,
And if so, a long time or less.

"She has," said Liz, "some little while,
Kept him so he can live in style;
I don't quite know how they first met,
That story's not been told just yet."

"You know, of course, that she is aunt,
To Darcy who does not enchant,
And like as not her daughter will,
In time wed Darcy – what a thrill!

As you know, both are stinking rich,
So, though when wed, the two might bitch,
It will unite their two estates,
And make Darcy extremely great."

"Well, bless my soul!" Eliz replied,
"I knew not this and more beside;
Until just now I had not heard,
Of Lady de Bourgh, not a word.

And now it seems that Caroline,
Has really just been wasting time,
While all the time she's making eyes,
And hoping for her wedding ties.

But Mr Collins speaks so high,
I think he's confused as to why,
For he's misled by patronage,
That helps him keep stocked up his fridge;
She is, it's true, so very rich,
And just a fat conceited bitch."

"I'm sure you're right," Wickham said quick,
"I met her once, she made me sick;
For she is arrogant as well,
As anyone can surely tell,
If they had looked upon her face,
Or been round her enormous place.

She is supposed to be quite bright,
But I think that's not really right,
Her skills in life, I am afraid,
Come from the cash and golden braid,
That marks the wealth of this old crone,
As well as her enormous home."

The supper was served very soon,
The girls continued all to swoon
Over young Wickham, whom Liz thought,
Was nicer by far than she ought.

Then on the way home, no-one spoke,
'Xcept Lydia and that Collins bloke,
Who, though he wasn't much a slob,
Should really learn to shut his gob!

Chapter Seventeen

Next day Liz told the tale to Jane,
How Wickham had endured such pain;
She was glad to her mind relieve,
But this Jane just could not believe.

"I cannot think," she said at last,
"Ill of them both for actions past,
Perhaps bad folk of them hath lied,
Misrepresenting both beside."

"That may be so," now Liz again,
"But thinking ill doth give me pain,
So do not blame these random folk,
It was quite ill of them you spoke."

"But if we don't, Darcy is bad,
And I just can't believe he had,
Done dreadful things though he is proud,
He's not like that, I am avowed."

"I can more easily believe,
That Darcy might Bingley deceive,
Than Wickham lied and lied again,
About his childhood and his pain."

"One really knows not what to think,
For it, for sure, will make a stink,
If Bingley has been used this way,
Quite possibly with hell to pay."

Just then but who should amble past,
Bingley and sisters, both typecast,
Armed with the invites for the ball,
For Bennets and their daughters all.

But they spoke just to daughter Jane,
They found the others quite a pain,
And as for Mr Bennet's prose,
They tried to avoid it like those
Germs which back then were pretty vague,
And lumped together as the plague.

The girls and Mrs Bennet could
Not wait, for the ball would be good,
And Mrs B was really chuffed,
That Bingley had not simply stuffed,
His card into an envelope,
But had himself spruced up with soap,
And brought it round so personally,
For her and daughters two plus three.

The girls all now began to dream,
About how they might get the cream,
Of male companions who weren't pissed,
So, if you like, here is their list.

First, Jane was really pretty keen,
On Bingley – man not girl, I mean –
While Liz with Wickham longed to dance,
And hoped that then she would perchance,
See Darcy's scowling look of hate,
Confirm what Wickham did relate.

Now, Kate and Lydia were not fussed,
Whom they might dance with but he must,
Be from society's upper crust,
And thus prove worthy of their lust.

Mary, meanwhile, studious and dim,
Cared not whether the men were trim;
She would just come along she said,
Though she was not inclined to wed.

Elizabeth, though, was really thrilled,
And asked of Collins if he willed,
Himself to come attend the ball,
Or if he wouldn't go at all.

RHYME AND PREJUDICE

"I will be there," he said outright,
"Upon this coming Tuesday night,
For I believe that balls are good,
And so one well and truly should,
Attend and dance with girls galore,
And sweep their feet right off the floor.

And so upon this pleasant night,
To dance with all is surely right,
And to begin, if you are free,
Perhaps you would first dance with me."

"Oh, bloody hell!" thought Lizzy then,
"Of all the old and boring men,
Who could have danced and played the part,
It had to be this silly fart.

I should have kept my mouth quite shut,
And not asked him the question but,
I s'pose even if I had not,
He might still just have lost the plot.

How very kind," she said at last,
"To ask me to dance first, not last.
I will accept, 'twill be a treat,
But watch out where you put your feet."

At this point Lizzy had a thought,
That maybe Collins thought he'd caught,
A mistress for his parsonage,
Who could wash up and play at bridge.

Her mother, she sensed, was quite keen,
But really, Lizzy did not mean
To marry Collins, not at all,
Before or after Bingley's ball.

So she ignored the thought for now,
It might just go away somehow,
And 'til the question had been put,
It just remained a feeling, gut.

From then until the Tuesday night,
Torrential rain came down all right,
And if there hadn't been a ball,
They'd have had nought to do at all.

Chapter Eighteen

The ball came round, Liz said, "I fear,
I can't see Wickham now I'm here;
I've dressed and preened to look my best,
And all I see in here's the rest.

Oh, it's too bad, it is a shame,
I'd like to know who is to blame,
For I had planned to him seduce,
And now my efforts are no use.

I bet I know who is behind,
Thinking that I would never mind,
It's that man Darcy who has quite,
Told Bingley to send no invite.

I am so mad, I will not speak,
To Darcy for at least a week,
So my friend Charlotte Lucas must,
Hear what I must get off my bust.

But, Oh my God!, that's Collins there,
This instant rising from his chair,
To come and claim me twice, not once –
He really is a stupid ponce.

EBENEZER BEAN

I s'pose I'll have to dance with him,
   His footwork will be really grim,
   He shouldn't be here at the ball,
   Because he cannot dance at all."

Dance number three was better and,
   The officer who took her hand,
   Told her that Wickham really was,
   Well-liked by everyone because,
   He was so pleasant and refined,
And good with manners when he dined.

While Liz was talking to her friend,
   And trying to her ear bend,
   About her latest hat and frock,
   She got a really dreadful shock,
   For standing there, so very grand,
   Was Darcy, asking for her hand,
   In the next dance around the floor –
   At least he wasn't such a bore.

Before she knew, she'd muttered "Yes,
But keep your hands off my new dress."
   Then she to Charlotte did complain,
   "I really should have used my brain.
   I cannot stand him, he's so proud,
      To avoid him I am avowed,
   And now, to you, I must confess,
   I've got myself in quite a mess."

"Oh, don't you fret," Charlotte replied,
"You do not know until you've tried;
I've seen him dancing here tonight –
Much better that that Collins sh*te."

"You make it worse, him I can't stand,
He is the worst in all the land,
So if I find he's not too bad,
It would be the worst thing I've had."

The band struck up, her beau stepped out,
He really had a lot of clout,
And everyone was quite amazed,
As on the pair they fixed their gaze.

They danced in silence, not a word,
Passed once between them, quite absurd,
So Liz then made to break the ice,
They both spoke, little more than twice,
With words, it seems, intended to,
The other one perhaps outdo.

At length Liz mentioned Wickham then,
Darcy said, "He can make friends when
Ever he likes, he's rather cool,
But often, maybe as a rule,
The friends he makes might be quite fleet,
And seldom long term be complete."

"He's been unlucky," Liz replied,
"To lose your friendship, more beside;
You really have the man decried,
And this may, long as he reside,
Upon this earth be to his loss,
Because your wealth makes you the boss."

Her partner offered no reply,
And was about to say, "Oh why ...?"
When old Bill Lucas then appeared,
And as he Mr Darcy neared,
Gave such a bow, so very low,
And said that Darcy's dancing show,
Was really good, in fact first class,
And also was that of his lass.

He looked across at Bingley, said,
"I hope those two may soon be wed;
But let me not distract your eyes,
From Lizzy's which are large in size."

At this point it now seems to me,
That Darcy, absentmindedly,
Considered that the two might wed,
But then he turned to Liz and said,
"When Lucas interrupted so,
I forgot what I was 'bout to go
And say to you, what words were next,
It really does make me quite vexed."

RHYME AND PREJUDICE

"I do not think that at this ball,
We really said that much at all;
We've tried three times without success,
Our small-talk's really just a mess,
And what I should next say to you,
I really do not have a clue."

"What do you think," he gave a look,
"About that thing we call a book?"

"A book? Such things are rather flat,
What sort of conversation's that?
But anyway, you once did say,
If your respect was lost one day,
It never could be won back quite,
I'm pretty certain that is right.
And if that's so you should take care,
This situation is quite rare."

"Quite so," said Darcy, "tell me, though,
Where these questions are leading so."

"I am trying," 'Lizbeth then said,
"To see what goes on in your head;
Your character is there no doubt,
But I just cannot make it out."

EBENEZER BEAN

"What people say I can't control,
No matter English, French or Pole,
But if reports like that you trust,
Then you believe them if you must."

They parted then, not such good friends,
But Darcy soon would make amends,
He was, with die soon to be cast,
Besotted with this girl at last.

Miss Bingley now sticks in her oar,
Said, "That George Wickham who is poor,
Is good-for-nothing I would say,
And it has always been that way.

My brother on this point was glum,
But was relieved he couldn't come,
And you should know if you do not,
That Darcy likes him not one jot.

He can't abide to hear his name,
For folk think he should take the blame,
For what took place some years ago,
But really he is blameless so."

"Just mind your nose," Liz then replied,
"Perhaps you're taking the wrong side;
You're not accusing him of much,
And he has told me such and such."

RHYME AND PREJUDICE

"Well excuse me!" Carol said quick,
"I always thought that you were thick;
To inform you was my intent,
My interference was well-meant!"

"The cheeky sod," then whispered Liz,
Whose mind was getting in a tizz,
"You are so thick, that's you not me,
And not much different from Darcy."

Liz stormed off then to seek out Jane,
From whose expression it was plain,
That she'd been snogging with her beau,
But might still have some way to go.

"I did ask," Jane said to her sis,
"But Bingley does not know of this;
He says that Darcy's good and so,
Wickham's the one that has to go."

"Does he not know George Wickham then?"
"No, he does not, he does nae ken."

"Then he knows just what Darcy said,
About the lives these two have led."

"So I'm inclined to keep my view,
Based on what Bingley said to you,
So while old Bing's an honest soul,
Darcy is dreadful, on the whole."

These things now said, the talk moved on,
To Bingley whom you know's the one,
That Jane is keen on and might wed,
At least that's what the writer said.

While these two spoke, Bingley sat down,
So Lizzy left Jane on her own,
While she with Charlotte Lucas spoke,
And into conversation broke.

No sooner had the two sat down,
Than who should come in view – that clown,
Called Reverend Collins, whom you know,
Behaves like he is steeped in woe.

"I have found out just now," quoth he,
"Some news which could be good for me,
For someone here's related to,
Lady de Bourgh who, as you knew,
Provides for me with loads of dosh,
And you recall's extremely posh.

RHYME AND PREJUDICE

I must now go and introduce,
Myself to him and be obtuse;
How wonderful this happy chance,
D'you think I should ask him to dance?"

"Well, maybe not," the girls replied,
"Such is reserved for man and bride;
It isn't seemly men to dance,
And would not your image enhance.

For gayness is still years away,
One ought to keep it quiet today,
And if you plan to speak or shout,
For God's sake don't say 'Coming out!'"

"You need not fret," Collins again,
"Or worry that you might feel pain;
I'll simply go and say 'How do',
It is a pleasure meeting you."

So Liz began to panic now,
For first of all would come the bow,
And then the awful boring bits,
From Collins here who was the pits.

"I do think not," Liz tried to say,
"'Cos if you do so here today,
He will think you a total pratt,
And your entreaty will fall flat."

"I thank you for your wise advice,
I've weighed it up now once or twice,
But on this point I fear, old chap,
Your view is simply total crap.

For I'm a parson, good and true,
Church of England and not a Jew,
And status this bestows on me,
At least the equal then of he."

So saying, Collins, glass in hand,
Accosted Darcy as he'd planned,
And bowing like a restless ape,
He set about to bow and scrape.

Darcy, he seemed taken aback,
But no politeness did he lack,
So when it was his turn to speak,
He quickly turned the other cheek,
And with polite but distant words,
He told him he was not a turd."

Thus reassured, Collins returned,
He thought he'd not his bridges burned,
"I have to say, it went so well,
Darcy thought I was really swell,
And he was polite to a T,
So clearly impressed with me."

RHYME AND PREJUDICE

Liz looked at Jane and said, "He's mad,
To think Darcy could be so glad,
To be accosted by this twit,
Who's always talking downright sh*t."

With that disaster out the way,
The sisters settled down to say,
To each other how great it was,
That Jane might marry Bingley 'cos,
He was so nice, quite fine did dwell,
And had a lot of cash as well.

The only ointment round the fly,
Was Bingley's sisters whom she'd try,
To like p'rhaps just a little for,
Between them should be peace, not war.

Their mother had these same thoughts but,
Was not one to keep her mouth shut,
And so, throughout the evening meal,
She talked so loud it wasn't real,
To Lady Lucas about how,
Her Jane would soon be settled now.

"She'll soon be living here," she said,
"He's very rich so when he's dead,
And also in the years before,
My Jane will never want for more.

EBENEZER BEAN

Her status, too, will then ensure,
My other girls, so nice and pure,
Will have their husbands soon as well,
And will in great big houses dwell.

But I would like to say to you,
Your Charlotte surely will come through,
With equal fortune and be wed,
To someone who can earn his bread,"

Liz could not stand it any more,
Embarrassment, more than before,
And Darcy was, of course, close by,
No doubt just thinking 'My oh my!'

So Liz then tried to shut her up,
Hoped in her mouth some cake to stuff,
But then it all just got still worse -
She carried on but now in verse.

"I do not care," she said out loud,
"That Darcy's listening in the crowd;
If he likes not my verse and parse,
He can just stick it up his arse."

"For heaven's sake, do shut your gob!
'Cos this won't help you do your job,
Of marrying your daughter Jane,
If Bingley thinks you are a pain."

But no effect, she would not stop,
And now was also in a strop;
Liz knew it was not her to blame,
But still she nearly died of shame.

And Mr Darcy, she could tell,
Was listening to it all as well,
His countenance gave all away,
And surely there'd be hell to pay.

At length, however, she shut up,
Looked round for some more wine to sup,
But silence would not last too long,
'Cos someone said, "Let's have a song."

So here was more for Liz to dread,
He sister, Mary, slow in head,
Got up without a mo's delay,
And she began to sing and play.

Liz tried and tried and tried her best,
To tell her she should take a rest,
But all this was to no avail,
For Mary, with complexion pale,
And, really, who was none too bright,
Thought that her singing was all right.

So when she heard the people clap,
Although they all thought it was crap,
She sang again without delay,
As if 'twas a one girl relay.

Liz looked for someone to assist,
But short of breaking Mary's wrist,
There was no help, no help at all,
And Bingley's sisters, by the wall,
Derided with their looks so bad,
The middle daughter Bennet had.

It fell to Mr Bennet then,
He the most sensible of men,
To bring this singing to an end;
So he did Mary's ear bend,
By saying, "That's enough, my girl,
Now let the others have a whirl.

You have delighted long enough,
And now you must be out of puff,
So others now must take a turn,
But don't now get all taciturn."

But taciturn she did become,
Because her singing was now done,
And other folk were pressed to be,
The next great singer just like she.

Next, Collins steps up to the mark,
And in a loud voice like a bark,
"My efforts next to that would pall,
For I just cannot sing at all.

Although music is rather good,
So, too, for clergy as it should,
A vicar who is just like me,
Has other things that he must see
Are done and properly complete,
As he doth earn a crust to eat.

He has got sermons he must write,
By day and, too, some in the night,
And if this bores you all to hell,
It's time I shut my mouth as well."

Ms B piped up, "I will be bound,
The speech you gave does really sound,
Like common sense and more as well,
It's good of you such words to tell."

And then to Lady Lucas she,
Remarked that, "This man, Collins, he
Is so clever and so divine,
And might just wed a girl of mine"

But Liz detested all of those,
Ways her relations did expose,
Themselves and all their foolish ways –
She'd not get over it for days.

Bingley, she thought, had missed it all,
Through snogging Jane o'er by the wall,
But Darcy had seen it all through,
As well as Bingley's sisters, two;
And now all three, of upper class,
Thought that the Bennets were just crass.

Things then continued just as bad,
'Cos Collins designs on Liz had,
And though he no more tried to preach,
He did stick to her like a leech.

He asked to dance, she did refuse,
To try his plans to disabuse,
But she could not, it didn't work,
And she could not shake off the berk.

Now Darcy was engaged elsewhere,
And of this Lizzy did not care;
He did not speak, he was stuck up,
And she had really had enough.

Now Mrs Bennet, scheming cow,
Had planned a subterfuge for now;
She'd made sure that the carriage was,
Coming quite late for them because,
She wanted to see how they waved,
And how to the Bennets behaved,
As they took leave with everyone
Else at the hall already gone.

They were quite civil – no surprise –
With compliments all shapes and size,
And Mrs Bennet, not reserved,
Told Bingley, really, she preferred,
That he might come round for to eat,
For this would be a real treat.

"Why, yes indeed," he answered quick,
"We really must a date soon pick.
Then when I'm back from London soon,
I'll come round on one afternoon."

So Mrs Bennet was quite pleased,
Her wedding problems had been eased,
For Jane would very soon be wed,
And long before Bennet was dead.

And Lizzy, perhaps, she did hope,
Might get hitched to that stupid dope,
The parson who, perhaps with luck,
Might learn to keep his cakehole shut.

For Jane this was a perfect match,
With Bingley very rich with cash,
Whereas for Liz, girl number two,
A vicar would just have to do.

Chapter Nineteen

The next day Collins thought he should,
Propose to Lizzy if he could,
So after breakfast – tea and toast –
He addressed Mrs B, his host.

"I wonder, Madam, if I may,
Have private words with Liz today."

"Why, yes of course," she answered quick,
"Kit and I will go in a tick,
So then you can with Liz converse,
And don't you dare, Liz, be perverse."

Liz spoke up now in great alarm,
Expecting not to come to harm,
But, guessing what Collins might say,
She didn't want to go that way.

So she protested to her mum,
About this fate which would be glum,
But this was all to no avail –
Her mother had her up for sale.

The two now gone, Collins began,
He was, he said, of her a fan,
And her reluctance him to like,
Really, truly, him did strike,
As rather more attractive than,
If she'd already been his fan.

"You cannot doubt," he said, "My Dear,
For I have made it pretty clear,
By my attentions and kind words,
Which you have surely seen and heard,
That I would like you as my wife,
And that for the rest of my life.

I picked you out when I arrived,
Expecting pleasure to derive,
From marrying a girl like you,
For whom the converse must be true.

But more than this, the reason why,
I want to do so by and by,
Can easily be set out now,
In advance of our making vows.

RHYME AND PREJUDICE

The first is to example set,
For people who are single yet,
The second I disclosed above,
To be so happy with your love,
And for the third as I tell you,
My patroness has told me to.

She said, during a game of cards,
"Collins you must just shift your arse,
And get a wife who well can speak,
And live on just ten bob a week.

She must be useful, active too,
So that she can look after you,
She really has to play the part,
So don't just get an idle fart.

And when you've found one bring her round,
So I can see just what you've found,
And if I think she looks the part,
Then you can go and wed the tart."

EBENEZER BEAN

"There's one more reason I am drawn,
To one of the girls of Longbourn,
And that's so when your dad is dead,
If I have then his daughter wed,
The entail on this house so fine,
Which means it will by then be mine,
Will less affect you than it might,
And so you will all be all right.

I also know he's got no cash,
So some will think to wed is rash,
But I don't mind that you are poor,
To marry you I am still sure.

I'm told your mum has got some cash,
Not much, so we cannot be flash,
We'll get it when she pops her clogs,
And it might buy a few new togs.

But all throughout our married life,
I'll take care to create no strife,
And won't refer, even by stealth,
To your apparent lack of wealth."

Well, Collins was of himself full,
This was a red rag to a bull,
And now although it was abrupt,
Liz really had to interrupt.

She spoke up loud, "Just wait a mo,
I've not agreed so don't you go,
And get ideas that we may,
Walk up the aisle in church one day.

I'm deeply touched by your request,
To be your wife at your behest,
But I decline, I have to say,
It can't be any other way."

"I know," said Collins, "girls say no,
When really they intend to go,
And accept when they're asked again,
So your refusal does not pain."

"Upon my word," Liz said out loud,
"To answer no I am avowed.
You could not make me happy and,
I'm the last woman in this land,
No matter what I try to do,
Could ever make you happy too.

And I am sure that Lady Cate,
Will say you should not have a date,
With me whom she will think is crude,
And, on occasion, can be rude.

So you must really sling your hook,
Go elsewhere for a wife to look,
And now you have the offer made,
You'll not deserve a big tirade,
About our estate you shall own,
Though mother will still curse and moan."

But Collins would not take the hint,
Began another doubting stint,
And then he said if she said no,
There might not be another beau,
Would deign to ask her for her hand,
And so her marriage would be canned.

Now Lizzy at this point gave up,
It seemed to be a right cock-up,
And she decided to rely,
On her dad if Collins were sly,
And asked her dad to overrule,
That ought to work – he was no fool.

He'd surely take her side in this,
Both sober and when on the piss,
He would tell Mr Collins 'Nay',
And so would not give her away.

Chapter Twenty

Now Mrs B, you've heard before,
Was snooping there outside the door,
When Liz came out she was in thrall,
But, in fact, didn't hear it all.

Liz rushed on past like lightning greased,
The conversation having ceased,
And Mrs Bennet rushed inside,
Expecting Liz to be the bride,
Of Reverend Collins who was dull,
But, of himself, a shade too full.

She said, "Well done!" he answered, "Thanks,
I didn't fall for Lizzy's pranks.
When she refused my kind request,
I knew that she just spoke in jest,
And though she was inclined to tease,
It was just to her conscience ease."

But Mrs B was not so sure,
She wanted now one daughter fewer;
She knew her Liz was strong of head,
Direct and plain in what she said.

"Now Reverend, please depend on me,"
Again here speaking, Mrs B,
"The girl has really been too bold,
And will do just as she is told.

As well as headstrong she's a fool,
Though shows it little as a rule,
So I, or possibly her dad,
Will change her mind or I'll be mad."

"If she is foolish and strong-willed,
Maybe I should have better grilled
Her when I spoke to her just now –
I do not want an awkward cow.

So if she really does mean 'No',
Perhaps it's better you not go,
And try to force a change of mind,
I don't want a wife of that kind."

Now Mrs B was thinking quick,
He mustn't now another pick,
So she said, "No, perhaps My Dear,
I did not make myself quite clear.

She's daft in matters of the heart,
But otherwise a pleasant tart,
So if she was wedded to you,
She'd do the cooking, cleaning too."

So off she rushed, with Collins stirred,
Before he said another word,
And called out for her husband who,
Would surely know just what to do.

"Oh, Mr Bennet," she intoned,
"That Lizzy with the head that's boned,
Turned down the chance of wedded bliss,
And now the stupid little miss,
Who has got too much intellect,
Might find Collins will her reject."

"Now calm down and just wait your sweat,
I cannot understand you yet;
Now tell me clearly what it is,
That's got you in this bloody tizz."

"It's very clear, I am quite plain,
But still I'll say it all again;
To marry Collins she's refused,
And though he was at first bemused,
And used to think her pretty swell,
He might now tell her, 'Go to hell!'"

"I'm sure that he will not do that,
He is a parson, short and fat,
If he instructs his flock like this,
He will his monthly targets miss.

But, anyway, tell what I am,
Supposed to do in this log-jam;
'Tis womankind, so often fickle,
That's got us in this bloody pickle."

"Go after her and then insist,
That Collins she must not resist."

"Then bring her in and I will see,
What will be best for us and she."

Liz duly came, he sat her down,
His wife still wore her bloody frown,
"Come here," said Bennet, "tell me if,
Twixt you and he there is a rift."

"You bet there is, you might have heard,
He is a fat obnoxious turd!"

"Your mother, none the less, insists,
You marry Collins, he the pits."

He turned to his wife, "Is that so?
And if not, then what things might flow?"

"It surely is, she is a pain,
And I will not see her again!"

RHYME AND PREJUDICE

Bennet now played his master-stroke,
He knew his wife would nearly choke,
But he knew best how to resolve
This, round which their lives might revolve.

"Lizzy, you've an unhappy choice,
So listen clearly to my voice,
From this day forth you will not see,
One of your parents – her or me.

If you refuse you'll not see she,
Should you accept it will be me."

As Lizzy smiled, her mum went mad,
She laid straight into her old dad,
"You turncoat!" she accused him so,
"We really have to let her go."

"My Dear, at the end of the day,
You must just let me have my say;
And also to myself I'd like,
My library so on your bike!"

But Mrs B did not give up,
She saw this just as one hiccup,
And pestered Liz and all the rest,
To persuade her to do what's best.

Collins, meanwhile, did change his mind,
Looked round to seek another kind,
There were more girls and quite a few,
So maybe one of them would do.

So next time Collins came around,
His feet more firmly on the ground,
He told her mum, despite the ball,
He did not want her after all.

"I really very sorry am,
Especially to you, her mam;
I thought she liked me at the ball,
And now I don't want her at all.

I'm sure she'll find another bloke,
With luck one who declines to smoke,
She should now go and have a look,
And when she does I wish him luck!"

Chapter Twenty-one

This had now put the kibosh on,
Collins's offer which had gone,
And though he did not much complain,
He made it really very plain,
By being stiff and silent that,
He was annoyed and would not chat.

And luckily, for some at least,
Collins, the all-attentive priest,
Turned his attentions to their guest,
Miss Lucas, maybe his next best.

Next day things were still much the same,
And Collins would not change his aim,
Of leaving on the day he'd planned,
Despite his plans had just been canned.

With breakfast done, the girls went out,
To Meryton or thereabout,
To see if Wickham was around,
Or, if not, if he might be found.

They were in luck, he was in town,
And with a great regret and frown,
He told the party, one and all,
Why he had not been at the ball.

"I was concerned," he said to Liz,
"That getting Darcy in a tizz,
By being there on Tuesday night,
Might end in some sort of a fight."

Liz was, by these words, quite impressed,
She, too, thought it was for the best,
And Wickham then walked home with she,
To meet her parents and have tea.

Later that day a bombshell dropped,
Which sister Jane in her tracks stopped,
A letter had just been received,
Which little did to them relieve.

Jane read it to avoid suspense,
In present, past or future tense,
It was from Bingley's sister who,
Described what they had had to do.

Liz could tell something was not right,
For Jane was looking quite uptight,
So once they'd got rid of their guest,
The two went to this news digest.

"The Bingleys have all gone away,"
Said Jane upon this fateful day,
"They've gone to town, that's London, see,
And without telling poor old me.

She says they are not coming back,
Though happiness they did not lack,
   Especially – she says it here –
With you and me, so, too, the beer."

Liz thought this was a load of balls,
   From Caroline as she is called,
For she thought Bingley would retain,
   A place from which to visit Jane.

"No, no! You're wrong! It says it here,
   He'll stay in London, that is clear;
She says I'll not see him again,
   Oh, really, this will be a pain."

"Don't be too sure, she says it's true,
What she wants Bingley boy to do."

"There's more," said Jane, "I'll read it out,
   And this will banish any doubt,
That this is final, I'm afraid,
And scuppered all the plans I'd made.

She says Bingley will go to stay,
   With Darcy's sister far away;
He likes her too, I must take care –
She is another girl that's spare."

"That isn't quite what Carol means,
Not looking after you it seems,
When she says Bingley doesn't feel,
His love for you is really real,
She's telling lies, she has to be –
His love is there for all to see."

Jane thought a bit then shook her head,
"I think you're wrong, I'm right instead."

"You are mistaken, she's quite wise,
And devious behind those eyes,
She surely sees her brother's love,
For you and so she wants to shove,
You out the picture so she can,
Now execute her little plan.

I'll tell you what she wants to do,
She wants Charles, who is known to you,
To marry Darcy's sister so,
That she won't have so far to go,
To marry Darcy then herself,
Before she gets left on the shelf.

And it might work, the girl is spare,
But his love for you is still there,
And so you should still persevere,
Although he isn't living near."

RHYME AND PREJUDICE

"But I don't think I should, you know,
When all his family says no."

"You have to make up your own mind,
By judging whether being kind
To him and you is worth more points,
Than putting noses out of joint.

And if, when you add up the score,
The first is small, the second more,
Then do be done with this young toff,
And tell him just to bugger off."

"How can you say this," Jane again,
"To do so would cause me such pain;
If he should ask me in a dance,
I really would jump at the chance."

So after all this, Jane, it's plain,
Thought she might see her man again,
But when this wish might just come true,
They neither really had a clue.

They did not say much to their mum,
Who was at this news pretty glum,
But she as well thought he'd return,
And end her spell of taciturn.

And she recalled, she'd asked him round,
To dine on dishes quite renowned,
On that day she would take great care,
There was enough with some to spare.

Chapter Twenty-two

Collins was still the Bennets' guest,
And making himself quite a pest,
But Charlotte Lucas, Lizzy's friend,
Did now a friendly ear lend,
To absorb most of Collins' words,
A lot of which were quite absurd.

Liz was quite grateful for this fact,
For she was lacking still in tact,
But what she did not realize,
Was that the girl him up had sized,
And was determined him to wed,
To protect her and buy the bread.

So she encouraged him a lot,
So her plans would not go to pot,
And when, next morning, he did dodge
His cousins, en route Lucas Lodge,
Charlotte said, "Well, I do declare,
I think that's Collins over there.
I realize he is a pain,
But I will meet him in the lane,
And there perhaps he will me woo,
But only if he's wanting to."

EBENEZER BEAN

Well, well before he reached the door,
She got more than she bargained for,
For Collins with his speeches long,
Said that his feelings were so strong,
And down he went on bended knee,
To ask if she would marry he.

Within a mo it all was set,
But he must ask her parents yet,
So in they went at Lucas Lodge,
Where he hoped not his lines to bodge.

He asked her parents, they said, "Yes.
This happy union we will bless;
We think her happiness you'll give,
For just as long as you may live."

So Charlotte now her husband had,
Although a fool he wasn't bad;
He would provide for her at least,
From his good living as a priest.

And since she was, in fact, quite plain,
So no prize in the marriage game,
She really was quite much content,
Her satisfaction evident.

RHYME AND PREJUDICE

Charlotte began to worry though,
That Lizzy would soon have to know,
And she might really not approve,
If she and Collins did remove.

So he to secrecy was sworn,
'Til he departed in the morn;
To not tell all was such a strain,
And Collins found it quite a pain,
For he wanted of it to boast,
To the five daughters of his host.

That night Collins said his goodbyes,
And Mrs Bennet, not so wise,
Said she hoped he would come again,
Although he'd been a real pain.

To her surprise and others' too,
He said that's what he'd like to do,
The seven panicked, wondering what,
They must do to of him get shot.

So Mr Bennet spoke up quick –
Do not you think that he was thick –
"Perhaps," he said, "if you come here,
It might just cost you very dear.

For Mrs Bloggs, of whom you spake,
Might possibly exception take,
When she is sitting in the pews,
And you're not preaching sacred news."

"I thank you, Sire, for pointing out,
But I should not return without,
My patroness being on board,
Not to's more than I could afford."

"But one cannot too careful be,
About the likely wrath of she,
So you should really stay at home,
Where you can read the sacred tome.

And if you can't upon us call,
We will not be upset at all,
And if my words make little sense,
I mean we will not take offence."

"Thank you again, you are so kind,
And if you really wouldn't mind,
I'll write to you when I've returned,
With compliments you all have earned.

And I wish all my cousins fair,
Good health, perhaps with some to spare,
And I include in this good wish,
Lizzy, for I am not churlish."

RHYME AND PREJUDICE

Ms Bennet tried to make some sense,
In present, past or future tense,
And came to the conclusion he,
Might want one of the other three.

She thought, perhaps, she might persuade,
Mary, who might just make the grade,
For, though she was indeed well-read,
Was not quite all there in the head.

While Mrs Bennet thought on this,
The girls' friend, Charlotte Lucas, Miss,
Turned up and standing there quite sage,
Said she and Collins were engaged.

"You can't be, that's a stupid thing,
That you have done. And where's the ring?"
Then realizing what she'd said.
She said she hoped when they were wed,
That they'd be happy as can be,
And might invite her round to tea.

"I see your feelings," Charlotte said,
"But thinking of the life I've led,
I'm not romantic, you can see,
So Collins might just do for me.

I only ask for simple things,
I'm not expecting many flings,
And I expect, with little strife,
I'll have a happy married life."

Charlotte departed, Lizzy thought,
Collins had probably just bought,
A wife in exchange for some wealth,
And done it with a bit of stealth.

She could not see how Charlotte could,
Think that this matchmake would be good,
And she was certain as could be,
E'en she would get fed up with he.

Chapter Twenty-three

Sir William Lucas soon came round,
And announced that on the rebound,
That Collins from whom Liz had fled,
Would, in due course, his daughter wed.

He really was of himself full,
Had no concerns Collins was dull,
And though he said it as a plus,
The rest were quite incredulous.

You will not be surprised to learn,
That Lydia waited not her turn,
Not much inclined to wait her sweat,
She blurted out, "You're wrong, I bet,
For do you know that Collins plans,
With Liz to read the marriage banns?"

Sir Lucas was taken aback,
By this quite unprovoked attack,
But good breeding made him polite,
Taking with forbearance this sh*te.

And Mrs Bennet joined the fray,
Said he must be quite wrong today,
Then Lizzy thought that she should speak –
She'd known the best part of a week –
For she'd been told by friend Charlotte,
That they would surely tie the knot.

She complimented Mr L,
So pleased about the wedding bell,
And hoped that her kind words and frown,
Might get the others to pipe down.

'Til Lucas left, it worked all right,
He mother near speechless with fright,
But once Lucas was out the way,
She determined to have her say.

She wanted to make several points,
Would put folks' noses out of joint,
For first she just would not believe,
This event she could not conceive.

Then she said Collins was deceived,
He really must be quite naïve,
And then she said the two would fight,
By day if not also by night,
And, last, with this man of the cloth,
The whole thing might be broken off.

RHYME AND PREJUDICE

She then went on to blame poor Liz,
Who was still Miss, not yet Mrs,
And to her girl she would not speak,
For over three months and a week.

Now calm, collected Mr B,
Said he was very pleased to see,
That Charlotte was a foolish as,
His wife and more so that his lass.

"It makes," he said, "quite little sense,
In present, past or future tense."

As for the rest, the youngest two,
Quite pretty but with brain cells few,
Had low opinion of this match,
A parson being a poor catch.

So it was left to Jane to say,
What luck she wished them anyway;
She hoped they would so happy be,
And now it must be time for tea.

And, finally, I want to say,
That Lady Lucas day by day,
This news to Mrs B would point,
Which put her nose right out of joint;
But Mrs B just wished her ill,
And likely does to this day still.

EBENEZER BEAN

Now consequent upon this news,
Charlotte and Lizzy shared few views,
And Liz spent more time in converse,
With Jane as you'll learn here in verse.

Now Jane had, as you will recall,
Written to Carol post the ball,
But no reply had been seen yet,
Which left her in a state of fret.

A letter, though, from Collins came,
That dowdy parson, just the same,
And in it he, although inept,
Said Bennets' invite he'd accept.

He would so do without delay,
On the forthcoming fourteenth day,
For Lady Catherine had agreed,
For him to marry with all speed.

And with this he s'posed Charlotte would,
Agree the date on which they could,
Be united as man and wife,
For all of the rest of their life.

The Bennets did this visit dread,
Disturbance of the life they led,
For they the better could him dodge,
If he would stay at Lucas Lodge.

RHYME AND PREJUDICE

The wife complained most every day,
She didn't like guests, by the way,
She was convinced the visit would,
Do her nerves not a lot of good.

The other thing that stressed them up,
Was Bingley's not coming to sup
With them for he had not returned,
And likely he sweet Jane had spurned.

This was a touchy subject so,
Liz did then out of her way go,
To not discuss this awful mess,
So not to cause undue distress.

She didn't fear Bingley cared not,
And of Jane wanted to be shot,
Her worry was that awful sis,
Was masterminding all of this.

Her mum, though, was not so inclined,
And daily, hourly, she opined,
That Bingley who had lots of cash,
Was treating her now just like trash.

She constantly would Jane remind,
Which daughter one now found a bind,
But she was calm, all this she heard,
Without a sharp or nasty word.

The day came round, Collins arrived,
Again he greeted cousins five;
But his time, luckily, he spent,
At Lucases whose girl he meant,
In church up to the altar go,
But this you do already know.

We can now see one reason more,
Than, recall you, the other four,
For Mrs B had now worked out,
That Charlotte Lucas without doubt,
Would take her place, the dirty louse,
As mistress of the Longbourn house.

And when she did this dreadful deed,
She was unlikely then to heed,
The needs of her and daughters five,
Whom she would from the estate drive.

So she addressed her husband then,
"It's difficult to imagine,
That tart as mistress in my place,
It really is a big disgrace."

"Look on the bright side," Bennet said,
"It might be you that is first dead."

Ignoring this, she carried on,
"This entail should not have been done;
It is too bad what comes to pass,
The whole damned thing is really crass."

Chapter Twenty-four

The letter from Carol arrived,
With proof for Liz she had contrived,
To keep Bingley away from Jane,
Because she was a bloody pain.

The letter now dashed all Jane's hope,
That she might marry or elope,
With Bingley whom she liked a lot,
But now for her was not so hot.

The letter spoke at greatest length,
Of Darcy's sister whose great strengths,
Included piano, you recall,
And others, she might list them all.

She boasted that her brother might,
Marry her to her great delight,
And she proclaimed how nice it was,
That she with Darcy stayed because,
It would improve her chance you see,
To Darcy wed eventually.

Liz realized this mostly was,
A fabricated tale because,
She knew that Bingley's love for Jane,
Was genuine and caused her pain.

RHYME AND PREJUDICE

And she despaired that he was caught,
By others whom she really thought,
Could influence by what they said,
Because he was weak in the head.

Although he was a trifle weak,
Liz thought he really ought to seek,
To think about poor Jane's distress,
Instead of leaving such a mess.

Now Mrs B still spoke each day,
Of Bingley and about the way,
He'd treated Jane so very bad,
And quite behaving like a cad.

"I wish," said Jane, "my mother would,
Not speak of this, it does no good;
She always has her nose to stick,
And is now getting on my wick.

For Bingley now is in the past,
His memory will scarcely last,
Whatever might have been in store,
We'll soon be as we were before."

"Oh Sister Dear, you are naïve,
If such as that you do believe;
The world is full of dreadful sh*ts,
A lot of whom get on my t*ts."

EBENEZER BEAN

"But Lizzy dear, you must not think,
All people like to make a stink,
Example: Charlotte, your friend who,
Will marry Collins as you knew.

He is respectable, if glum,
And Charlotte who could be a mum,
Has done quite well, himself to chuse,
So we should give the girl her dues."

"I do not want to be obtuse,
But Collins there is not much use;
He's pompous, conceited and daft,
And I doubt that he's ever laughed.

So don't pretend he's such a catch,
For his new bride a perfect match,
'Cos doing so you redefine,
Words that have stood the test of time."

"Enough of this, let us change tack,
Not speak of folk behind their back,
I know that Carol you would blame,
But I just cannot do the same.

They surely do want Charles to chuse
Miss Darcy, which means I will lose,
But surely they do all this would,
For Bingley's happiness and good."

RHYME AND PREJUDICE

Liz now gave up, could say no more,
Jane was behaving as before,
While mum continued to complain,
Each time she heard Charles Bingley's name.

Now Mr B, old, sage and grey,
Addressed his daughter late one day,
"Your sister's crossed in love I find,
And really she should never mind,
It will give her a status which,
Will be a source of discourse rich.

And now, perhaps, it is your turn,
To get yourself a man to earn,
So off you go, try Wickham out,
He's nice but doesn't have much clout.
In spite of this, he dresses neat,
And I think it will work a treat."

Well, this endorsement paved the way,
For people generally to say,
What a fine fellow Wickham seemed,
And just the thing for girls who dreamed.

Chapter Twenty-five

A week went by, then Collins left,
Of his beloved now bereft,
But all was not despondent gloom,
His wedding day would be fixed soon.

As soon as he'd taken his leave,
The house was readied to receive,
Brother and wife of Mrs B,
Who came for Christmas annually.

Now Gardiner was this man's name,
As Mrs B was not the same,
For he was sensible, polite,
Not like his hostess, queen of spite.

He definitely made the grade,
His living mainly came from trade,
He was agreeable, well-bred,
And sensible within his head.

No sooner had their aunt arrived,
Than Mrs B and daughters five,
Were eager, while they all sat down,
To learn of fashions in the town.

This bit soon done, then Mrs B,
Related what had annoyed she,
Especially, no surprise here,
That Jane and Lizzy had been near,
To getting settled down and wed,
And might be if Liz had not said,
She'd not accept her suitor for,
He was indeed a dreadful bore.

"Her swift reply was quite perverse,
As I am telling now in verse,
And now that she's refused his bed,
He'll marry Lucas' girl instead.

And so embarrassing is it,
The Lucases are full of sh*t,
They came round here, they rub it in,
Their words are just a load of spin;
I can't now stand to see her face,
'Cos they've won in the wedding race."

But Mrs G, she knew all this,
From letters writ by Jane and Liz,
And when she got Liz on her own,
She tried excuses to intone,
Reminding Liz to this dismiss,
'Cos such things often go like this.

EBENEZER BEAN

"I thank you for your kindly words,
But in this case it's quite absurd;
The two were so much deep in love,
It only happened with a shove,
By Bingley's sister, she's a bitch,
Determined so to queer the pitch.

Their love was there for all to see,
He almost went on bended knee,
And at the dances he refused,
The other girls, leaving them bruised."

"Well, I can see," said Mrs G,
"Jane is deserving of pity,
For with her disappointment she,
Will take it more to heart than thee.

For you will always take the piss,
To put behind you things like this,
But, say, do you think that Jane would,
Come back with us, 'twould do her good?"

"I'm sure she will, she'll find relief,
Her mother here just gives her grief;
But while in London she won't see,
Darcy, Bingley or sis of he;
To visit you would give them fits,
They'll think your borough is the pits."

RHYME AND PREJUDICE

Despite these fine and feisty words,
Liz thought p'rhaps 'twas not too absurd,
That they might meet one day or night,
And their love thereby reignite.

When put to her Jane did agree,
She would go there quite happily,
But still she longed his sis to see,
Hoping that Charles elsewhere would be.

While visiting with Mrs B,
The Gardiners were bound to see,
That Mr Wickham from before,
With other folk – perhaps a score.

Her aunt watched how she did behave,
With Wickham who looked like a knave,
And she thought she should clear the air,
Advising Lizzy to take care;
She cared not 'bout a heart of flint –
He might be well and truly skint.

Chapter Twenty-six

"So do be careful when you woo,
He needs to have a fortune too,
And your dad will on you depend,
To make the right choice in the end."

"I know he does and I'm resolved,
That all your doubts should be dissolved,
And though young Wickham is quite hot,
Right now I'm in love with him not.

My dad, however, thinks he's good,
To marry him perhaps I should,
And while I'll try not to upset,
You or my dad who's still here yet,
I have observed when people flirt,
They really seldom are alert,
To whether their beloved man,
Has got his own insurance plan,
To pay out cash upon the day,
One's no longer described as née.

So how can I since not so old,
Do opposite of what I've told?
All I can promise you, our guest,
Is I will try to do my best,
And if I find I have a crush
On him, at least I will not rush."

RHYME AND PREJUDICE

"Perhaps," continued Mrs G,
"He shouldn't come here you to see,
Since often as I have observed,
You should be a touch more reserved."

"And so I was the other day,
I told him to be on his way,
But really you should not much fear,
'Cos when we have guests staying here,
My mum thinks there should be a queue,
Of other folk to talk to you."

"Well that's OK, I have to say,
You've eased my mind on this today;
It has been good to clear the air,
But please don't do it for a dare."

No sooner had the Gardiners gone,
Back came the one like Herbert Lom,
But as he did with Lucas stay,
It mattered not much anyway.

Now Mrs B, still full of spite,
Wised that the two would be all right,
But as she said it, most could tell,
She really wished they'd go to hell.

Then on the eve before they wed,
Charlotte went up to Liz and said,
"I will be wed tomorrow see,
Then you must come and visit me.
I will be in my house in Kent,
The staircase there is old and bent,
My dad and sister will come soon,
Come too and you'll have the spare room."

Liz didn't want to turn her down,
But wasn't keen to meet the clown,
To whom she would by then be wed,
And filled her with foreboding dread.

Once they were wed and had both gone,
They carried on to correspond,
But thoughts in letters were reserved,
As Lizzy thought they now deserved.

C wrote with optimistic hand,
So Liz would not misunderstand,
How very nice it all was now,
E'en when she had to scrape and bow,
To Lady Catherine 'cross the way
Who did, of course, her husband pay.

RHYME AND PREJUDICE

The tone was much like Collins, Sir,
And neither dared to make a stir,
For it would likely cost them dear,
As they'd be turfed out on their ear.

Miss Jane, meanwhile, arrived in town,
Hoping to track the Bingleys down,
But despite writing there before,
Miss Bingley'd not knocked on the door.

A week went by, Jane got annoyed,
That Carol tried to her avoid,
And so she went on her to call,
Because she'd not seen her at all.

The visit done, Jane wrote again,
Expressing thoughts by means of pen,
"Carol," she wrote, "was out of sorts,
She proclaimed that I really ought,
To have told her I was in town –
I did write before I came down;
My letter, then, had not arrived,
So of it she had been deprived.

Her brother seldom was at home,
Had now a tendency to roam,
With Mr Darcy whom you know,
Is always out there making dough.

EBENEZER BEAN

That evening, though, I was there told,
Miss Darcy who is not so old,
Would be expected there to dine,
Arriving about half past nine.

And then I had to quick depart,
For both the Bingley girls were smart,
And on the point of going out,
That she was truthful I've no doubt."

As she read Lizzy shook her head,
Jane's treatment just made her see red,
For this was all a pack of lies,
And Lizzy did Carol despise.

It proved to her carol would keep,
Jane out the way which was so cheap,
And with this underhand deceit,
It would be hard for them to meet.

A month went by, Jane changed her mind,
She now thought Carol quite unkind,
And this she wrote to sister Liz,
Who always saw it as it is.

"My Dear Liz I have been a fool,
The object of deceit most cruel,
But do not sit and crow all night,
Because, of course, you were quite right.

RHYME AND PREJUDICE

After a month she came to call,
Did not enjoy to come at all,
And she does not, it is quite plain,
Want ever to see me again.

When I look back I see that she,
Always made the approach to me,
And now after her dreadful trick,
She makes me well and truly sick.

But more than this Charles Bingley must,
Get just a bit of my disgust,
For he must know I am in town,
So why did he not call around?

These thoughts cause me a lot of pain,
I will not think of them again,
These thought I must now try to banish,
So that in time they will all vanish.

I don't expect that Charles will come,
To Netherfield with his posh chum,
But you must have as your intent,
To visit our friends down in Kent."

To some extent Liz was relieved,
To find her sister now believed,
The truth about the Bingley clan,
And he who'd seemed to be her man.

EBENEZER BEAN

She hoped he'd marry Darcy's sis,
So he'd find out what he had missed,
When he departed in a rush,
And gave Miss Bennet there the push.

But back to Lizzy's suitor who,
Was Wickham – you know, yes you do,
Liz could by now her aunt advise,
He'd found himself another prize.

A girl, Miss King, he'd come across,
And Lizzy couldn't give a toss;
In fact she could to aunt report,
He wasn't marrying for nought,
For this Miss King was pretty flash,
And had come into loads of cash.

"My Darling Aunt, I do recall,
I haven't been in love at all,
So if my chap's another found,
Result of looking all around,
It suits me fine, I have to say,
For he is now out of my way.

I am quite grateful to Miss King,
And wish her well in her new fling,
So when things are all done and said,
I hope they'll be OK in bed."

Chapter Twenty-seven

In Jan and Feb the days were cold,
And Charlotte, Lizzy's friend of old,
Had asked her as you may recall,
On her in her new house to call.

Although at first Liz was not keen,
She did not want to be too mean,
And since she'd not seen her for weeks,
The prospect did not look too bleak.

And also, though perhaps unjust,
Time had so weakened her disgust,
Of Mr Collins so it would,
Be tolerable if not good.

And anyway she would be free,
For one month, maybe two or three,
Of her mother and sister too,
Without whom she could nicely do.

The plan, so that you will it know,
Was that Elizabeth would go,
With Lucas and his daughter two,
Whose name is not yet known to you.

And on the way they would call in,
For tea, perhaps a glass of gin,
On Jane who, recall, had gone down,
To stay with friends in London town.

The only regret that she had,
Was leaving at home her old dad,
Who might fall ill or even worse,
With mum and sisters to converse.

To Wickham she now said goodbye,
He was a pleasant kind of guy,
And though she'd been his first new friend,
The fact that he soon did intend,
To wed another meant that she,
Could part now on good terms with he.

So next day her companions would,
Be Lucas and his brain of wood,
And Maria, his daughter who,
Was pretty empty-headed too.

The trip in miles was twenty-four,
By noon they'd reached her aunties door,
And dearest Jane, her sister fair,
Was in the window waiting there.

RHYME AND PREJUDICE

She seemed to be in quite good shape,
Before you knew it donned her cape,
And both set off to do the shops,
Which they would do until they dropped.

The day went by, the evening came,
They sought some shelter from the rain,
Then to the theatre they went,
Which always had been their intent.

Her aunt, at length, did then explain,
The mental state of sister Jane,
Which was not good, despite her smile,
Still suffering from Carol's guile.

But aunty wanted to learn more,
Of Wickham whom she'd known before,
And whether him she should distrust,
Because he'd his intentions thrust,
On Miss King who had not been flash,
But just acquired a pile of cash.

On this point they both disagreed,
Eliz'beth thinking that such greed,
As might now influence his view,
Was generally all right to do;
Whereas her aunt was keen to know,
About this girl he had in tow.

"Of Miss King I cannot speak ill,
There are no beans that I can spill."

"But he ignored her, wasn't brash,
Until he heard she'd got some cash."

"Why should he," Liz replied once more,
"Be interested if she were poor?
A man without wealth of his own,
Perhaps because he has it blown,
Has not the time to worry that,
He might get mixed up in a spat,
About his motives – good or bad –
Dependent on the cash she had.

And if the girl does not object,
Not chusing to her man reject,
She may be foolish – who would know -
It's she must make her mind up so."

"No, Lizzy, you have missed my point,
It's not my nose that's out of joint,
But Wickham's – listen if you would –
From Derbyshire so must be good."

RHYME AND PREJUDICE

"Well excuse me! I have to say,
I don't like men from up that way,
And intimates of theirs down here,
Are no improvement now I fear.
They really all do me appall,
And I am so sick of them all!

Thank goodness," - Liz now in full flow -
"That on the morrow I shall go,
To meet a man who has no sense,
And one might say is pretty dense.
It really, truly seems to me,
Such fools are all it's worth to see."

The play all done, her aunt enquired,
If she'd come with them to admire,
The countryside, perhaps the Lakes –
They planned to a vacation to take.

"My Darling Aunt, I do declare,
I cannot wait for such fresh air;
A trip like this will be so fine,
No doubt there will be food and wine?

And we will not be like dim folk,
Who don't know of what they have spoke,
Because their days get jumbled up -
Result of all the ale they sup.

No, we'll remember what we've seen,
No matter mountain, lake or dene,
So when we tell our folk back home,
They'll know just where we went to roam."

Chapter Twenty-eight

Next day the three set off for Kent,
To visit Charlotte their intent,
The parsonage the house they sought,
Because that's what they had been taught.

They drove around the Rosings' fence,
So long and really quite immense,
Until, at last, I can tell you,
The parsonage hove into view.

Charlotte and husband manned the door,
Four feet there standing on the floor,
And when they stopped there at the gate,
They really had no time to wait,
Ere Collins with formality,
Asked all about her family.

The questions done, they went inside,
Where Collins happily applied
Himself to describing the place,
Which all had quite a bit of space.

Liz thought that Collins made the point,
She wasn't mistress of the joint,
But that, in fact, she could have been,
If on his person she'd been keen.

EBENEZER BEAN

As Collins said, it was quite nice,
And after he'd described it twice,
He asked them all to take a stroll,
But Oh! his narrative was droll,
As he dissected every view,
And pointed out the Rosings too.

Liz could not see how Charlotte could,
Think living with him any good,
Because he was a dreadful bore –
Something you've heard me say before.

The men walked on, the girls turned back,
For walking shoes they all did lack,
And Liz was shown the whole affair,
Better when Collins wasn't there.

The house was small but quite OK,
Convenient for the modern day,
And later on at evening meal,
The husband said that a big deal,
Would be them meeting Lady Cath,
At church on Sunday on the path.

RHYME AND PREJUDICE

"It will an honour be," quoth he,
"You will, with her, delighted be,
For she will surely condescend,
Some moments of her time to spend,
Conversing with you at the door,
No matter she's rich and you're poor.

And I think it is likely too,
She'll include Maria and you,
Within our little dining clique,
Most likely once or twice a week.

And when the dining is complete,
We do not need to use our feet,
To walk back home or use the bus –
She sends a carriage just for us."

At this point Charlotte spoke up loud,
"Although Her Ladyship is proud,
She is quite wise and clever too,
Always with some advice for you."

"I do agree," Collins again,
"She is fantastic in the main,
And, really, it makes such good sense,
To regard her with deference.

This def'rence can't be overdone,
It's practiced here by everyone
Who knows, if their mind isn't gone,
Which side their bread is buttered on."

Not much more took place that first day,
They much discussed news and the way,
Charlotte put up with her new mate,
Or appeared to at any rate.

Next day, it must have been at noon,
A great commotion broke out soon,
With people calling her to look,
At this event the house had shook.

Liz ran outside but all she saw,
Was others standing round in awe,
For Lady de Bourgh's daughter was,
At the gate in her coach because,
Her duties and her tasks were few,
So this is what she used to do.

Maria then exclaimed, "How thin!"
"She is, but seldom comes she in.
For so to do would surely be,
An honour great bestowed by she."

RHYME AND PREJUDICE

At this point Lizzy gave a smile,
Wondering if she would beguile,
That Mr Darcy who, 'twas said,
This sickly heiress might just wed.

Collins, Liz easy could discern,
And mindful that he had to earn,
Was with the women in converse,
With some bits he'd had to rehearse.

At length the man ran out of words,
And some he spoke were quite absurd,
So then the carriage pulled away,
To come back on another day.

The priest came back, he couldn't speak,
For later on that very week,
They were invited, he advised,
To dine at Rosings – no Levis.

Chapter Twenty-nine

Now Collins, as you know by now,
Always the one to scrape and bow,
Was quite beside himself with joy,
That his guests could so soon enjoy,
The pleasure of an audience,
And Lady Catherine's radiance.

"I had expected now," quoth he,
"That Sunday next we would all be,
Invited round to Rosings see,
To meet Her Ladyship for tea,
And then, perhaps, an hour to spend,
Until the evening had its end.

But who could ever this have guessed,
That we'd be Lady Catherine's guests,
So soon post your arrival here,
To take tea but, alas, no beer.

Sir Lucas then spoke up quite clear,
"I'm less surprised for I did hear,
That well-bred folk can often be,
Extreme polite while taking tea."

RHYME AND PREJUDICE

Now as you can imagine well,
The waiting time was just like hell,
For Collins took time to explain,
Over, over, over again.
What they should expect there to see,
When they all went to tea with she.

He thought they might be terrified,
And one of them might just have died,
Because they might be overawed,
Or, worse, that they might yawn if bored.

And then to Lizzy he applied,
"Her Ladyship will not you chide,
If you just wear the best you've got,
Though it might not have cost a lot.
In fact it's not a big disgrace,
And shows her just where is your place."

The girl's response we do not know,
But she was pretty headstrong so,
Jane Austen doesn't even hint –
Most likely 'twasn't fit to print!

It's well established ladies take,
Eons of time themselves to make
Respectable for going out,
Even when only round about.

And Collins, quite aware of this,
Perhaps from his new wedded bliss,
Kept urging them all to be quick,
So not to get on Catherine's wick.

For should they be a trifle late,
For this quite unimportant date,
And Lady Cath became annoyed,
He could not her great wrath avoid.

The dressing done, the five set out,
With Lucas last – he had the gout,
And Collins gave a running talk,
On what they could see on the walk.

"The windows, if I may point out,
Are numerous without a doubt,
And their cost when de Bourgh did buy,
Was really quite extremely high.

They are the finest in the land,
Fit by the glassmaker's own hand,
So if you should pick up a stone,
Do please make sure it isn't thrown."

Inside, their apprehension rose,
As I could have writ here in prose,
But so you will get it first time,
Instead I'll write it down in rhyme.

RHYME AND PREJUDICE

The house with servants overflowed,
The china on display was Spode,
And when they came into the room,
As I record here with my plume*,
Her Ladyship rose up and stood,
Just like a caring hostess would.
* French pens were popular in the early nineteenth century

Now, luckily, I have to say,
Charlotte had told her man that day,
She'd introduce them in the hall,
So he would need not speak at all.

They all might then perhaps be spared,
The crap her husband always cared
To utter when at Rosings, lest
His present living might go west.

The Collins' had seen this before,
But Lucas bowed right to the floor,
And his girl who had lost her wits,
So very nearly had the sh*ts.

Our heroine, though, made of steel,
Did not emotions like this feel,
So there she sat and did observe –
No danger *she* would lose her nerve.

EBENEZER BEAN

As she surveyed the genteel scene,
She thought that Lady Cath was mean,
For though she was quite handsome still,
Her daughter looked like she was ill.

And her demeanour – mère not fille –
Calculated to make guests feel,
That they should always know their place –
If not, she'd tell them just in case.

They sat for five minutes at least,
And then they all, including priest,
Were sent to stand and then look through,
The windows to admire the view.

The gong rang out, they took a seat,
Because it was now time to eat,
And Collins, as you may have guessed,
Was seated farthest from the best.

He bowed and scraped throughout the meal,
With compliments his only spiel,
And Lucas echoing his thoughts,
From soup right through until the port.

Liz thought her hostess would despise,
These compliments, none in disguise,
But as she did there eat and sup,
The compliments – she lapped them up.

RHYME AND PREJUDICE

The dinner passed in silence 'til,
The eating rate had dropped to nil,
And then the ladies all retired,
To listen to advice inspired,
From Lady Cath who always would,
Tell everybody what they should
Do as they went about their lives,
And woe betide them if they skived.

She quizzed Liz 'bout her family,
How many sisters – one plus three;
What sort of car her father had,
And was it very good or bad?

Liz answered well and bit her tongue,
The inquisition wasn't long,
And then – Oh! quite a nice surprise,
As Lady Catherine did advise,
That to a girl's estate entail,
Was really quite beyond the pale.

She then went on to this observe,
Which really was a bloody nerve,
That Liz and, too, her sisters four,
Should all have learnt to read a score,
To draw and paint and also sing –
She thought they'd not learnt anything.

But then a really dreadful shock,
When Lizzy said she and her stock,
Had not a governess then had,
Which Catherine though extremely bad.

"I wish," said she, "I had but known
Your mother, she who ran your home,
For I would then have her advised,
That it is really most unwise,
To bring you up nevertheless,
With no help of a governess.

For many people round here know,
That out of my way will I go,
To match up mothers with young girls,
Who, as respectable females,
May as young governesses work,
As long as they don't swear or shirk.

And did I not say, Mrs C,
How grateful these folk are to me,
For helping them in this regard,
And making their lives far less hard?

But tell me, Liz, your sisters four,
Are any out though they are poor?"

"Why yes, Maam, they are all at large,
Acquaintances to thus enlarge."

"Well bless my soul, this will not do,
Some shouldn't be at large 'til you,
Are married or betrothed at least,
Or else, I s'pose, perhaps deceased."

"But surely," Lizzy then replied,
"To keep them all, or some, inside,
Might lead them to the elders hate,
Or p'rhaps be unaffectionate."

"Upon my word, you are quite rude,
With such opinion of your brood;
So tell me, I entreat you pray,
How old are you upon this day?"

What Liz replied, politely said,
Still made Her Ladyship see red,
For she afforded her short shrift –
I'm pretty sure you get my drift.

The men returned stinking of smoke,
One carried still his can of Coke,
And so the card tables were set,
Liz hadn't played at cards here yet.

EBENEZER BEAN

The games they played, long since forgot,
Were played back then an awful lot,
And while they played the talk was bad,
Because quite stupid folk they had,
Within the playing groups that night,
And most of it was pretty trite.

Collins, I can tell 'cos it's true,
Although at risk of boring you,
Kept paying compliments, none slight,
And carried on like that all night.

At length his patroness got bored,
And consequently she implored,
By infecting a polite cough,
Her guests at last to bugger off.

They drove home, Lizzy's praise was slight,
About their hostess on that night,
So Reverend C said, "This won't do,"
And chipped in with his comments too.

His words, of course, were quite absurd,
As anyone would think who heard;
This was what he was expert at,
But really he was just a twat.

Chapter Thirty

A week after they had arrived,
Sir Lucas by himself contrived,
To go back home to Lucas Lodge,
Wherein his wellies he could splodge.

He was, I'd say, quite satisfied,
To learn his daughter, Collins' bride,
Was well set up in comfort so,
It was OK for him to go.

While he was there his host would drive,
Him every day and would then strive,
To show him all there was to see,
Especially that house of she.

Now he had gone, routine returned,
To things so that folk money earned,
And Collins, parson as you knew,
Engaged himself in things quite few.

He sometimes wrote and sometimes read,
Attended to his flower bed,
And when he tired then of his book,
He would out of the window look.

EBENEZER BEAN

His bookroom was one of the best,
Surveyed the road, the view was west,
While Charlotte's parlour round the back,
Commanding, pleasant views did lack.

Liz wondered why she chose this room,
Which often had a touch of gloom,
But then she realized one day,
'Twas 'cos her husband stayed away.

As I've just said, they could not see,
Much further than the closest tree,
But Mr Collins - God knows why –
Would tell them when Miss Bourgh drove by.

It's not as if it was so rare,
Or even that his wife should care,
For she passed by most every day,
But very seldom did she stay.

Most every day Rev Collins went,
To Rosings where he some time spent;
His wife, Charlotte, most days went too,
And just occasionally in lieu.

On rare occasions Lady Cath,
Departed Rosings' splendid garth,
And condescended then to call,
Upon the parson, wife and all.

RHYME AND PREJUDICE

When once inside she looked at all,
The things in progress, big and small,
And in each case she found some fault,
Then followed with verbal assault.

"You shouldn't do the stitch that way,
And why's that mirror on there, pray?
And why've you such a joint of meat,
With only two or three to eat?"

Liz found she was a magistrate,
So did some good at any rate,
For if the residents rebelled,
Were quarrelsome or short of geld*,
She gave them a piece of advice,
And woe betide they got it twice.
* money

Around about two times each week,
With scarcely any change or tweak,
At Rosings they all had to dine –
At least she generally served wine.

And after dinner as before,
The card table stood on the floor,
Comprised the entertainment that,
After some weeks was pretty flat.

So Liz sought out one quiet path,
Where she could walk and maybe laugh,
And seldom did folk there intrude,
So she could stroll in solitude.

And one that she'd not want to see,
Was Rosings' very own queen bee,
So she could generally avoid,
The questioning that so annoyed.

Then coming up to Easter – news!
On which Elizabeth could muse,
For Mr Darcy was soon due –
One of the very wealthy few.

Though Liz did not this Darcy like,
She thought his presence might just spike,
The evenings with a bit of zest,
Which really must be for the best.

And she'd observe and watch with glee,
How the designs of Miss Bingley,
Would be shown to be hopeless for,
Her Ladyship had sunk her claw,
Into this man who was so grand,
And sure to take her daughter's hand.

RHYME AND PREJUDICE

Collins, of course, was right up there,
When this potential Rosings' heir,
Arrived by carriage as he would,
And Collins bowed low as he could.

He rushed back home, no time to lose,
Announcing to the girls his views,
That Darcy and his colonel mate,
Had been seen by him at the gate.

Next day, though it was pouring rain,
The parson just could not contain,
His excitement and hastened round,
To pay respects to those renowned.

His duty done, he hastened back,
By now his mind was quite off-track,
For Darcy and the colonel too,
Came back with him which was a coup.

They were first seen by Charlotte, wife,
Who then got the shock of her life,
As she the gentlemen espied,
And opened wide the door with pride.

They call came in, compliments paid,
Fitzwilliam conversation made,
But his friend Darcy from the hall,
Stood there and said no words at all.

EBENEZER BEAN

After a pause he ventured to,
Ask if her parents, sisters too,
Were well in body and in mind,
"Why, thank you, yes," she said, "that's kind."

But as she said it Lizzy thought,
So confident perhaps she ought
Not to be for, as has been said,
Her mum was not right in the head.

"And by the way, my sister Jane,
Who's recently been under strain,
Has been in town in London where,
Are you sure you've not seen her there?"

"I am afraid," he said at length,
"That drawing on my mental strength,
I am quite sure that I have not,
And that, Dear Liz, is the upshot."

Chapter Thirty-one

Fitzwilliam was a great hit with,
The girls who then declared forthwith,
That he their evenings would improve,
When they to Rosings did remove.

But now that Rosings had new guests,
The Collins group were second best,
And not 'til Easter did they get,
A Rosings invitation yet.

And even then it wasn't grand,
No formal invite card in hand,
But after church, in Sunday best,
A simple casual request.

And also throughout that same week,
Not much news of which one might speak,
For only Fitzwilliam had,
Come round to see them which was sad.

They went at the appointed hour,
But found things had turned slightly sour,
For Lady B spoke most the time
To Darcy, but not much in rhyme.

EBENEZER BEAN

The colonel, though, was rather keen,
On Liz and new upon the scene,
So he sat with her and conversed,
Though principally prose not verse.

Quite curious, Darcy observed,
And possibly was quite unnerved,
For he perhaps had sweet designs,
On Liz whom he'd met several times.

The next to get a bit uptight,
Concerned things might not be all right,
Was Lady Catherine who called out,
But not so loudly, didn't shout,
"Fitzwilliam boy, of what do you
Speak, come on now and tell me do."

He did ignore her for a while,
Notwithstanding her huge great pile,
But in the end he had to say,
Their subject was music today.

"Then do speak up, I want to hear,
And you're not sitting very near;
It is, you know, my greatest love,
And I do like it way above,
What other folk in England do,
Both Moslem, Christian and Jew.

RHYME AND PREJUDICE

If I had learnt I would be good,
And just the same my daughter would,
But she is ill so can't apply,
And as for me I didn't try.

But Darcy, now, your sister fair,
Who plays the keys without a care,
Do tell her she will hopeless be,
Save that she practice constantly."

"She does do this, do I not know?
For when to her house I must go,
Her playing doth keep me awake,
And sometimes causes earache."

"I'm pleased to hear," Catherine again,
"That she doth practice in the main,
And all young ladies should, I think,
Learn then they can all play in sync.

In fact, I've told to Mrs C,
That she can play in any key,
On my grand piano over here,
Provided she is not too near.

This she can easily attain,
For we do have one room quite plain,
Where she could play most every day,
And won't at all be in the way."

EBENEZER BEAN

The coffee came, they drank it all,
Then Liz sat down with Fitz in thrall,
And as he watched she played a song,
At which Catherine, ere very long,
Resumed her talking, which was rude,
Thus not displaying rectitude.

Darcy, quite soon, had had enough,
Of all his aunties pointless guff,
So he moved close so to observe,
Liz and maybe her to unnerve.

"A-ha!" said Liz, "You mean to scare,
By standing with superior air;
But I will not while there you dwell,
Although your sister plays so well.
And should one try to me upset,
I'm stubborn and grow stronger yet."

"I'm sure you're right," Darcy replied,
"For I have seen your other side;
For some time I have yourself known –
Your thoughts might not all be your own."

Liz then turned round to Darcy's friend,
Intending to his ear bend,
"Listen to that, he says today,
Do not believe a word I say.

RHYME AND PREJUDICE

I am unlucky that he can,
Apparently my whole brain scan,
And, really, he should not reveal,
My faults which he believes are real,
And which he learnt from meetings past –
Behaviour that leaves one aghast.

I can retaliate for this,
If he will not such thoughts dismiss,
For I can say a thing or two,
And to his nature give a clue."

Darcy said, "I am not afraid,
Of observations you have made."

Fitzwilliam then spoke up once more,
"Do let me hear what is in store."

"OK," said Liz, "but do prepare,
'Cos something dreadful I can share,
For at a dance we both were at,
He several times turned down quite flat,
The possibility to dance,
And – who knows – maybe take his chance,
With females, not in short supply,
And to this day no-one knows why."

"The problem was," Darcy spoke now,
"On that occasion I avow,
I did not know the ladies there,
And hence which ones were going spare.

Maybe I should have asked a friend,
A dating service there to vend,
And find me there a girl to dance,
Perhaps one who had come from France."

"Shall we now ask him to explain,
Why he is like this in the main?
For he is clever, good and smart,
And should not be without this art."

"I can give you the reason" (Fitz),
"For this is getting on my t*ts.
The explanation is not odd –
Darcy is just an idle sod."

"At this point p'rhaps I should confess,
That talent other folk possess,
Of conversing quite easily,
Is something not possessed by me.

I really do find it quite hard,
To try not to just disregard,
What folk in conversation say,
And then join in along the way."

RHYME AND PREJUDICE

"My fingers," said Liz, thinking deep,
"Get wrangled up or go to sleep,
When music I might try to play,
For they just will not go the way,
They should whether by day or night,
To play music the way that's right.

I've always thought this was down to,
My practice hours that have been few,
And I'd be better, there's no doubt,
If I had pulled my finger out."

"You are so right, but anyway,
The playing that I hear today,
Is pretty good, I have to say,
No-one could think another way."

Their hostess now at this point spoke,
Out loud to these three talking folk,
And said that she would like to know,
The gist of talk round the piano.

To stave off more intrusive Qs,
Liz resumed with no time to lose,
The playing in a minor key,
In hope of thus distracting she.

She listened for some moments few,
And then proclaimed it was her view,
That Liz would have played better notes,
If she had better learnt by rote,
And had a London teacher who,
Knew how to play and what to do.

"Of course," said she, "my daughter would,
Be superb at this if she could
Have learnt, but sadly she could not,
Because of the bad health she's got."

Liz looked at Darcy to observe,
If he thought this praise was deserved,
And was there any sign of love,
Between these two, together shoved.

She concluded that there was not,
Which did not surprise her a lot,
And so Miss Bingley might not be,
Disadvantaged compared to she.

The rest of the time was now filled,
With advice with which none was thrilled,
But, probably, all this you knew,
For that's what she was wont to do.

Chapter Thirty-two

Elizabeth there sat waiting,
When on the doorbell came a ring,
She put away paper and pen,
In case it was Lady Catherine,
For she so wanted to avoid,
An inquisition which annoyed.

To her surprise Darcy came in,
He was alone, he gave no grin,
"I'd been assured," he said, "that you,
Were at home with the other two.
I must apologise to you,
But can I please go to the loo?"

Ablutions done, the two sat down,
Liz knew not should she smile or frown,
And when a silence then befell,
She said, "Pray, Mr Darcy, tell,
If Mr Bingley will return,
To Hertfordshire – I'd like to learn?

And while I'm on the subject now,
Perhaps you would just tell me how,
The Bingleys are all getting on,
If you know pray enlighten one."

"They are quite well, I can inform,
But he is pretty well lukewarm,
About returning to that place,
For he thinks London's pretty ace."

"Then if he plans not to return,
Perhaps he should his bridges burn,
And sell up quick so there can be,
Some other folk in place of he."

"I would perhaps," Darcy replied,
"Think that he would maybe decide,
As soon as any offer's made,
And the new occupant has paid."

Elizabeth made no reply,
Determined now to make him try,
To speak and openly converse,
No matter whether prose or verse.

A moment later he began,
Remarked the house was nicer than,
It was before Collins arrived,
And how he would have been deprived,
Of this save for his aunt's largesse,
Which he thought right now to profess.

RHYME AND PREJUDICE

"How very true, I think you'll find,
Collins thinks she's been very kind,
And there can surely never be,
An object more grateful than he.

For he does always bow and scrape,
Which surely must be his inscape,
And compliments to her he pays,
In lots and lots of different ways."

"I also think, beneath this thatch,
His wife was quite a lucky catch."

"I think she is, though what's unclear,
Is why Charlotte, his wife's still here;
For most would surely not remain,
With Collins who's a dreadful pain,
For most, when all is said and done,
Would by now have got up and run."

"At least," said Darcy," she's quite near,
Her family not far from here,
'Tis not much more than fifty miles,
And that's by road, not paths and stiles."

"Why, fifty is a long long way,
For folk with not much cash to pay,
I think as I my words now parse,
That you are talking through your arse."

EBENEZER BEAN

He took offence at this repost,
With words selected to his cost,
So not quite knowing what she meant,
He changed the subject round to Kent.

They talked about it for a bit,
The place to which Charlotte had flit,
Until the other girls came back,
And found them, but alas alack,
For back then in the days of yore,
It wasn't done for a señor,
To be alone with a female –
To be so was beyond the pale.

So Darcy tried then to explain,
What he'd intended in his brain,
And after he had had his say,
He just got up and went away.

"Well fancy that! It's surely true,
That he must be in love with you!
For otherwise, I have to say,
He wouldn't call on you this way."

But when Liz explained what he'd said,
So few words coming from his head,
The two concluded from this clue,
He must have had nought else to do.

RHYME AND PREJUDICE

The sporting had come to an end,
And one might well go round the bend,
At Lady Catherine's where were books,
And one girl who had not much looks.

And so it was most every day,
These two gentlemen came to pay,
A call on those within the house,
Could they be seeking each a spouse?

They came in pairs, sometimes alone,
And now and then with the old crone,
And Fitzwilliam it was plain,
Came to be social in the main.

Liz he with Wickham did compare,
He had a less appealing air,
But as for that beneath the thatch,
Wickham was not for him a match.

But as to Darcy none could tell,
Why to the house he came as well,
He often sat and didn't speak –
You could have heard the floorboards creak.

Charlotte did not know what to make,
Of this rich man who seldom spake,
She thought and hoped that he might be,
In love, at last, with friend Lizzy.

EBENEZER BEAN

But no matter how hard she tried,
To see what was his mind inside,
His expression gave nought away,
And it was thus just every day.

He looked at Liz with earnest stare,
But meaning in his gaze was rare,
And sometimes he just vacant looked,
As if, perhaps, he had been spooked.

She did suggest to her friend Liz,
"D'you think maybe the reason is,
That he could be in love with you,
And all his staring is a clue?"

But Lizzy would have none of this,
Thought her friend did take the piss,
And so she tried to think and plan,
For Colonel Fitz to be her man.

He certainly was of the best,
With politeness and manners blessed,
But though he was considered hot,
Of fortune he'd not got a lot.

Chapter Thirty-three

You may recall that Liz was fond,
Of walking in the park with pond,
And she found unexpectedly,
That walking also there was he.

By time that this had happened twice,
She worried it was not so nice,
And quite improper one would say,
At least it was back in that day.

So with propriety in mind,
And seeing that it was a bind,
She thought it would be better that,
She told him so that he could scat.

But Darcy would not take the hint,
And kept bumping into the bint,
And yet his talking was quite sparse,
With words quite few for him to parse.

And though he had not much to say,
He did not then just turn away,
But walked back with her which was odd,
So keen, it seemed, with her to plod.

In semi-silence they both walked,
Liz not much listened, nor yet talked,
Yet on the third time noticed she,
That of the questions posed by he,
Most of them seemingly implied,
That should she come back to reside,
Again in Kent maybe she'd stay,
At Rosings each and every day.

This was, she thought, distinctly odd,
That she might stay there on her tod,
And all that she could think he meant,
Was that it must be her intent,
To shack up with his cousin who,
Was Colonel Fitzwill as you knew.

Well, not long after, as she walked,
One other caught her up and talked,
It was not Darcy, not this time,
But Colonel Fitz who spoke in rhyme.

"I did not know," Lizzy did say,
"That you would ever walk this way."

"I have been making," Fitz replied,
About now to our Liz confide,
"A tour of this park every year,
And this time, if OK, My Dear,
I plan to close it with a call,
Round at the parsonage and all.

But did you intend," he went on,
"To walk much further when I'd gone?"

"Why no," said she, "for without doubt,
I would have turned back hereabout."

So saying, that is what she did,
And so the two now like-minded,
Back to the parsonage did go,
They both walking not fast but slow.

As they walked back Liz asked him, "Well,
How long more do you plan to dwell,
At Rosings for I hear that you,
May leave this weekend, is that true?"

"Quite possibly, but it depends,
On what friend Darcy then intends,
For he decides and I fit in –
In such things he will always win."

"Another like him I don't know,
That has the power of choice like so."

"That he likes to have his own way,
Is plain on each and every day,
But then so many people's aim,
Is oft to do the very same.

But since he is so very rich,
When he does it most folk don't bitch,
And I, myself, the younger son,
Must accept he gets all the fun."

"A younger child, though, of an earl,
No matter whether boy or girl,
Can little know of hardship for,
Of money you can't want for more."

"You may be right, I am not poor,
And don't depend on daily chore,
But when the need for cash is great,
I don't control a grand estate,
So then when marriage comes in view,
One must consider cash then too."

RHYME AND PREJUDICE

Liz wondered if this was a pass,
If so, it was completely crass,
But she continued, asking what,
Sort of a dowry he had got
In mind for the younger son's hand –
Should not be more than fifty grand.

A silence then developed 'til,
Liz spoke up in a voice quite shrill,
"Your cousin Darcy, I would think,
Should get wed, maybe to a Chink,
For it's convenient, he'd find,
To have a wife who will be kind.

But I suppose his sister can,
Take a wife's place for this young man."

"Not really so," Fitz did reply,
"His sister must on both rely,
'On both' means him and also me,
For her guardians both are we."

"Well fancy that, does she give you,
Some trouble or perhaps argue?
She is a Darcy, I dare say,
She likely likes to have her way."

But as she spoke his earnest look,
Led her to think her not mistook,
And that she must be near the truth,
About this gifted teenage youth,
So she thought she had better say,
Some more to take concern away.

"Please do not fret, I never heard,
Against the girl an awkward word,
And she's been a good friend some time,
Of some acquaintances of mine.

Miss Bingley, Mrs Hurst they both,
Have confirmed although not on oath,
That they have a soft spot for her,
And so they are friends as it were."

"I know them both, their brother is,
Young Darcy's friend, that's how it is,
And Darcy generally takes care,
Of Bingley now because the pair,
Are very close, Darcy's the ace,
And Bingley often gets in scrapes.

RHYME AND PREJUDICE

There is a recent case, in fact,
It's delicate, requires some tact,
And I don't even know it was,
For certain Charles Bingley because,
Darcy did not confide in me,
The name and therefore who 'twas he.

But if you will swear on your mum,
And also promise to keep schtum,
I can disclose the problem was,
An ill-advised marriage because,
Although of this he makes no hobby,
The future in-laws were too gobby.
They had attracted Darcy's ire,
And there is no smoke without fire.

Of course, I cannot be so sure,
It could be someone more obscure,
But Bingley often goes amiss,
Especially when on the piss.

As well as that the two did spend,
The summer and did condescend,
To engage with the local folk,
And of them Darcy may have spoke."

Elizabeth then answered nought,
But carried on now deep in thought,
Until the colonel asked her why,
And maybe could he now just pry,
Into her thoughts which seemed intense,
And didn't really make much sense.

"Of what you told I'm at a loss,
And it all makes me rather cross,
That he should dare to poke his nose,
Into private affairs of those,
Who might be thinking to get wed,
And now are separate instead."

Back in the house and in her room,
Her thoughts were pretty full of gloom;
It wasn't credible to her,
That Darcy's dreadful, wicked slur,
Could be about another name,
Instead of elder sister Jane.

She had for some time well believed,
That Darcy, Jane and Charles had cleaved,
But the main culprit in her eyes,
Was Caroline she did surmise.

RHYME AND PREJUDICE

But now, it seemed, he was to blame,
For upsetting her sister's aim,
And that of Bingley also for,
He had between them stuck his oar.

Liz mused upon the colonel's words,
Which she had so recently heard,
And thought which of her family,
The problem relative might be.

It could not be dear Jane herself,
For she was a delightful elf,
But her uncles perhaps just might,
Have cast her in a lowly light;
One was a lawyer in the sticks,
The other trading then in bricks.

Her father should have been OK,
For though he has his own sweet way,
He is good-natured through and through,
And very respectable too.

But then, alas, she was more glum,
When – yes, you guessed it – it's her mum!
But even then she thought it true,
That Bennet's good connections few,
Would count more in the future tense,
Than her old mother's lack of sense.

And so she concluded that he,
Was full of pride which liked not she,
Plus he determined to retain,
His Bingley friend, one Charles by name,
So that he would his sister wed,
And not some other girl instead.

After all this a headache came,
And so Liz was forced to proclaim,
That she could not to Rosings go,
Although it might just spoil the show.

And Darcy would be in that place,
Today she just could not him face,
So she decided home to stay,
While others went there anyway.

Chapter Thirty-four

The others gone, now Liz sat down,
The task she had now made her frown,
For she was reading once again,
The letters from her sister Jane.

She noticed, reading them this time,
Although they did not really rhyme,
That every sentence, every page,
Which had before been hard to gauge,
Was full of worry and unease,
Not quite the thing to make her pleased.

This was not like her Jane at all,
The one you heard of at the ball,
For Jane – please listen if you would –
Considered everybody good.

And now, aware of Darcy's deeds,
Sure to make her heart break and bleed,
Liz saw with greater clarity,
Effects of his barbarity.

But soon he would be gone from Kent,
Which was for certain his intent,
And better still Liz would soon see,
Her sister Jane back home with she.

EBENEZER BEAN

She very nearly shed a tear,
For Colonel Fitz, not likely queer,
Would go as well and so would be,
 No longer wont to visit she.

But though he was so much polite,
 Both in the day and on a night,
He really had made it quite plain,
He didn't want her hand to gain.

She wiped the tear, the doorbell rang,
 Or on the door there came a bang,
 I do not know just which of these
 It was, both probably Chinese.

"Oh gosh! I'm wondering if it's,
My new acquaintance Colonel Fitz."
But then she stood there quite amazed,
For standing there looking half-crazed,
 Was Mr Darcy, Oh my God!
 He'd come round calling on his tod.

He asked about her health – polite,
 And got an answer pretty trite,
 He sat and then got up again,
 Aware, perhaps, of her disdain.

RHYME AND PREJUDICE

Eventually he stopped and spoke,
With words that almost made her choke,
"Against my better judgement I,
Must say I love you, God knows why.

I've tried and tried to no avail,
For it's almost beyond the pale,
For me, a gent with loads of wealth,
To be in love with you yourself,
For as is obvious to see,
You are inferior to me.

No matter, though, I do not tease,
I really can do as I please,
And so I have come round to see,
If you'll consent to marry me."

From such a man, such a request,
Left Lizzie feeling quite impressed,
And as she listened and he spake,
'Twas clear that there was no mistake,
And he was certain as could be,
That she would answer 'Yes' to he.

EBENEZER BEAN

His words trailed off, then Lizzy spoke,
"Is this some awful kind of joke?
Although I should politely say,
I'm grateful for your words today,
I am afraid that I cannot,
And certainly won't tie the knot,
For your opinion of me,
Is pretty poor as one can see."

On hearing this the man went pale,
Though he'd not had a drop of ale,
And after quite a little time,
That it doth take to think in rhyme,
He said, "Well, excuse me I'm sure,
Why, your reply has been so dour,
With no attempt at civil words,
At least none such that I have heard.
So you reject me, that's your loss,
And now I couldn't give a toss."

"Might I enquire," said Liz at last,
"Why you have left me so aghast,
By telling me you liked me, though
Against your better judgement, so
If this had been your fault alone,
Though of contention quite a bone,
I may to you more civil be,
And offer you a cup of tea.

RHYME AND PREJUDICE

But you've provoked me one more way,
It pains me now to have to say,
But you my sister's life have wrecked,
Which is why I am now so vexed.

Your role in this you can't deny,
And these who wouldn't hurt a fly,
Are now embarrassed, upset too,
All, as we know, because of you."

Darcy now he no excuse made,
In response to the girl's tirade,
As he took in the words of she,
He stood in incredulity.

"These claims of yours I can't deny,
To separate them I did try,
And though I know 'twas for the best,
I don't rejoice in my success."

"There is some more," Lizzy again,
"Which once again has caused me pain;
You have also cost Wickham dear,
See - I have got his letter here,
It's pretty damning stuff, I'd say,
So can you explain it away?"

"On Wickham you seem very keen,
Accusing me of being mean,
His misfortune's indeed been great,
That's why he's in his present state."

"And it is all because of you,
Depriving him of his fair due,
And so he is now in a mess,
And pretty nearly penniless!"

"So this is of me what you think,
That I am just a dreadful stink,
And all because I have explained,
In truthful words that have you pained,
Rather than in deceitful way,
Expressing what I have to say.

You really could not expect me,
To rejoice in the things I see,
For your connections are much worse,
Than mine in either prose or verse."

"If you think that, you are so thick,
And have the wrong end of the stick,
(As angry sewage workers know,
This is not where you want to go.)
For I'd have still rejected you,
Although your bad manners, it's true,
Have made it easy under strain,
To say 'No' in spite of the pain.

There really is not any way,
You could have got me now to say,
That I'd accept your hand tonight,
For you are such a dreadful sh*te!"

Darcy was hurt and quite upset,
But Lizzy hadn't finished yet.

"Right from the start, although polite,
You were so very much uptight,
And you with arrogant disdain,
Would insult folk, including Jane.

From this things went to worse from bad,
And after a few weeks I had,
Decided that there was no way,
That I could marry you one day."

EBENEZER BEAN

"You've said enough, I understand,
Why you will not give me your hand;
I am ashamed that I spoke thus,
So now I'll go and catch my bus,
But ere I do I must digress,
And wish you health and happiness."

And that was it, the wealthy toff,
Then turned his back and buggered off.

By all this Liz had not been fazed,
But still she was so quite amazed,
That, first, a man with so much land,
Would deign to ask her for her hand,
And this despite objections which,
Already queered her sister's pitch.

She was quite pleased, I have to say,
That she'd affected him this way,
But his unkindness and great pride,
Meant she must give a berth that's wide.

She was still thinking on this track,
When all the other folk came back,
And dreading what might now be said,
She upped and buggered off to bed.

Chapter Thirty-five

Next day Liz could not concentrate,
After Darcy's attempted date,
So she decided on a walk,
Where, hopefully, she need not talk.

She set off on her favourite way,
But recollected Darcy may,
Decide to walk that way as well,
And that disaster might then spell.

So she turned back and up the lane,
Less likely there to feel the pain
Of meeting Darcy, so she thought,
Which really would be pretty fraught.

She'd walked along the lane three times,
As you are learning in these rhymes,
When she thought that she might tempt fate,
And take a look in through the gate.

As she did so, what should she see,
A branch or possibly a tree?
But no, a gentleman was there,
Like her, walking to take the air.

She backed away quite quickly, lest
It might be Darcy, well-known pest,
But he had seen her by this time,
The same in either prose or rhyme,
And as she heard him call her name,
She knew 'twas Darcy just the same.

They reached the gate together and,
Towards her he held out his hand,
And she, as in Jane Austen's book,
Instinctively the letter took.

"I have been waiting hours today,
In hope that you might walk this way,
So now you've got my letter thin,
Please would you read what's writ within."

So saying, this quite wealthy gent,
Bowed then put on his hat and went.

Liz did not know what to expect,
From he whom she sought to reject,
She opened up the letter wide,
And found two paper sheets inside.

It had been written on that morn,
With quill pen then so freshly worn,
And adding to her state of shock,
The time, it said, was eight o'clock.

RHYME AND PREJUDICE

The letter was so very long,
But written in the English tongue;
Such things are easier in prose,
So cross your fingers and here goes.

"Be not alarmed, expect no pain,
Thinking I might propose again,
For now it is so very clear,
That you would like me out of here.

Before then, though, I must explain,
The origin of your disdain,
Within your mind there must be doubt,
So please read on and hear me out.

So, two things of which you complain,
With both quite bad but not the same;
The first concerns your sister Jane,
The other Wickham in the main.

And so I think I have a right,
To explain now and not tonight,
The accusations you have made,
That put my image in the shade.

The two for which you lay the blame,
Are unequal and not the same,
The first was that I did detach,
Your elder sister from her catch.

The second, really much more worse,
As I can now relate in verse,
That I ruined Wickham's prospects,
Since he himself came to expect,
That as my old father's best friend,
He should be able to depend,
On our help to give him his life,
Which otherwise would all be strife,
For he did have no other way,
Of getting by from day to day.

So I will now start to explain,
About these things that give you pain,
And I must apologise yet,
If what I say makes you upset.

In Hertfordshire I saw, I heard,
That my friend Bingley much preferred,
Your sister Jane to others who,
Might also have been known to you.

But it was not until the ball,
That certain I became at all,
That he was serious on this,
And she might change, Mrs from Miss.

RHYME AND PREJUDICE

I met Sir Lucas while in there –
You know the one, with not much hair –
And his discourse did me alert,
That people thought it was a cert,
That after all is done and said,
My friend and Jane would soon be wed.

Then as I watched, it was quite plain,
That Charles was much in love with Jane,
But while by no means taciturn,
She seemed not to his love return.

On this point we do disagree,
And you know her much more than me,
So if you're not in error here,
It's likely me that's wrong I fear.

Though indifference was what I sought,
At this point I should really ought,
To say my view had not been skewed,
For so to do would one delude.

It's true connections were quite bad,
Because of all the friends she had,
But worse than this I think you'll find,
And really quite an awful bind,
Is how your sisters, parents too,
Your eldest sister's chances blew.

EBENEZER BEAN

I should, however, now explain,
That you and, too, your sister Jane,
Conducted yourselves with aplomb,
Not like the others and your mom.

So I'd no choice than to protect,
My friend of modest intellect,
So when he left for London town,
His sisters and me too went down.
And as we three were of like mind,
We did, though it may seem unkind,
Explain to him why he should not,
Get hitched up to one of you lot.

To make sure he was not confused,
We also sought to disabuse,
His belief that your Jane, quite slim,
Was ever much in love with him.

He really had thought that she was,
And I convinced him not because,
He always believes what I say –
Or he did this time anyway.

He was persuaded that it would,
Be pointless and would do no good,
For him to go back whence he came,
And to your sister make a claim.

But there is one thing I must say,
Of which I am ashamed today,
Which is I did a thing quite bold,
And did from Bingley then withhold,
The fact your sister was in town,
In case he tried to track her down.

You may think me a dreadful cad,
And maybe it does make you sad,
And though she was your aunty's guest,
It really was done for the best.

And that's it, let no more be said,
Let's turn to Wickham now instead.

The story here is quite complex,
And clearly it does you vex,
So I must tell the story whole,
In order to achieve my goal.

I do not know, I am afraid,
What accusations he has made,
But of what I will now relate,
I can find many who will state,
As witnesses that I am right,
And not just acting out of spite.

EBENEZER BEAN

George Wickham's father was quite good,
And therefore quite right my dad should,
Show kindness liberally bestowed,
A sort of duty that he owed.

He paid for him to Cambridge go,
Essential, and it must be so,
For Mrs Wickham used to moan,
And shopped until the cows came home.

My father liked him very much,
He was polite, his heart did touch,
And it was all planned out you see,
That Wickham would a parson be.

But all was not quite as it seemed,
For though the girls all of him dreamed,
He had a darker side to boot,
Which wasn't nearly quite so cute.

I will this other side relate,
Although I know you don't him hate,
And so 'tmight not be welcome news,
That I express now in these views.

My father died five years ago,
No longer could the garden mow,
And he left word, left word that I,
Should help George Wickham by and by.

RHYME AND PREJUDICE

This should include, I have to say,
My family would provide and pay,
A living in the Church for he,
So he'd not have to work for free.

As well as this, a thousand pound,
I tidy sum I will be bound,
Would be bequeathed to him as well,
So he'd not have to clothes pegs sell.

Well, not long after father died,
I found that Wickham did decide,
Against the Cloth and so now he,
A priest or parson would not be.

He wrote to me some words in ink,
To say he hoped that I should think,
It reasonable for me to pay,
All of his dues without delay.

I really was quite unsure, though
He did assure me he would go,
To study law and would need more,
In pounds than fifty times a score.

So with grave doubt still held by me,
I sent a thousand pounds times three,
And that was it, I'd washed my hands,
And he was now well off my lands.

The next three years I little heard,
Though time to time a little bird,
Told me he was an idle sod,
Unsuited as a man of God.

After a while our vicar died,
And Wickham then to me applied,
To be considered for that role,
For he was now a desperate soul.

He promised he'd a priest become,
Which I though really pretty rum,
And so, when I my hat did doff,
I told him just to bugger off.

He did not like this sage advice,
I s'pose it wasn't very nice,
But when one's mind is in a haze,
There is no better turn of phrase.

But there is more that I must tell,
So hear me now and listen well,
My sister now comes centre-stage,
Though she's much younger than my age,
And Wickham convinced her with hope,
To consent with him to elope.

She was at this time but fifteen,
So Wickham really was quite mean,
And just by chance I found the plan,
And managed then to stop the man.

His purpose, really, was quite clear,
And I can say quite without fear
Of contradiction he was brash,
And really wanted all her cash.

And that is all I have to say,
I hope you read it all this day,
And, reading every part of it,
Accept that Wickham is a sh*t.

Things like this you would not suspect,
And so none of these things detect,
But if so doubtful you still am,
Please ask Colonel Fitzwilliam.

For he can vouch for all of this,
Lingering doubts he will dismiss,
And then you will believe the truth,
Of Wickham who is bad, by strewth!"

Chapter Thirty-six

The letter which Liz did receive,
She just could not at all conceive,
What it might be contained therein,
Unless more offers made by him.

That he should be disposed to make,
Apology in words he spake,
Was certain not this girl to faze,
But it would truly her amaze.

She read with care no words to miss,
Her mind quite full of prejudice,
And she quite galloped through the text,
Impatient for what might be next.

His belief Jane was not sincere,
To her seemed really very queer,
So she dismissed it in a trice,
And didn't even read it twice.

No great regret did he express,
For having started all this mess,
No sorrow could there be espied,
But only haughty words and pride.

But as she 'cross the page did speed,
Wherein about Wickham could read,
Her thoughts became alarmed instead,
Because the sentiments she read,
Were really awful if all true,
And cast a dreadful light anew,
On Wickham, whom she though was great,
Even if he'd refused a date.

So prejudiced was she by now,
Repeatedly she said, "I vow,
That all this sh*t cannot be true –
Such things I thought he could not do.

But this account's so like his own,
That maybe his story's been blown,
And the opinion that I had,
Might have to change from good to bad."

The letter now she put away,
But folded up it would not stay,
And so it was, oh damn and drat,
Back out in thirty seconds flat.

Reading with forensic intent,
The trace of ink that had been spent,
She took in all that Darcy said,
About the life Wickham had led.

The first bit exactly the same,
Described no fault and laid no blame,
But when the will came into view,
The two accounts could not be true.

The key point was the living and,
Alternately the three thousand,
That he allegedly received,
And maybe she had been deceived.

She weighed up all the cons and pros,
But serious doubts still arose,
And she was getting more uptight,
For only one man could be right.

That Darcy slagged him off is true,
Which is by now well known to you,
And she was shocked, quite shocked indeed,
That in the words that she could read,
If they were false she had no proof,
So they could even be the truth.

Wickham was popular, quite so,
But maybe it was only show,
For as to background to recall,
There was not much more than sod all.

The Georgiana bit she read,
A bad event it must be said,
And this had partly been confirmed,
By what she recently had learned,
From Fitzwilliam, colonel he,
In conversations, past, with she.

Darcy had said, she did recall,
"Go if you like and check it all,
With Colonel Fitz, a friend of mine,
Whom I have known a long long time."

She wondered if she should apply,
Regarding Darcy's alibi,
But she might just embarrassed be,
To raise the subject now with he.

For Darcy'd not his image wreck,
By advising that she should check,
Unless his witness would agree,
With everything he'd said to she.

She was now coming to the view,
That Wickham's story had a few
Inconsistencies, low he'd stooped,
And, in fact, she might have been duped.

EBENEZER BEAN

Considering him in this light,
Wickham's account did not seem right,
For then she did recall Miss King,
With whom George Wickham had a fling,
And married her for little cash,
With motives that now seemed like trash.

And then a bit more close to home,
The preference that he had shown,
To her, despite her poor estate,
Pretending she could be his mate.

His propositions came to nought,
Most likely 'cos Miss King had bought,
Unknowingly, I have to say,
The need to use the posh word 'née'.

Darcy, by now, was looking good,
Maybe, she now thought, as he should,
For one of the apparent trends,
Was in his own circle of friends,
He was considered as the cream,
And always held in high esteem.

As well as this he always spoke,
Well of his sister and that bloke,
Called Bingley who, as you all know,
With Jane began to have a go.

RHYME AND PREJUDICE

By now Liz really was ashamed,
That Darcy for this she had blamed,
"Oh, how despicable," she said,
"That I have let my mind be led,
To that conclusion which was bad,
Decrying Darcy as a cad.

I have been prejudiced, absurd,
Accepting almost every word,
And without question, without doubt,
To try to help me make it out.

I've often said Jane was naïve,
And very easy to deceive,
And now I find, Oh bloody hell!
The same applies to me as well!
I really have been very vain,
I will not fall for that again."

Her mind turned back to sister Jane,
Was Darcy all that much to blame?
For thinking 'bout it in this light –
On some points he was clearly right.

Jane's feelings were reserved, it's true,
Quite easily mistaken too,
Then as for mother's role, Oh God!
She really ought to shut her gob.

EBENEZER BEAN

Our Liz by now was so ashamed,
That Jane's life chances had been maimed,
By her own mother, stupid fart,
Who knew not how to play the part,
Of future in-law to a dude,
Extremely rich and seldom rude.

The formula is pretty clear,
Don't spend too much time very near,
And so that you won't drop a blob,
It's critical to shut your gob!

Chapter Thirty-seven

Fitswill and Darcy left next day,
And Collins, his respects to pay,
Was hanging round where they would pass,
For he was such a silly ass.

He hurried home directly then,
To tell them that he thought the men,
Were in good health and spirits high,
Despite the ointment round the fly,
That he'd so recently observed,
And surely had not been deserved.

Then on to Rosings he repaired,
Where consolations could be aired,
And he learnt that the lady there,
Now bored and with some time to spare,
Had asked them all to come and dine –
They should be there for half past nine.

By now Liz might have been engaged,
Which would the lady have enraged,
And she amused herself to think,
She could have made a dreadful stink.

Her Ladyship, of course, spoke first,
"This day is really quite the worst;
For I feel very sad you know,
That for them it was time to go.

I really like them very much,
And now their absence doth me touch,
For, as I will confide in thee,
Much more than this they both like me.

Since Darcy likes to come here so,
It's so sad when he has to go,
And though he's been these five years past,
He seems more keen this year than last."

The dinner o'er, while guests kept schtum,
He Ladyship said Liz looked glum,
And ventured then the cause to tell –
That she would soon depart as well.

"You must write to your mum by hand,
And ask that your trip back be canned,
So you can stay two weeks at least,
Thereby your holiday's increased.

Your mother surely can spare you,
If this is what you'd like to do;
There cannot be reason nor rhyme,
Why you must leave here at this time."

RHYME AND PREJUDICE

"My mother does not give a toss,
But back home father is the boss;
He wrote last week and in words few,
Said, "Shift your arse and come home too!""

"Your father may be short of cash,
But please don't give me all that trash,
Despite whatever he might say,
He doesn't need you anyway.

And if you'll stay for four more weeks,
I'll take you both to have a peek,
Round London town, the place is ace,
With parks and lots of open space."

"You are all kindness," Liz replied,
"But for my father, who's not died,
And is a kind and pleasant man,
I think we must stick to our plan."

"Oh, very well," she now gave in,
"But Collins, it would be a sin,
For them to travel post alone,
So you must send a chaperone.

It definitely would not do,
For them to travel – just the two,
The chaperone's not just for fun,
And sometimes you need more than one.

I'm really pleased I thought of this,
A point so many people miss,
And though you may be of class low,
Alone by post you must not go."

"My uncle who's in London town,
Has planned to send a servant down."

"OK but when you change your steeds,
In Bromley – nowhere near Leeds –
Just mention me there at the Bell,
And you'll be treated very well."

The letter from the one she'd spurned,
Now over in her mind she turned,
And her thoughts ranged from good to bad,
About the way that Darcy had,
Behaved towards her, then again,
Sometimes herself she had to blame.

Her fam'ly, though, were all a mess,
Redemption – far beyond hopeless,
Her father just would not restrain,
His younger girls who were a pain,
While mother's manners were so poor –
I think I touched on them before.

And although Liz and Jane might try,
Their bad behaviour to decry,
And try to get them to improve,
'Twould easier be to mountains move.

Kitty was weak and as I tell,
Completely under Lydia's spell;
The two were ignorant, idle, vain,
And, as I said, a constant pain.

About Jane, Lizzy worried still,
Not so much that she might be ill,
But since her suitors had been few,
And Bingley's intentions quite true,
It really had been a cock-up –
Her family had screwed it up.

To this I think we can now add,
George Wickham's character, so bad,
Which she had once thought was the best,
And all this left her quite depressed.

The last week of their holiday,
They went to Rosings, I would say,
As often as in weeks of yore,
Which means those that have gone before.

The topic now for their discourse,
Was their forthcoming trip by horse,
And Lady Catherine did advise,
How, for a gown of any size,
The folding should be done quite straight,
Or mostly so at any rate.

So on the next day they both left,
Rosings was now of guests bereft;
The ladies, two, wished that they would,
Now have a journey that was good,
And since it was not far away,
Perhaps again they'd come to stay.

This invite was a blessing mixed,
And Liz was in-between and twixt,
For though she liked the Rosings food,
She found it hard not to be rude.

Chapter Thirty-eight

Next morning about breakfast time,
Collins, not then the worse for wine,
Said, "Lizzy Dear, before you go,
We really have to thank you so,
For gracing our small portal here,
Which really is a touch austere.

Our home is humble and it's plain,
Has very small rooms in the main,
And though our servants are quite few,
We have tried to be kind to you.

We know that Hunsford's not the hub,
We see so few folk, there's the rub,
So for your visit we're thankful,
'Cos probably for you it's dull."

"I can assure you," Lizzy said,
That from the daybreak until bed,
I have enjoyed most every day,
Just every aspect of my stay."

Now Collins' chest swelled up with pride,
He really was quite gratified,
"I am so pleased you have enjoyed,
Your stay for we have both employed,
Our best devices as you know,
So that you would not wish to go.

And on this point we have had luck,
So you've not in the house been stuck,
For you have been to Rosings where,
There dwell that lady and her heir.

And you must be so very pleased,
That there your entrance I have eased,
For as you know I need not say,
But I go up there every day.

I really must to you now stress,
Her Ladyship does always bless,
Ourselves and also all our guests,
Including those who're sometimes pests.

And so I hope you will convey,
A good report about your stay,
When you get back home to your friends,
And say Collins his wishes sends.

RHYME AND PREJUDICE

I think most likely you can tell,
That your friend Charlotte's chosen well,
We are like one in what we do,
Which can be said of couples few.

An I do wish when it's your time
To marry, as I say in rhyme,
That you will chuse as well as she,
And very very happy be."

Liz thought it best she did not speak,
The prospects for her friend looked bleak,
Holed up with Collins, what a louse,
And then those two at Rosings House!

But though she seemed to have regret,
Her guests would soon not be there yet;
She did not seem at all to mind,
That she had taken on the kind,
Of life that Liz could not abide,
And done so with eyes open wide.

It seemed to Liz that she must still,
Enjoy those things her time did fill,
Like housework, hoovering and such,
All things that I don't like too much.

At length the carriage came in view,
With seating for the ladies, two,
And Mr Collins, so polite,
Expressed views that they'd be all right.

He also, for the umpteenth time,
Sent compliments, though not in rhyme,
To Lizzy's relatives he'd met,
And others he had not seen yet.

The door closed, Collins stood without,
Then suddenly he gave a shout,
"I do declare I think that you,
Have something else you ought to do.

You have not sent a message to,
Rosings House and the ladies who,
Have condescended to invite,
You to their home most every night.

I will be pleased to them convey,
The thanks I'm sure you want to say,
It is the best to do I think,
For we don't want to make a stink.

Then off they went, Maria spoke,
She wasn't one to crack a joke,
"We dined at Rosings night and day,"
Was all that she could find to say.

RHYME AND PREJUDICE

"It will take me a lot of time,
To tell folk about it in rhyme,"
But Liz thought that it might be wise,
Some of her secrets to disguise.

Now later on that self-same day,
They stopped in London on the way,
And Liz was pleased to see that Jane,
Was pretty happy once again.

She was quite dying to relate,
About Darcy's intended date,
But worried that it might remind,
Jane of Charles Bingley – not so kind.

Chapter Thirty-nine

It was in May, the second week,
The girls set of from Gracechurch Street,
Back home to Longbourn where they'd find,
Their family was still a bind.

The plan was at an inn they'd stop,
The coachman would there drop them off,
And Bennet's coach would pick them up,
But after they had dined and supped.

The further plan – they would be met,
By sisters who'd not grown up yet,
And when they got there, there they were,
As usual making a stir.

"Look at this food, it's all laid out,
And it should really cost you nowt,
But there's a problem 'fore you eat,
For we went there across the street,
And in the shop our money blew,
While we were waiting here for you.

The bonnet that I bought is crap,
It's really ugly, has no strap,
But I'll re-sew it once or twice,
So then it might look really nice.

The upshot of all this is that,
Our money all went on that hat,
So if you want to eat this lunch,
You've probably now got a hunch,
The food's not going to be free,
And you must pay instead of me."

Lydia continued as she did,
Although by neither she'd been bid,
"The regiment is leaving town,"
She tried then to disguise a frown,
"But guess what? They're in Brighton next,
And I shall really be quite vexed,
If we don't all go and stay there,
This summer – there'll be men to spare!"

She carried on, "I want to say,
I have more news for you today,
Concerning someone we all know,
And I can't wait to tell you so."

Concerned at what Lydia might say,
They told the waiter, "Go away",
For they might quite embarrassed be,
It he heard words retailed by she.

"I do not care if he should stay,
He'll have heard worse some other day,
But goodness! he's an ugly face,
So better in some other place."

Decision made, the waiter gone,
Lydia at talking carried on,
And told that Wickham's future wife,
Miss King, was escaping from strife,
Though this was much more Lizzy's view,
Than Lydia's who had not a clue.

Jane, of course, she the thoughtful one,
Said "I hope when the friendship's gone,
That these two who may be ill-matched,
Were not, in fact, strongly attached."

Young Lydia then piped up in French –
She really was a callous wench –
"I think," said she, "she was a pain,
That he looked on her in disdain,
For she was freckled, small and fat,
And really not worth looking at."

All very soon had had their fill,
One sort of started feeling ill,
So after Liz and Jane had paid,
The four the final journey made.

RHYME AND PREJUDICE

They were all crammed in space quite small,
And so none could avoid at all,
The dreadful sound of Lydia's words,
The most of which were quite absurd.

"We're all crammed in," she said, "and so,
We will be snug as home we go,
So Sisters Dear, now tell us pray,
What you've been up to while away.

Have you found any pleasant men?
And did you flirt at all with them?
I had been hoping one of you,
Would by now have a lover true.

For Jane's approaching twenty-three,
Which would be much too old for me,
I really must now get wed soon,
That is if I can find a groom.

My aunt says Liz should Collins take,
That would, though, be a big mistake,
For he's no fun, he is a bore,
But then we've all said this before."

She thus continued all the way,
The only one with things to say,
And mostly this was such a pain,
Because the girl had little brain.

And all throughout the journey long,
The chatter caused by Lydia's tongue,
Included often Wickham's name,
So intentions of hers were plain.

Then when they were at home again,
Their mother was pleased to see Jane,
While Bennet said, "Alas alack,
I'm so pleased Lizzy that you're back."

At dinner, then, that self-same day,
Lucases came, respects to pay,
And Lady L said, "Tell me pray,
About our Charlotte on this day.

Is she quite well? Has she still chicks?
Such poultry would get on my wick,
And if the birds should get the flu,
I hope she knows just what to do.

For it's quite bad I think I've heard,
If such as that infects the birds,
They'll all die in horrendous pain,
And we'll have the Black Death again."

But Mrs B just did not care,
That there might be germs in the air,
Her interest lay in ladies' clothes,
Especially fine gowns and those
That Jane had seen in London town,
But preferably not ones in brown.

And every snippet Jane re-told,
This Mrs Bennet, fairly old,
Retailed to Charlotte's sisters there,
And any other ear spare.

Of all this Lydia heard no word,
And carried on with things absurd,
Telling her sister Mary that,
She'd bought a new exciting hat,
And paid for lunch, which she had not,
But Mary didn't care a jot.

"These things," she said, "of which you speak,
In English, Latin, French or Greek,
While they may suit some empty minds,
For me are simply just a bind.

I do not criticise such folk,
Who like the words that you have spoke,
But I with this will have no truck,
And always much prefer a book."

But Lydia heard none of this,
Did just her sister's thoughts dismiss,
And then she went on to suggest,
The thing to do she'd like the best,
Was going out to look for oats,
Which meant some soldiers in red coats.

Liz was determined not to go,
Did not want to see Wickham so,
And it was really in poor taste,
That Lydia should be in such haste,
With officers to go and flirt,
Just like a tawdry bit of skirt.

In two weeks they would all be gone,
And as for going to Brighton,
Liz saw, despite what mother said,
'Twould be over dad's body, dead.

Chapter Forty

Next day did Lizzy spill the beans,
And tell of the surprising scenes,
That recently had come to pass,
Between young Darcy and this lass.

Jane surely was surprised at first,
But neither could she see the worst,
And soon she felt quite sorry for,
Darcy who had been shown the door.

"He was," said Jane, "wrong to assume,
That you would make a bride and groom;
He's landed himself in a mess,
Assuming that you would say yes."

"I'm sorry too," then Liz replied,
"But he has feelings deep inside,
Which likely are important yet,
And surely will make him forget.

But tell me, Jane, you do not blame,
Me for refusing him – a pain?"

Jane, as expected, answered, "No,
You really don't want him in tow."

Thus reassured, Liz spoke again,
"What of my view of Wickham then?"

"Your view of him was very warm,
Sentiments that should be the norm,
And likely right I would surmise,
Views that I could not criticize."

"I thank you for your kindly view,
But something I must tell to you,"
And Liz related word for word,
The letter of which you have heard.

In fact she just of Wickham told,
How he was bad and very cold,
Jane listened but could not believe,
How one could so the world deceive.

She said, "There must be some mistake,
Perhaps some bits of this are fake,
For no-one could be bad as this,
And maybe Darcy takes the piss."

But Liz replied, "This will not do,
You have to make a choice it's true,
And you cannot have it both ways,
So everything one of them says,
Must be quite false and total crap,
So you should not believe that chap.

RHYME AND PREJUDICE

I for myself think Darcy's right,
And Wickham's just a little sh*te,
But you must now say which is right,
And please don't take all bloody night!"

At length Jane gave a sort of smile,
"The more I think of this the while,
I think it's pretty shocking for,
I've never been this shocked before.

That Wickham's bad, perhaps a thief,
Must really be beyond belief,
And Darcy you did disappoint,
Put his nose really out of joint,
Especially as he'd to tell,
About his sister's life as well."

"Although he after me might lust,
I can't say I am all that fussed,
That he might be so much upset,
'Cos your compassion helps him yet.

It is strange one of the two had,
Appearance of good but was bad,
Whereas the other, I surmise,
Was like an angel in disguise.

I did not like Darcy one bit,
Told everyone he was a sh*t,
I had no reason, that was bad,
For most then thought he was a cad.

But just as bad as slagging him,
I did, upon an idle whim,
Pay compliments to Wickham tall,
Who did deserve it not at all.

So tell me, Sister, if I should,
Tell people now that he's no good,
Or should I now from day to day,
On this one topic silent stay?"

"I think not to create a stink,
But tell me what it is you think."

"I do agree we shouldn't say,
Folk won't believe us anyway,
And also Darcy did entreat,
Me not to gossip in the street.

Folk won't accept that Darcy's good,
They really would not think they should,
And George will soon be gone from here,
The sun still shining from his rear.

In time folk might just learn the truth,
We'll feign surprise and say 'By strewth.
Did you not know he was the pits?
You really are all stupid nits!'"

Jane then did have another thought,
She said, "You and me really ought,
Not try his good name to destroy,
For it might really harm the boy.
And if on this we both agree,
I'd really like some bloody tea!"

This was a weight off Lizzy's mind,
But still it was an awful bind,
That she could not her sister wise,
On what Darcy'd Bingley advised.

Now as Liz watched her sister Jane,
She could see that she was in pain,
For on Charles Bingley she was keen,
Though recently she'd not him seen.

She really wanted him so much,
To hear his voice, to feel his touch,
And his rejection of her hand,
Was really more than she could stand.

She had so missed him, missed him still,
Was very close to being ill,
And it was Lizzy's firm belief,
Her sister might just die of grief.

But things now went from bad to worse,
As I will tell you now in verse,
For Mrs B sticks in her oar,
As she has often done before.

"Well, Lizzy," said she in a fit,
"Tell me what do you make of it?
I am resolved of this affair,
No more again to it refer.

Jane did not see him while in town,
And people say he won't come down,
To Netherfield where he could see,
Your sister Jane and also me.

He has used Jane extremely ill,
She should not put up with it still,
But it might just a comfort be,
If Jane should die for want of he,
For he will then see that he's erred,
The stupid little greasy turd."

RHYME AND PREJUDICE

Liz did not know quite what to say,
But kept her mouth shut anyway,
And then her mother, acting strange,
Decided to the subject change.

"So how is Charlotte? She's quite shrewd,
Is careful, throws away no food;
So she'll manage her budget right,
Because she's really pretty tight.

I expect that they talk a lot,
About their entail on our plot,
It really does make me see red,
That they'll get it when father's dead."

"They did not mention it to me,
For it would cause distress you see."

"It's not surprising, I suppose,
But I just bet that Collins goes,
And gloats about this bad entail,
Which really is beyond the pale.

I really hope they sleep at night,
For this entail just is not right;
They know it's not, they are the pits,
And just two greedy little sh*ts!"

Chapter Forty-one

A week went by, the soldiers were,
About to go which caused a stir,
For local females, almost all,
No longer on them could then call.

The elder Bennets did not care,
There were no soldiers going spare,
But Kate and Lydia, you know,
Were really quite consumed by woe.

Their mother also shared their grief,
She said, "It's really my belief,
That more than twenty years ago,
A regiment then had to go,
And though there were then soldiers fewer,
I cried for two days I am sure.

Their going nearly broke my heart,
For I had then to wed that fart,
Who is your father so intense,
And hadn't really any sense."

"My heart is broken just the same,"
Said Lydia, she a real pain,
"But if to Brighton we could go,
I would be shot of all this woe."

RHYME AND PREJUDICE

"I know but father does refuse,
And so our suitors we will lose."

Liz listened to this childish rant,
From siblings with brains rather scant,
And she concluded Darcy might,
In his view of them have been right.

And then Lydia some fresh luck had,
Though others might have thought it bad,
For Mrs Forster asked her down,
To go with them to Brighton town.

Lyd rushed around the house with glee,
Oblivious to the fact that she,
Had been invited but not Kate,
Who now got into such a state,
And also in a dreadful stew,
Because she wanted to go too.

She really could not be consoled,
My her siblings who were more old,
And Liz feared that if Lydia went,
Their reputation would be spent.

So off she went to see her dad,
Said, "This will really be so bad!
She'll be just like a common flirt,
And will our reputation hurt."

Her father gave a great big sigh,
"No matter how hard I might try,
And whether I am kind or stern,
Your sister there will never learn."

"But what she does affects us all,
Our suitors she does sore appall,
And she's already put some off,
Because of her they've had enough."

"Already?" Bennet said out loud,
"Some lovers has your sister cowed?
If they're put off by one like her,
They're not much good you must infer.
So come on, let me see your list,
Of these youths that she off has pissed."

"I do not have a list to say,
But, really, there'll be hell to pay,
If you won't keep her now in check,
Our family's good name she'll wreck.

She really must by you be told,
That though she isn't very old,
She must behave and must not flirt,
Just like the meanest bit of skirt.

You know she's lazy and doth shirk,
And flirting will be her life's work;
  She's also stupid, also vain,
Seeks compliments, too, in the main,
And Kitty follows where she leads,
Not just in thought but also deeds."

"Oh, do not fret," her father said,
  "For you are sensible instead;
  So too is Jane, your sister wise,
And quite delightful in folks' eyes.

If she goes not we'll get no peace,
  Her silliness will just increase,
  So let her go and she will find,
That with her really empty mind,
  The officers won't give a hoot,
Unless she wears a bathing suit.

In town she'll less important be,
Right at the bottom of the tree,
  And as I tell you now in verse,
She really cannot get much worse."

Liz left, at least she had been heard,
Although the outcome was absurd;
She'd told her dad what was in store,
And sadly, now, could do no more.

If Lydia or her mum had known,
Into a rage they would have flown,
For Lydia thought Brighton was gay,
And that she would most every day,
The centre of attention be,
And flirt with soldiers, two or three.

Liz now saw Wickham one more time,
They spoke in prose, not much in rhyme,
And Liz now Wickham did despise,
Since Darcy'd opened up her eyes.

He dined at Longbourn one more day,
And Lizzy there contrived to say,
That she Fitzwilliam had met,
And had he ever known him yet?

He looked surprised, displeased, alarmed,
And for a moment lost his calm,
But then he said, "I've seen him oft,
He's a polite and pleasant toff."

But tell me, Liz," he said to she,
"Did you, in fact, like me like he?"

"He is quite nice as you do say,
I met him almost every day,
And though his manners aren't the same,
As the other, Darcy by name,
I have to say I think it's true,
That Darcy can just grow on you."

"Indeed," said Wickham, "may I ask,
If it's 'fore or behind the mask,
That he's more civil day to day,
When people come respects to pay?
For, fundamentally, I'd say,
He hasn't changed in any way.

"Oh no," cried Lizzy, "I think he,
Is quite the same as used to be,
And when I said he was more good,
I meant he's better understood."

Wickham by now, upon my word,
Concerned at what Liz might have heard,
Was worried she might know the truth,
Of him and Darcy in their youth.

EBENEZER BEAN

"You know I've been ill-done by him,
And what he says is really spin,
But when to Rosings he doth go,
He likely does put on a show,
For his old aunt and daughter too,
Who he is rather keen to woo."

Liz gave a smile at this remark,
For he was quite wide of the mark,
The prospect of more talk looked bleak,
So any more she did not speak.

They parted as the clock struck ten,
She thinking him one of the men,
She would not want again to meet,
And she was voting with her feet.

The group split up, Lydia then went,
With Mrs Forster whose intent,
Was to be Brighton bound next day,
With lots of chance for girlish play.

She was wished well by Mrs B,
And Jane and Liz, both calm you see,
But Kitty was sad as can be,
Not off to Brighton by the sea.

Chapter Forty-two

The Bennets were a group apart,
The father, who was fairly smart,
Had made the error of his life,
By picking this one for his wife.

She was quite pretty, that is true,
But quite soon this he came to rue,
For though she didn't have affairs,
   She hadn't got a lot upstairs.

With Bennet's happiness thus canned,
He sought his solace from the land,
And complimenting his wife's looks,
   He also read a lot of books.

The story says not what he did,
   So on such I can't lift the lid,
He liked to spend time on his tod,
   Or maybe was a lazy sod.

He seldom grumbled, didn't moan,
   Accepted what went on at home,
And when his wife said something daft,
You can be sure he always laughed.

EBENEZER BEAN

You might say it was rather mean,
To hold her in such low esteem,
But when there isn't that much fun,
You must make do with what is done.

Liz knew he should not act this way,
But seldom did she want to say,
That he his wife should well protect,
Including her low intellect.

And now she worried laissez faire,
Not quite the same as couldn't care,
Was damaging his daughters' chance,
Of getting hitched now at a dance.

Such things he might perhaps affect,
But as for his wife's intellect,
It took only a moment's pause,
So see that that was a lost cause.

Liz was pleased to see Wickham go,
He had turned round from friend to foe,
But otherwise life was now glum,
And emphasized as such by mum.

Mum and her little sister were,
Intent on glumness I infer,
Though Kitty might just be improved,
Now that the youngest had removed.

She'd gone to Brighton you'll recall,
With officers, to see them all,
And Liz was fearful that she would,
Be getting up to not much good.

Jane Austen's words now get involved,
The meaning not so lightly solved,
But what I think she means is this:
That when there isn't that much bliss,
And 'specially when other folk,
The melancholy fires stoke,
The best thing anyone can do,
Is have things to look forward to.

In Lizzy's case this was the traipse,
Up north and including the Lakes,
And, strangely, there was just one point,
Which would her always disappoint,
And would make her feel slightly glum –
It was that her Jane couldn't come.

"This disappointment is quite good,
It means, in fact, I really should,
Against such backdrop happy be,
Although she will not come with me.

When Lydia went she'd promised to,
Write often – you know, like you do,
But all her letters were quite terse,
And rather short but not in verse.

But tittle-tattle all that they,
Contained on each and every day,
For that was likely all she did,
With not much underneath her lid."

In time the glumness wore away,
And I think perhaps I can say,
That on this tranquil, rural scene,
Life went back to what it had been.

The northern tour just weeks away,
A letter came which, sad to say,
Announced that it would be delayed,
And also shorter would be made.

The Lake District which had been planned,
Unfortunately was now canned,
And Derbyshire was all that they,
Would see when they now went away.

RHYME AND PREJUDICE

Liz was upset at this late change,
Her holiday a shorter range,
And then, of course, she realised,
As you may also have surmised,
That in those parts was Darcy's seat,
A man she did not want to meet.

"But surely," said she, "I can go,
To Derbyshire, seat of my foe,
Without his knowing I am there,
So I don't need to have a care."

The last weeks passed, the Gardiners came,
They had four little brats in train,
Who were left with her sister Jane,
Which must have been a right old pain.

Rid of the kids, they made a start,
Liz and her aunt plus one old fart,
And as they went I have to say,
They stopped at places on the way.

It's not my job to write a list,
Excluding any I have missed;
To know the routing they all took,
You'll have to read the proper book!

To Lambton, though, they bent their steps,
A phrase that sounds somewhat inept,
And also it just does not rhyme,
I'll get it right another time.

Her aunty now produced a trick,
Liz wondered if she had been thick,
For Pemberley they'd like to see,
Inhabited sometimes by he.

"My love, surely you'd like to go,
To this place that you've heard of so;
It's where George Wickham spent his youth,
Believe me for this is the truth."

Liz was distressed, she'd seen enough,
Of big grand houses full of stuff,
But Mrs Gardiner said, "You're daft,
Outside the house both fore and aft,
There are fine gardens, lovely woods,
And cows that sometimes chew the cud."

Liz did not like this one small bit,
Came close to having then a fit,
And so she asked her chambermaid,
Who brought a glass of lemonade,
If folk were living in the hall,
Or was there no-one there at all?

RHYME AND PREJUDICE

The answer when it came was, 'No'
So Liz though she might as well go,
And have a nosey all around -
The price would be less than a pound.

Chapter Forty-three

They drove along and easy found,
The entrance to the house's grounds,
They carried on up through the wood,
As people back in those days could.

And there at the top of the hill,
A view which really was so brill,
For there across the valley floor,
A view she hadn't seen before.

The house looked really very grand,
Set right across the valley and,
With woods behind and stream before,
You really couldn't ask for more.

The scene was all to nature due,
With colour shades of every hue,
And though the gardeners must have toiled,
The natural beauty was not spoiled.

She surveyed the amazing scene,
Of which she could have been the queen,
Save for one all too recent fact –
She'd failed to show sufficient tact.

RHYME AND PREJUDICE

They approached, stopped outside the door,
   Six feet there firmly on the floor,
   And they applied to look around,
   At cost of much less than a pound,
Something one could do in that day,
If one the housekeeper would pay.

   The lady came, she said, "Hello,
   Around the house we all can go;
   The dining parlour here is roomy,
   Big windows stop it being gloomy."

Liz thought it was all pretty good,
With views out as far as the wood,
And other rooms in which they came,
Had views all pretty much the same;
The hills, the stream, the sky, the lake,
Enough one's breath away to take.

   The furniture was nice as well,
He had good taste, she could just tell,
   And all was in far better taste,
Than in that grand old Rosings place.

   "Just fancy if I had said 'Yes',
   Of all this I might be mistress,
And showing aunt and uncle round,
With no need to collect a pound.

But no, alas, it would not be,
For they are lower class than he,
I'd not be 'llowed to let them in,
For doing so would be a sin."

She would have liked to ask their guide,
If Darcy was out or inside,
But she was nervous, nothing said,
Then uncle questioned her instead.

"The master presently we lack,
Tomorrow, though, he will come back,
We think that is what he intends,
And will bring, too, a lot of friends."

Liz was pleased this was her belief,
The news came as a big relief,
She was glad they'd not been delayed,
Or she'd have really been dismayed.

Her aunt then spied some pictures there,
Wickham and Darcy, likeness fair,
The housekeeper said Wickham had,
Gone in the army but gone bad.

RHYME AND PREJUDICE

Liz dared not speak when this was said,
She knew about the life he led,
And when Ms Reynolds pointed to
Another picture, like you do,
And said that it was Darcy's face,
Aunty proclaimed she thought it ace,
And asked Liz if 'twas likeness fair,
At which their guide asked if she'd care,
To say if Liz her master knew,
Because she hadn't got a clue.

"I have met him, he's pretty cool,
And over him some girls might drool."

The housekeeper with this concurred,
Which Liz thought just a touch absurd.

And then the conversation turned,
To Darcy's sister who, they learned,
Was an accomplished little tart,
At playing, singing and at art.

Then, more of Darcy, Reynolds spoke,
"He really is a lovely bloke,
But half the time he is away,
And I would really like to say,
No matter if in prose or rhyme,
I wish it were a shorter time.

Perhaps if he would take a wife,
He'd spend a bit more of his life,
Round here but then he'd have to see,
A girl quite good enough for he."

Reynolds continued to heap praise,
On Darcy which did Liz amaze,
She carried on, "You could not meet,
One better – he's a real treat,
And has been since he was a kid,
Because of the good things he did."

Liz really was gobsmacked at this,
High praise she just could not dismiss,
And despite what had gone before,
She was now desperate for more.

After a bit of info on,
The rooms' contents and dimension,
About her master she resumed,
So further praise now likely loomed.

"He's the best landlord, master too,
Never a better will find you."
(And if you think this rhyme's not good,
Then you yourself to try it should!)

"His tenants will all speak out loud,
To work for him they are so proud,
And no-one will of him speak ill,
'Twas always thus and it is still."

Liz pondered, "If all this is right,
It shows him up in a good light;
It seems this is to be believed,
So surely we were all deceived."

The next room has been done out for
The sister – yes, the one before –
And it seemed that Darcy would do,
Whatever she might ask him to.

By now Liz had well changed her mind,
Believing Darcy must be kind,
And all his servants did agree,
That only good was done by he.

He did control so many lives,
Of tenants, children and their wives,
And did, it seems, care for their good,
As any wealthy landlord should.

EBENEZER BEAN

The tour all done, the gardener came,
It's not explained what was his name,
Then as they passed the stable block,
Liz got the most tremendous shock,
For there stood Darcy, bright as day,
Not more than twenty yards away.

Their eyes all met, their cheeks went pink,
He looked like he could use a drink,
Then he advanced towards the girl,
His mind completely in a whirl.

She was upset as well she might,
But his words were extreme polite,
She turned away, her eyes cast down,
Not knowing should she smile or frown,
For she did not know his intent,
Amid her own embarrassment.

The others stood some yards away,
She didn't know quite what to say,
As he enquired so politely,
About her dreadful family.

She really knew not what to say,
About them on this fateful day,
And although Darcy was polite,
He really wasn't thinking right.

RHYME AND PREJUDICE

He flustered on, mind in a tizz
From meeting, unexpected, Liz,
And she was so embarrassed for,
She hadn't been round there before.

Quite sudden he bid them goodbye,
And left Liz wondering then why,
He'd been so civil and polite,
When she'd thought him a dreadful sh*te.

Some moments passed, they carried on,
About their walk with Darcy gone,
And Liz was desperate to know,
If Darcy might still like her so.

She puzzled on this for some time,
Could make no reason nor no rhyme,
So in the end she thought that she,
Had better for now forget he.

They wandered on, now in the wood,
Along the paths as walkers should,
But in a while Eliza's aunt,
Whose walking stamina was scant,
Said, "Really, I have had enough,
Of all this country walking stuff.

We must now to the house proceed,
Because my body has the need,
To be conveyed by means equine,
Instead of on these legs of mine."

They set off but progress was slow,
Her uncle faster would not go,
For he was watching jump the trout,
Though he had not his tackle out.

As they progressed Darcy appeared,
And then as he the party neared,
Liz thought that it would do no harm,
If he should speak, to remain calm.

She thought she should be first to speak,
In English, not in ancient Greek,
And she began to compliment,
His house built of stone and cement.

But then a dreadful thought occurred,
Which you may now think was absurd,
That all the praise that she now meant,
Could be construed with bad intent;
She did not want insults to lob,
So pretty quick she shut her gob.

He then asked if she'd honour do,
And her friends introduce him to,
So she did but was quite concerned,
That when who they were he had learned,
He might think they were rather low,
And then perhaps off he would go.

He was surprised, Lizzy could tell,
But still he behaved rather well,
Better by far than she could wish,
And with uncle he discussed fish,
Saying that it would be all right,
For him to fish by day, not night,
And he would lend him tackle too,
So he could maybe catch a few.

Ms G was mightily impressed,
His manners really were the best,
And Liz wondered why this should be,
"It surely isn't just for me.
My words in Kent near made him ill,
He surely cannot love me still."

The two walked on, now side by side,
And Lizzy, not yet Darcy's bride,
Explained they'd thought he was away,
And so had visited that day.

"This is quite true," he said, "although,
Back home quite early I'd to go,
My other guests will come quite soon –
Most likely in the afternoon.

You have met some – Bingleys – before,
Another in the group – a score –
Is Georgiana, sister who,
Is very keen to meet with you."

At this Liz really was impressed,
To meet her was quite for the best,
And they walked on in silence 'til,
They reached the house set on the hill.

"Do come inside," he said, "and sit,
To rest your weary feet a bit."

"I thank you for your kind invite,
But, really, I am quite all right."
So they stood outside anyway,
Not quite sure what they ought to say.

They had to fill the time somehow,
The Gardiners not arrived by now,
And searching subjects for discourse,
She thought, "Why, silly me, of course,
I've travelled all around the dales,
So can recount some of my tales."

RHYME AND PREJUDICE

So they talked on but it was stiff,
The others came, not in a jiff,
And once again the four were pressed,
To take refreshment inside, lest
The walking had been too intense,
So doing this would make some sense.

They all declined, he helped them in,
Their carriage, now off for a spin,
And as they left, I have to say,
Liz saw him slowly walk away.

As they drove off the Gardiners spoke,
"He is a really lovely bloke;
He's very kind and quite sedate,
But tell me why you did him hate,
For I would say, though not out loud,
That he is anything but proud."

Liz shuffled her feet, did not know,
Quite why she had disliked him so,
And so she said, "Each time I see
The man, he simply grows on me.
And now today I like him more,
He hasn't been this nice before."

But Mrs G was still not sure,
If Wickham or Darcy were truer,
She said, "If he's done Wickham ill,
And yet his servants praise him still,
 Perhaps his servants only say,
 What he wants them to anyway."

Liz wanted to say she was wrong,
First thought she'd better hold her tongue,
But then decided to explain,
That Wickham was the one to blame,
Rather than Darcy whom she knew,
 Was very good and polite too.

At these new facts she had just learned,
 Mrs Gardiner was concerned,
But now they were so very near,
To places she held very dear,
And where when younger she would play,
 Right back then in a former day.

So she was occupied in full,
With memories, mostly quite dull,
And after dinner, great relief,
When she'd finished using her teeth,
She set off then old folk to meet,
Which was, for her, a real treat.

But Liz, meanwhile, in wonderment,
Was pondering Darcy's intent,
In being civil now to her,
And introducing his sister.

Chapter Forty-four

Next day when Liz was at the inn,
Thankfully none the worse for gin,
And dressing to go out to eat,
She heard a carriage in the street.

She looked outside, the badge was his,
They were all getting in a tizz,
And aunt and uncle thought this was,
An honour for them all because,
Darcy had come of his will free,
And so must be quite fond of she.

By Now Liz had got in a state,
Darcy had said that she was great,
And maybe he had overdone,
His praises with the little one.

She wanted so much to impress,
So she would like her – more or less,
And she paced up and down the room,
Just like a bride without a groom.

The door opened, the two came in,
She was tall but not really thin,
And though Liz did not quite know why,
The girl seemed exceedingly shy.

RHYME AND PREJUDICE

She didn't say much, that's for sure,
Compared to Liz her words were fewer,
But she was gentle, kind and smart,
Liz wasn't frightened of this tart.

Darcy then spoke, he said, "My friend,
Whom you know – Bingley – doth intend,
To call on you, perhaps today,
Or in a few days anyway.

But hark! I hear him on the stair,
I'd know that footstep anywhere."
And in a jiff, Bingley came in,
Just as Liz knew him but more thin.

He said to see her he was glad,
And asked about her mum and dad,
For he was pleasant, not a bore,
Just as she recalled from before.

The Gardiners were all agog,
Could tell that Darcy'd like a snog,
But Lizzy's plan it did appear,
Was probably not quite so clear.

Lizzy was keen to please them all,
Determined not to trip or fall,
This really would just be a breeze,
For all three wanted to be pleased.

Liz now thought about sister Jane,
Did Bingley like her in the main?
He asked, it's true, about her health,
And not especially by stealth;
He could recall at any rate,
The date when they had their first date.

By such was Lizzy now much cheered,
And then as she at them now peered,
(That's Bingley and the Darcy Miss,
Liz had to know if they might kiss,)
She noticed – you know like you do –
Their interactions were quite few.

The message really was quite clear,
Assuming neither one was queer,
(Which I think was not in those days –
It must just be a modern craze.)

With others out of earshot,
Bingley asked Liz, though not a lot,
If *all* her sisters were at home,
And she could tell then from his tone,
That though he might not speak her name,
His question really was 'bout Jane.

RHYME AND PREJUDICE

Liz also now watched Darcy's mood,
Since he had well stopped being rude,
And she discovered with delight,
He was now being most polite,
And none of her friends did he slight,
On each and every day and night.

She'd never seen him so at ease,
Or so determined one to please,
Not even in those former times,
Which I've recounted in these rhymes,
At Netherfield or Rosings where,
He'd friends and suitors going spare.

Before they parted, now polite,
The Darcy's offered an invite,
To Lizzy's party for to dine,
At Pemberley with food and wine.

So unexpected, for a min,
This put Mrs G in a spin,
For she'd no wish to seem a twit,
And knew not what to make of it.

She looked at Liz as if to say,
Should we all accept this today?
But Liz, now unsure more than wise,
Decided to avert her eyes.

EBENEZER BEAN

She took this that it should mean 'Yes',
And also, as you might well guess,
Her husband, though he seldom rude,
Was keen on any sort of food.

So she accepted I can say,
And there and then they fixed the day,
It was, and this bit is quite true,
Into the future by days two.

As Lizzy thought about the way,
That things had all played out that day,
It all did really seem to prove,
Bad thoughts of him she should remove.

All through the night she lay awake,
Not really sure what she should make,
And what her feelings now should be,
About the character of he.

She was quite grateful she now thought,
Because she really didn't ought,
To have been prejudiced so bad,
As to denounce him as a cad.

RHYME AND PREJUDICE

Although he did have lots of pride,
It really wasn't justified,
And that he could now forget all,
She had heaped on him since that ball,
Made her think maybe that she could,
Love him as any woman should.

There was one other thing to do,
For protocol I s'pose it's true,
So on the morn of the next day,
They should go round respects to pay,
So after out of bed they'd slid,
That is, in fact, just what they did.

Chapter Forty-five

Now Lizzy knew that jealousy,
Was twixt Carol Bingley and she,
And she was curious to see,
How civil she would be to she.

Inside the house they were both shown,
Down past the staircase made of stone,
To the saloon whose windows tall,
Were lovely summer, spring and fall.

There Georgiana said, "Hello,
My two friends here I think you know;
There's Mrs Hurst here in this chair,
And Carol Bingley over there."

The girl was nervous, rather shy,
And though we do not know quite why,
It might be 'cos she was not old,
And consequently not so bold.

Low class folk might think it was pride,
That made her act as here described,
But it was not, she was quite nice,
And shy as I've now told you twice.

RHYME AND PREJUDICE

Two ladies curtseyed, all sat down,
On cushions mostly coloured brown,
And then a silence did descend,
No speech there which the air could rend.

The girl's minder was first to speak,
Or they'd have sat there for a week,
And Mrs Annesley her name,
Just minding Miss Darcy her game.

It was clear from her form of speech,
She could things to the others teach,
For she was clearly quite well-bred,
The other two morons instead.

In conversation now were three,
Ms Gardiner, Lizzy and she,
While Miss Darcy tried to join in,
Though her contributions were thin.

Liz noticed now after a while,
That Caroline who failed to smile,
Observed most everything she said,
Trying in her to instill dread.

This did not Liz intimidate,
Nor put her in a silent state,
But inconveniently I'd say,
Miss Darcy was some yards away,
Which made the talking quite a strain,
So Liz then soon shut up again.

She wondered if men would return,
And join this scene so taciturn,
And if so whether Darcy would,
Be with them and for ill or good.

She hoped he might come and be near,
But then again was wont to fear,
His presence, handsomeness and pride,
For she was all mixed up inside.

Some minutes later Carol spoke,
To break the silence of the folk,
Who in the saloon sat around,
All stressed up there without a sound.

She asked with cold civility,
About Eliza's family,
Liz thought she wasn't very nice,
So answered her in tones like ice.

RHYME AND PREJUDICE

The servants were next on the scene,
With food the far extreme from mean,
Comprising fruit, cold meats and cake,
And types for fish but nowhere hake.

The servants gone, they all dived in,
As if to leave some was a sin,
And after they had had their fill,
A couple started feeling ill.

Elsewhere Darcy was doing fish,
While Lizzy knew not what to wish,
At length he learnt Liz was inside,
So, having now consumed his pride,
He excused himself then shot off,
To find her and his hat to doff.

Liz had by now resolved to be,
Not embarrassed or cowed by he,
But as he came not in disguise,
Within the room all pairs of eyes,
Were focused on this man and Liz,
Though it was not part of their biz.

Now Caroline was first to speak,
She must have practised for a week,
For what she said was really mean,
Back then bordering the obscene.

"Eliza," said she, "tell me pray,
If all the soldiers down your way,
Now that they have all slung their hooks,
Mean that you're back to reading books?"

Though she did not George Wickham name,
She was attempting just the same,
To get Liz to refer to him,
Perhaps assuming she was dim,
And so by reference thus made,
Into her hands perhaps have played,
For speaking thus with Darcy there,
Was sure to cause the man to glare.

Imputed mention of this name
Though, upset Darcy just the same,
So for Carol in hatred mired,
Her little scheme had now backfired.

It also Georgiana hurt,
For the girl was, of course, alert,
Since their attempted elopement,
When she'd been living back in Kent.

So upset was the younger girl,
Her mind went straight into a whirl,
She couldn't look, it had been bleak,
And for a while she didn't speak.

RHYME AND PREJUDICE

The visit coming to an end,
Carol tried Georgie's ear to bend,
By criticising Lizzy's frock,
Which she said looked like bargain stock.

But Georgiana wouldn't play,
This nasty game I have to say,
For it, to her, was very plain,
Her brother liked Liz in the main.

Darcy had been to see them off,
To bow, also his hat to doff,
Then he returned, what do you know?
She tried to have another go.

"How crappy Lizzy's looking now,
She's such a frumpy little cow,
I don't know if she has been ill,
But all her looks have gone downhill."

Darcy at this point held his tongue,
But said he thought Miss Bingley wrong,
"She is, I think," he said, "the same,
But maybe tanned – the sun's to blame."

"Her face is thin," she continued,
With comments which were really rude,
"Her nose is odd, the teeth are bad,
Her eyes look shrewish, maybe sad,
And, really, she lacks fashion sense,
In present, past or future tense."

"It seems you do not find her great,
But maybe I should put you straight,
For I have thought for many weeks,
That with her lovely dimpled cheeks,
Concerning looks I can attest,
She is perhaps, one of the best."

This wasn't quite what she had planned,
While trying to secure the hand,
Of Darcy whom she hoped to wed,
For he'd now put her down instead.

RHYME AND PREJUDICE

Chapter Forty-six

Some time had passed back at the inn,
When Liz received two letters thin,
One was quite new, the other old,
For as I have before not told,
The one had gone astray – a shock –
'Cos the address was all to cock.

They were, of course, from sister Jane,
Who wrote quite good ones in the main,
But one of these was writ in red,
And here's the gist of what it said.

The first part was just normal stuff,
Some tittle-tattle, lots of guff,
But then the last bit, if I may,
I will recount to you today.

Jane wrote this bit with great alarm,
Said Lydia might come to harm,
For she and Wickham had eloped,
And might well by now have been groped.

(I must apologise right now,
A rude word has crept in somehow,
I do not use them in the main,
And won't let it occur again.)

EBENEZER BEAN

The news had come about midnight,
She wasn't sure that it was right,
But some folk thought that it did mean,
The two had gone to Gretna Green.

Liz was not much surprised to hear,
Her mum, distressed, had shed a tear,
And then a bit worse did it go,
She was beside herself with woe.

She's left a note for Forster's wife,
About the next bit of her life,
And so the colonel, I should say,
To the Bennets' was on his way.

One letter read, she got the next,
Devouring eagerly the text;
It said the pair had not been found,
They might, perhaps, have gone to ground,
And then for Bennets such a scare,
In Gretna they'd not been seen there.

Back then this outcome was quite bad,
For whatever the two then had,
Done or intended – not the same –
On all the Bennets brought great shame.

RHYME AND PREJUDICE

In fact the best that they could hope,
Was that their daughter and that dope,
Might marry and so Gretna Green,
Was the best place they could be seen.

The last place they had been espied,
Was Clapham where the streets are wide,
They'd buggered off amid the fuss,
On board the Clapham omnibus.

Since then by no-one they'd been seen,
And nothing since then could one glean,
And Colonel Forster whom you knew,
Has said he didn't have a clue.

"Our parents are all sad with grief,
And mother has now lost her teeth,
She must have put them down somewhere,
And, sadly, she's not got a spare.

She sits all day up in her room,
Her mind completely full of gloom,
And father, too, now fears the worst,
Today I heard that he had cursed.

Dear Liz, though you're on holiday,
I would entreat you, even pray,
That you might come home in a tick,
'Cos without you I'm feeling sick.

Quite soon the colonel will be gone,
From here and London to Brighton,
And dad in London on his own,
Won't be much good without a phone.

I think that uncle will be wise,
And help with this new bad surprise,
He is a kind and helpful gent,
And also generally well-meant."

"Oh, where is uncle," Lizzy cried.
"I think I heard him just outside."
But as she reached the bedroom door,
She got more than she bargained for,
For standing there about to knock,
Was Mr Darcy in coat frock.

"I beg your pardon, I must go,
And must be pretty quick not slow,
So please would you now me excuse,
There is, I fear, no time to lose."

"Good God!" said he, "What is to do?
You seem to be all in a stew;
I'll not detain you, this is true,
But maybe I could come with you,
Or, since we have man-servants few,
I'll send one – that's what servants do."

Liz thought upon this wise advice,
She wasn't needing to think twice,
So she the servant told to go,
And get on with it, not be slow.

She sat down, Darcy was concerned,
At recent facts he had just learned,
So he said, "Shall I call your maid?
Perhaps a glass of lemonade?
Or maybe wine, you look so ill,
Or, then again, perhaps a pill?

There are all sorts, for flesh and blood,
And one such which is really good,
Is aspirin though I can't it get –
It hasn't been invented yet."

"No, I'm all right, I am not ill,
Trying to digest bad news still;
It has exceeded my worst fears."
And at that she burst into tears.

The crying stopped, Eliza spoke,
"I am afraid this is no joke,
For Lydia's buggered off, you see,
With Wickham you know to a T.

EBENEZER BEAN

We have no clue where they both are
Going by bus or train or car,
And all we know to our disgust,
Is that the girl is likely lost.

For this I partly am to blame,
It really, truly is a shame,
That with knowledge I had of he,
I did not warn my family.

Although, in this case, though I could,
It really would have done no good,
For Lydia, though she is the titch,
Is really the most stupid bitch."

"I thank you for sharing this news,
And do concur with your own views,
But tell me, are you sure its right,
And not just done to cause a fight?"

"Oh yes, there's little doubt of this,
Wickham with stupid little miss,
Is probably there in the smoke,
Which means there's really not much hope.

My father's gone in search of she,
The last one in the family tree,
But, really, he has not much hope,
For he's a simple country dope.

RHYME AND PREJUDICE

My uncle needs to go as well,
Once he has heard the servant tell,
But even though this course is right,
The chances of success are slight."

Darcy now paced around the room,
As you can guess immersed in gloom,
And as Liz watched she realised,
That Darcy, she had thought her prize,
Would not now want herself to wed,
And would chuse someone else instead.

"I am concerned about your plight,
With Lydia now gone from your sight;
I would, if I could, put things right,
Though my influence would be slight,
And I must now say by the way,
You will not visit us today."

"You are right, please would you excuse,
Us and conceal now this bad news,
Although this bad news we'll not shout,
Eventually it must come out."

Darcy then left, Liz was quite sure,
Their future meetings would be fewer,
And Wickham's intent was not good,
He would not marry as he should;
The Bennets really would be hurt,
Their daughter just a bit of skirt.

Now when Elizabeth thought back,
Lydia's behaviour was quite slack,
She'd flirt with anyone at all,
But probably preferred them tall.

She didn't have a favourite beau,
Including George Wickham and so
That she for him did now have eyes,
Had come as quite a big surprise.

She had to get home pretty quick,
Her mother – no surprise – was sick,
And father gone off to the smoke,
Made then by burning coal and coke.

He aunt and uncle now arrived,
And Lizzy urgently contrived,
To tell them both the tale of woe,
And urge them now back home to go.

RHYME AND PREJUDICE

They both were shocked I have to say,
The worst news they had had all day,
And in an hour, or more or less,
They left to sort out all the mess.

Chapter Forty-seven

"I think," her uncle said at last,
As lots of countryside sped past,
"That although Wickham is a pest,
Perhaps we should hope for the best.

I do not think he'd be so dim,
As to take her out on a limb,
When she has friends now in her life,
And has stayed with his colonel's wife."

Her aunt then also waded in,
By now a bit the worse for gin,
"I do not really know the lad,
But think he can't be all that bad."

"I think he is a sod, though still,"
Said Lizzy, by now feeling ill;
For if they would get wed with grace,
Then surely Scotland is the place."

Then uncle had another go,
"Where they have gone we just don't know,
It could be Scotland where it's chill,
Or they might be in London still.

RHYME AND PREJUDICE

In London town they both could hide,
Potential bridegroom and his bride;
In Scotland wedding costs are steep,
In town one can wed on the cheap."

"But no, I really don't accept,
That Wickham would be so inept,
As to wed Lydia in a flash,
Because he hasn't any cash.

She's young and pretty, that is plain,
Which on young men can put a strain,
He might just take her for a spin,
And then they'll go and live in sin.

The problem is Lydia is young,
And though her praises might be sung,
To Mensa she is not much loss,
Because she is a idle toss.

She's been allowed to waste her time,
As I can tell you now in rhyme,
By soldier boys she's been bewitched,
And quite intent on getting hitched."

"But ... but," said aunty, "see that Jane,
Would never impugn Wickham's name."

EBENEZER BEAN

"Well fancy that," now Lizzy said,
"'Twould be over one's body dead,
That Jane of someone would think bad,
Even were he a proven cad.

But Jane knows just as well as me,
That Wickham's profligate you see;
He is deceitful, false as well,
And sometimes has an awful smell."

"And do you know these things are true?
How can it all be known to you?"
Thus spake her aunty, one of those
Females who sported a long nose.

"I do indeed," responded Liz,
Who was now getting in a tizz,
"But I may not reveal my source –
Unless you are a spy of course,
And it is really now past doubt,
That Wickham really is a lout."

"But can your sister be so thick,
That she has fallen for this prick?"

"I am afraid she has said Liz,
For Jane and I were in a tizz,
And thought we should not tell the folk,
The nature of this rotten bloke.

RHYME AND PREJUDICE

We did not think she'd be deceived,
Do things for which we all would grieve,
And though she is exceeding dim,
We thought she was not fond of him.

Once he'd arrived it was quite soon,
When after him we all did swoon,
So she, post an initial flirt,
Became another bit of skirt."

As they drove on, now headed south,
The only words they spoke by mouth,
Were on this subject I've disclosed,
Which really had some questions posed.

They made good speed, the man drove fast,
Eventually got home at last,
And Liz asked Jane while still in shoes,
That of the pair was there some news?

"Why no, we haven't heard a thing,
But now that you did uncle bring,
And as he will sleep here tonight,
I hope things will all be all right.

Our dad, as you know, has gone down,
To dirty, smelly London town;
He wrote once to say he'd arrived,
And all the journey had survived.

I also asked him his address,
While trying to sort out the mess,
And he wrote back but not in rhyme,
To say 'twould be a waste of time,
To write again and paper use,
Unless he had some better news.

And mother, Oh my God! I think,
Has very nearly took to drink;
She hasn't left her bed in days,
At least that's what the servant says.

She'll really like to see you all,
She thinks the sky's about to fall,
So when you go, do please my dears,
Just put your fingers in your ears."

The conversation continued,
Participants polite not rude,
And then they all went up the stair,
To Mrs Bennet's bedroom where,
The lady of the house was there,
All eager for her woes to share.

She said she's been used ill and bad,
But missed the point because she had,
By indulging her daughter Lyd,
Encouraged her in what she did.

"If I had gone," she carried on,
"To that damned place that's called Brighton,
I'm sure she would have been all right,
And never once out of my sight;
I really would not have been fooled,
But, as always, was overruled.

And now Bennet is gone away,
And it could be that any day,
If he finds Wickham on a night,
He will, for sure, the bugger fight.

If he does so, he will be killed,
His heart in consequence be stilled,
And then your cousin Collins see,
Will turn out of here you and me.

Oh it will really be so bad,
And I will be so very mad,
And we must then apply to you,
Brother to tell us what to do."

The others all poured scorn on this,
Said that her views were quite amiss,
And Gardiner said he'd go next day,
Down to the city built on clay,
And if their father didn't mind,
He'd help him to his daughter find.

EBENEZER BEAN

"Do not give way to false alarm,
She may not yet have come to harm,
And 'til we know she'll not be wed,
There isn't much more to be said.

Much information we have not,
They may be married, maybe not,
And till we do know more of this,
Such dreadful thoughts we must dismiss."

"Oh, Brother," Mrs Bennet said,
"If you find them alive not dead,
Force them straight down the church's aisle,
And tell the bloody girl to smile.

And don't you dare let Bennet fight,
I cannot sleep by day or night,
And please don't my afflictions mock –
I'm really in a state of shock."

These things all said, they went downstairs,
For dinner was by now prepared,
But upstairs remained Mrs B,
And quite unnecessarily.

The other two girls then joined in,
Sat with the others eating din,
Kitty was fretful without Lyd,
And dying to know what she did.

RHYME AND PREJUDICE

Mary, though, on the other hand,
So well composed and rather grand,
Said, "Lizzy, this affair is poor,
And folk must talk of it I'm sure.

We must stem this malignant tide,
Not hide at all but stay outside,
And in our bosoms we must pour,
The balm of consolation for,
It will help all of us be strong,
Provided it is not too long."

Elizabeth made no reply,
So in the twinkling of an eye,
Mary went on I can tell you,
With words which right back then were true.

"For Lydia this is pretty poor,
But there's a lesson we can draw,
Which is that if a girl has sex,
Such thing her whole life surely wrecks,
And so she really should stay clear,
Of undeserving men round here."

Liz looked up in amazement then,
For she could not remember when,
She had before heard words like this,
Quite blunt and not to be dismissed.

The elder two now on their own,
Began to each other to moan,
About the outcome this might have,
With Lydia gone off with this chav.

And Lizzy now her Jane beseeched,
Deep in her memory to reach,
And recount all there was to know,
About this dreadful tale of woe.

Jane said Forster was not to blame,
For he know nothing just the same,
He'd not suspected Lydia would,
With Wickham be up to no good.

But now the deed was likely done,
And both continued on the run,
Denny nor he had any clue,
What elopees now planned to do.

They all knew Wickham as a catch,
Was really, truly a bad match,
But if Lydia had sex today,
She really couldn't single stay.

"Kitty," said Jane, "had known of this,
Potential for true wedded bliss,
But she had kept her big gob shut,
Until her sister came unstuck."

"But what of Forster, does he know,
That Wickham is less friend than foe?"

"I think, although he does not shout,
That by now he has worked it out;
Wickham he used to think OK,
But he speaks ill of him today,
He says when Meryton he left,
He was so very much in debt."

"Oh Jane," said Lizzy in distress,
"Perhaps we might have stopped this mess,
By telling all and sundry that,
George Wickham really was a rat."

"But that was tricky, we'd be sued,
For saying things so very rude,
And we did act as we thought best,
E'en though we knew about the pest."

Jane then produced a written note,
Which had by her sister been wrote,
To Mrs Forster, colonel's wife,
At least for some years in her life.

"I have it here, there is no doubt,
And if you like I'll read it out."

EBENEZER BEAN

"Dear Harriet, I think you'll laugh,
When you find I have buggered off;
I'm off, you see, to Gretna Green,
Will set off in the night unseen,
And as to who's eloping too,
I shouldn't have to give a clue.

My family you need not tell,
For I shall write to them mysel',
And say I have a new name now,
But I think dad might start a row.

Pray tell to Pratt I've gone away,
So cannot dance with him today,
I really don't want to him spurn,
And will dance with him on return.

I'll send for my clothes when I'm back,
But please, before you up them pack,
Get Sally that great slit to mend –
It's not right now the latest trend.

I must end now and say goodbye,
Excuse me for I have to fly."

"Our sister," Liz said, "is a sh*t,
She shouldn't speak like this a bit,
My father was shocked and is still,
And mother very soon took ill.

RHYME AND PREJUDICE

Since then she simply has got worse,
At this rate she will need a hearse,
And dealing with her has been tough,
For her one cannot do enough.

Kitty is really not that strong,
While Mary just reads all day long,
I've looked after her without pause,
But she is almost a lost cause.

Aunt Phillips, Lady Lucas too,
Came round to see just like you do,
And they were really very kind,
So nobody would ever mind."

"It's best," said Liz, now in dismay,
"If one's neighbours just stay away,
Despite what they might do or say,
They've got one up on us today.

It's better that they gloat alone,
Instead of visiting our home,
Then they can cheer and laugh and grin,
And we need not get sherry in."

Liz said, "All this is very new,
Do you know what dad plans to do?"

"He's gone to Epsom, I believe,
For that is where they do relieve,
The horses which do draw the cart,
And I think this is pretty smart,
For if he finds the coach that they,
Used as they went upon their way,
He might be closer to them trace,
And put an end to this disgrace."

Chapter Forty-eight

Next morning but to no avail,
The Bennets waited for the mail,
To see if perhaps their dad might,
Have troubled to a letter write.

They knew he was a lazy sh*te,
And seldom had been known to write,
But they had hoped he might prevail,
And send a letter in the mail.

No letter came, their uncle went,
To London where his main intent,
Was to persuade his brother so,
That back to Longbourn he should go.

His wife thought this would mean the fool,
Would then avoid a nasty duel,
And if he managed to survive,
Collins would not dare to contrive,
To expel them from their abode,
And turf them out onto the road.

Their aunt stayed on a few days more,
Thank goodness it was not a score,
But while she stayed she was quite good,
Consoling people as you would.

Their other aunt, though, came as well,
With intention as I can tell,
Of cheering up the gathered throng;
But every day it wasn't long,
Before she'd to Wickham referred,
Which really was a bit absurd,
For this brought no cheer to the room,
And instead left them in more gloom.

At Meryton, folk rallied round,
Proclaiming that they'd all be bound,
That Wickham was a dreadful cad –
The worst guest that the place had had.

They all said that he was in debt,
He had seduced some people yet,
And most folk said they always knew,
That no good was the man up to.

Liz just did not believe it all,
Some bits were surely stories tall,
But with even half of this brewin',
She was sure of her sister's ruin.

And even Jane, inclined to doubt,
Malicious gossip thus put out,
Was now almost in deep despair,
They might to Scotland not repair,
For if they had and made their vow,
There would have been some news by now.

Three days now passed, their uncle wrote,
A letter – that's a kind of note,
And said he'd found that Bennet was,
In Clapham over there because,
He was enquiring if they'd been,
Around the place and had been seen.

Success eluding him so far,
He planned to ask at every bar,
And hotel in and round the town,
To see if he could track them down.

"I think this is a waste of time,
It makes no reason and no rhyme,
But since he will not change his mind,
I have to help him – what a bind!"

He also wrote that he had tasked,
That Colonel Forster now to ask,
Of Wickham's friends if they might know,
Just where the two of them might go.

EBENEZER BEAN

"I'm waiting now on his reply,
Am not keen to on him rely,
But wonder if Lizzy might know,
Some places where Wickham might go;
Or if she knows better than we,
If any relatives has he."

Liz said, "I do not have a clue,
In fact I know no more that you."

At Longbourn each and every day,
They did for news in the post pray,
For they had post but did not yet,
Have that thing called the internet.

One day there dropped onto the mat,
A letter which was thin and flat,
And it was from … but can you guess?
The Reverend Collins – No or Yes?

Now as you know this man's a bore,
In place of two words will use four,
So if you have now got all day,
I'll tell you what he had to say.
On second thoughts perhaps I ought,
To summarise and keep it short.

"Your youngest daughter is a slut,
This is a harsh description but,
It would be better, must be said,
If instead of this she were dead.

I think it's mostly down to you,
For letting her behave, it's true,
Just like a vulgar common flirt,
With any Harry, Tom or Bert.

I pity you in your distress,
And Lady Catherine, more or less,
Sends her thoughts which are much the same,
And also thinks you are to blame.

But let me give you wise advice,
It's necessary, if not nice,
Pray cast her off I do beseech,
And that will her a lesson teach."

At length their uncle wrote again,
Info from Forster in the main,
He said he no relations had,
And other news was pretty bad,
For he was very much in debt,
And had no means to pay them yet.

EBENEZER BEAN

The total was a thousand pound,
Mostly from gaming in the town,
He had, Jane Austen says in verse,
Some 'debts of honour' which sound worse.

Quite what she means is not too clear,
But given Wickham isn't queer,
It might mean, if my thinking's right,
He was out shagging every night;
But of such things that is enough,
So let's move on to other stuff.

Gardiner wrote that they all might,
See father back home Sat'day night,
For he had given up the chase –
Fed up of walking round the place.

Uncle, meanwhile, would go and look,
Except at night (afraid of spooks),
And try to find the naughty pair,
If they might still be staying there.

When Mrs B on this got wise,
Her reaction caused some surprise,
For she seemed not to be concerned,
That Mr B might be interred.

"Why is he leaving? It's not right,
He ought to stay to have a fight,
For Wickham must be made to pay,
By marrying Lydia one day."

Next to depart was Mrs G,
Along with children – two or three,
And on the journey she could not,
Work out the Darcy – Lizzy plot.

For though up north he had seemed keen,
She didn't know what it might mean,
For since returning back down south,
His name had just not left her mouth,
And correspondence had been none,
As if the man had simply gone.

You will not be surprised to know,
That Lizzy's spirits were now low,
And for this 'cos of sister loose,
She need not search for an excuse.

She was now having sleepless nights,
And Darcy made her more uptight,
The acts of Lyd, the stupid cow,
Seemed rather more important now.

EBENEZER BEAN

Bennet returned but did not speak,
Of what had happened all that week,
Until Liz said that she was sad,
About the trouble he had had.

"I only have myself to blame,
Which is to my eternal shame;
You warned me, Liz, some weeks ago,
And still I went and let her go,
I really should have made her stay,
P'rhaps Kitty will now run away."

"I will not," Kitty answered quick,
"Because I am not all that thick;
If off to Brighton I should go,
I wouldn't act like her you know."

"I would not trust you now at all,
No officers nor any ball,
And every day you have to spend,
Ten minutes when you do intend,
To act in a rational manner,
Or else you will be in the slammer."

At this the girl began to weep,
Thought that these sanctions were too steep,
So father said, "It's just a joke,
You will not cry too much, I hope,
And if a leaf you'll turn anew,
Ten years from now I'll this review."

Chapter Forty-nine

Two days after Bennet's return,
To Longbourn, still so taciturn,
Liz and Jane with some time to spare,
Were walking in the garden there.

They saw the housekeeper called Hill,
Approaching with her voice quite shrill,
And as she came in earshot,
She spoke as they expected not.

"I beg your pardon, Ma'am," said she,
"I wondered if news there might be,
For your dad has got an express,
Which surely is about this mess."

The girls ran off, too quick to speak,
Jane lagged behind 'cos she was weak,
And in the house they searched in vain,
Which simply just increased the strain.

The butler, though, stood by the door –
I thought the Bennets were quite poor –
He said his master had gone out,
Was walking somewhere thereabout,
He walked towards the little wood,
A scene that might do him some good.

RHYME AND PREJUDICE

So Liz and Jane, quite out of breath,
Though not in danger much of death,
Ran, both of them, fast as they could,
To look for him down in the wood.

Liz got there first for Jane was weak,
But even she could hardly speak,
"From uncle now have you got news?
And can you share with us his views?"

"I have indeed received this mail,
It really is beyond the pale,
The note has come by express post,
Arriving as I ate my toast.

Not DHL nor TNT,
Or Post Special Delivery,
This topic which our fam'ly wrecks,
Has just arrived here by FedEx."

"Well is the news there good or bad?
And should we laugh or remain sad?"

"To expect good is just too much,
So do not try at straws to clutch;
The letter here makes little sense,
In present, past or future tense,
So read it now and do not stall,
And we will listen to it all."

"My Dearest Brother, listen well,
To everything I will now tell,
And so that I'll not disappoint,
I will first get right to the point.

I have discovered where they are,
It isn't far by tube or car,
And so you'll trust what I will say,
I saw then both just yesterday."

At this point sister Jane cried out,
"They must be married without doubt!"

Liz carried on then with her prose,
Reading the words set out in rows,
"The two, alas, are married not,
And this was not part of their plot,
But Wickham who's a cunning sod,
Says he will not stay on his tod,
And will the wedding bells arrange,
If you will give him some loose change.

It is this dowry he desires,
And then to marry will aspire,
He wants about two pounds a week,
Which really is a real cheek.

But that's not it, he also said,
That when you and your wife are dead,
That money – it's five thousand pound –
Which for your daughters should be bound,
A fifth of it must come to him,
To keep him in his ale and gin.

Although this may not seem too nice,
Today my very strong advice,
Is right now round the bank to dash,
And send him all his bloody cash.

You really do not need come back,
Lydia will stay here in our shack,
And we will see her wed quite quick,
Before he does another pick.

So you must send to me today,
A summary of what you say,
And be aware it must be 'Yes',
If we are now to end this mess."

"Hip hip hooray," the girls both cried,
"Our sister is to be a bride,
You must write back without delay,
I'll write it for you if I may.

You must let uncle know your views,
Because there is no time to lose,
It may be hard such note to write,
That gives cash to that little sh*te,
And must we with these terms comply?
Perhaps to change them we could try."

"I am ashamed," their father said,
"The money now and when I'm dead,
Is not so much I have to say,
For him to take the girl away.

He really must have asked for more,
So uncle has settled the score,
I'm sure of this, I must repay,
The thousands he just gave away.

Uncle is kind I have to say,
We really have no chance to pay,
But now I must this letter write,
And get it sent before tonight."

"This really is fantastic news,"
Said Liz, expressing now her views,
"Although they will not happy be,
Marrying such a rogue as he,
The scandal we can now avoid,
And so we are all overjoyed."

RHYME AND PREJUDICE

Jane said, "Look on the side that's bright,
And I'm sure it will be all right,
He possibly loves her to bits,
So let us all now call it quits."

To both the girls it now occurred,
That Mrs B might not have heard,
So they said, "There's no time to lose,
We must now tell her this good news."

The other girls were there as well,
So just one reading would all tell,
They listened hard as well they might,
And quite erupted with delight.

Mum's pleasure could not be contained,
About the girl she should have brained,
When they heard Lydia would be wed,
And not be a disgrace instead.

And as to whether this girl she,
When married might then happy be,
The mother was, in fact, not cross,
And really didn't give a toss.

"It will be so good when we meet,
My happiness is now complete,
She will be married at sixteen,
That's really good – know what I mean?"

EBENEZER BEAN

Jane then enlightened her about,
The money uncle had shelled out,
Thinking if she explained to she,
Her mother might quite grateful be.

But mother's comment in reply,
Was really pretty poor and sly.

"It is his job like this to do,
He's not short of a bob or two,
And if he'd had no kids himself,
When he dies most of his great wealth,
Would come to us I have to say,
So he might as well pay today.

And anyway, he's pretty tight –
You know that what I say is right –
Although he's rich and we are poor,
We've never had that much before."

She now began to plan and plot,
The dresses for the wedding slot,
But Jane who a bit more sense had,
Said that she first should tell her dad.

"I'll go to Meryton," she said,
"And tell people, alive and dead,
About this new fantastic news,
Because there isn't time to lose."

"Oh! Here comes Hill, have you heard that,
Lydia will wed at sixteen flat,
And so then at the wedding lunch,
You shall all have a bowl of punch."

Liz now went off back to her room,
Knowing now there was much less gloom,
And though her sister's state was poor,
'Twas better than it was before.

Chapter Fifty

Now Mr Bennet wished he had,
In times of yore both good and bad,
Been rather careful with his cash,
And some of it away had stashed.

This money that he should have saved,
Would be useful in future days,
For to provide for kids and wife,
After the end of his own life.

If he'd done this he could right now,
Have paid for Lydia's marriage vow,
And would not now need to depend,
On money his brother would spend.

He thought that he should try to find,
So long as brother didn't mind,
Just how much then was the amount,
That Gardiner paid from his account,
Then he could get things back on track,
By paying all the money back.

RHYME AND PREJUDICE

Back when the Bennets were just wed,
And sleeping then two to a bed,
Economy just was not done,
For surely they would have a son,
And he if this plan did not fail,
Would simply cut off the entail.

This meant once old Bennet had died,
An inheritance would provide,
For widow and girls, maybe five,
Until they ceased to be alive.

But sadly it was not to be,
They started off girls one, two three,
The next one counted up to four,
Then five including one girl more.

By this time, though, wife was spendthrift,
Which in the marriage caused a rift,
But still they stuck together and,
The husband's spending was just canned.

Five thousand pounds was settled on,
Wife and girls for when dad was gone,
With sharing it determined still,
By statements in the parents' will.

But Lydia's part decided was,
And as you will recall because,
Bennet must now agree to pay,
The amount that Gardiner would say,
And now to Gardiner he would write,
To say the settlement was right.

Pragmatically this was quite good,
A hundred pounds to pay them would,
Be all that it would cost him now,
To be rid of the little cow.

Whereas the cost of board and bed,
Plus spending – always in the red –
Was very nearly much the same,
For he could not her spending tame.

So with this sweetening of the pill,
And cheaper now for good or ill,
He penned with haste his letter to,
His brother saying what to do,
And trying to politely find,
What brother paid in action kind.

But with Lydia he was irate,
That she'd got such a worthless mate,
And from such you might now infer,
He didn't write a note to her.

RHYME AND PREJUDICE

To people, then, this was good news,
For most folk then expressed the views,
That marriage was what mattered most,
With rings, bad speeches and a toast.

So folk said they were very pleased,
That Bennet's troubles were now eased,
And though they'd been spiteful before,
They need not be so any more,
For with Wickham folk thought indeed,
Her misery was guaranteed.

Upon this news our Mrs B,
Emerged from upstairs gleefully,
She'd got one daughter's wedding slot,
And more that that it mattered not.

She started to look for a house,
For Lydia and her new-found spouse,
And quite devoid of any sense,
Considered not the pounds and pence.

"Haye-Park might do or maybe Stoke,
But there the drawing room's a poke;
Ashworth is just a bit too far,
While attics in Purvis Lodge are,
So dreadful it must now be said,
I wouldn't be seen in them dead!"

Her husband let her ramble on,
Until the servants were all gone,
And then he said, "For sure, My Dear,
There is a house somewhere round here,
That they will never enter in,
Since they've been living now in sin.

This house, if you've not worked it out,
I'll not receive the girl and lout,
Is Longbourn House, that's this one here,
And they won't get in, have no fear."

An argument right then ensued,
The two were forceful but not rude,
And in the discourse the wife found,
Bennet would not advance a pound,
(It was a guinea at that time,
But such a word just does not rhyme)
For buying clothes and things like that,
So such requests were turned down flat.

She really could not comprehend,
Why he would not his money spend,
On things important such as this,
And her requests did just dismiss.

RHYME AND PREJUDICE

Liz now regretted that she had,
Told Darcy of all this news bad,
For since she would now married be,
She might have hidden it from he.

She worried not Darcy might speak,
Of this so constitute a leak,
But she was pretty sure that she,
Would have no chance to marry he.

This really was a dreadful mess,
Which now caused her acute distress,
For after thinking him a bore,
She did now like him more and more.

She really wanted him to wed,
You know this 'cos I have just said,
And now that this had come to pass,
That sister of hers, silly ass,
Had screwed it up for everyone,
And that was that, the deed was done.

From Bennet's brother, soon a note,
In which the writer had just wrote,
Wickham would the militia leave,
Which Gardiner thought a great relief,
And in the north to take a post,
Between the east and western coast.

EBENEZER BEAN

"I have told Forster I'll ensure,
That Wickham's debts will be far fewer,
For I of them am taking charge,
And will the chief of them discharge.

And you could have now as an aim,
In Meryton to do the same,
He ran up debts while he was pissed,
And of them I enclose a list.

I hope to us he hasn't lied,
And has not some more debts beside,
So we can now this chapter shut,
And rid ourselves of this bad nut.

And at this point, I ought to add,
That Lydia, though she's been bad,
Would like to come and see you soon,
As they embark on honeymoon."

Bennet and girls thought it was best,
To get rid of their sister pest,
To the far north where she was far,
From where the rest at present are.

But Mrs B thought it severe,
To send her very far from here,
Where she would have far fewer friends –
Perhaps as father now intends.

RHYME AND PREJUDICE

Lydia's request that they should call,
    At Longbourn got no truck at all,
    From Mr B who said they should,
Be banished to the north for good.

But Liz and Jane prevailed on him,
    Not just to follow his own whim,
    But to receive the wedded pair,
One day when he had time to spare.

Their father did as he was bid,
    And so this is what they all did,
    And Mrs B, you'll likely know,
At this time did her daughter show,
    To anyone who fancy took,
And might just want to have a look.

Chapter Fifty-one

The wedding day came round at last,
And happenings came rather fast,
For newlyweds the coach was sent,
To bring them back was its intent.

The elder girls stood there in dread,
At what might soon be seen or said,
For though it was not the intent,
There would be great embarrassment.

All stood there in the breakfast room,
Five minds now quite suffused with gloom,
Bennet was grave as grave can be,
His daughters anxious, uneasy,
But Mrs Bennet, standing there,
Was joyous – no surprises there.

In fact their mother was all smiles,
The best day she had had by miles,
And as the room door open flew,
She welcomed and embraced the two.

Her father, though, spoke not a word,
From which it's readily inferred,
That he did not like what they'd done,
While they were out there on the run.

RHYME AND PREJUDICE

Lydia, though, the brazen miss,
Was quite oblivious to this,
And she from girl to girl now went,
Demanding of them compliment.

All this now shocked both Liz and Jane,
Who was forgiving in the main,
And while all this was going on,
George Wickham, Bennet's latest son,
Had perfect manners, lovely teeth,
But Liz still knew him underneath.

Both Liz and Jane had blushed bright pink,
Consequence of what all did think,
But Lydia and her latest beau,
Behaved as if they didn't know.

The bride and mother talked non-stop,
Faster than in a fishwives shop,
And Wickham conversed now with ease,
Though Lizzy's words could start a freeze.

Lydia recounted lots of things,
Before they got their wedding rings,
About the life that she had led,
Which others thought should not be said.

And then as others spoke quite terse,
She started getting all the worse,
"Oh Mama, do the people here,
Know I have made my vows sincere?
I was afraid no-one would know,
And I would have to tell them so.

We did, as we came, overtake,
So very fast, the coach did shake,
William Goulding who you know,
And I just had to tell him so.

I lowered down the window glass,
Just at the point where we would pass,
And then I stuck my hand outside,
To show him that I was a bride;
He might to others this news bring,
Once he had looked and seen my ring."

At this point Liz could take no more,
She went out, running on the floor,
To stay away was her intent,
Until for dinner they all went.

And then, I'd say, to cap it all,
Lydia with mother in the hall,
Just said to Jane, "This is quite ace,
Because I can now take your place.

RHYME AND PREJUDICE

You've always been top of the list,
A privilege we all have missed,
You must go lower, maybe bow,
For I'm a married woman now!"

Lydia continued thus to boast,
Not mindful that there was no toast,
And she could really not await,
To tell the world of her new state.

She turned to mother, said, "You know,
Brighton is now the place to go,
For anyone who wants a man,
So take the others if you can."

"I know," said mother, "I'm upset,
I didn't take you all there yet;
But now just about any day,
You are both going far away,
I'd really like you both to stay,
So we can talk more like today."

"I am afraid we have to go,
But you must come and visit so,
And when you leave you can for free,
Let several daughters stay with me.

I am quite sure that I will get,
Husbands for several of them yet,
The officers there will be nice,
So it will be done in a trice."

"Why, thank you," Liz ventured to say,
"But I don't want a man that way."

To stay ten days the pair were set,
Her mum thought it was too short yet,
But all the rest, I have to say,
Could not wait 'til they went away.

Liz noticed Lydia was more keen,
On Wickham than he'd ever been
On her, so why should he elope,
Because he wasn't much a dope?

The answer was not hard to guess,
For with his big financial mess,
Escaping might have more success,
If he'd a partner in a dress.

(This last bit figuratively means,
She could still wear a pair of jeans,
But back then in Jane Austen's day,
Women just did not dress that way.)

And every time Lyd of him spoke,
He was a really gorgeous bloke,
To her he really was a star –
The best man in the world by far.

One morning Lydia to Liz said,
"I did not tell you when we wed,
Just what went on upon that day,
So now I must to you it say."

"No, really," Liz said, "tattle-tittle,
On this can never be too little."
But nonetheless she went ahead,
And here's the gist of what she said.

"'Twas at St Clements we were wed,
Because, as I have not yet said,
Dear Wickham's lodgings were right there,
And vicar had some time to spare.

Well, Monday came, I dressed and preened,
My aunt talked endlessly it seemed,
I think she wanted me to hear,
A lecture that was quite severe,
But I just thought of Wickham then,
And barely heard one word in ten.

In fact, while I was with my aunt,
Her pleasantness was rather scant,
And she and uncle – what a dude –
To me were really rather rude.

They would not let me go outside,
Before I was a proper bride,
I think they thought I'd find a toff,
And then with him might bugger off.

Well, just as we were due to leave –
You will find this hard to believe –
Uncle went off then on his own,
To talk shop with a Mr Stone.

I was, at that point, worried sick,
That this might be some sort of trick,
For after noon, it's always said,
Nobody is allowed to wed.

My uncle would give me away,
A simple task, I have to say,
But I recalled if this transpired,
I'd still have married as desired,
For Mr Darcy, also there,
Might just have acted as a spare."

"Darcy!?" said Liz in state of shock,
Trying of this news to take stock.

"Oh yes, he was with Wickham and,
Would see dear Wickham take my hand.
But goodness me, I quite forgot,
That I had promised quite a lot,
To say nought of his presence there,
Though I don't know why he should care."

"Do not say more," said Jane in verse,
"It only can just make it worse."

"Of course," Liz added, I as well,
Will not ask what more you can tell."
Though she was desperate to know,
Why Darcy to the church did go.

Liz ran off then to take the stress,
Off her mind and to try to guess,
But though the girl did try and try,
She really couldn't work out why.

So on a sheet of paper blank,
She wrote to her aunt quick to thank
Her for the recent holiday,
And could she tell her, by the way,
Why Darcy in a suit of grey,
Was at her sister's wedding day?

"Please write as quickly as you can,
I am tormented by this man,
Unless it's too secret to know,
Which will just be a bitter blow."

"But my Dear Aunt," she thought, "if you,
Will not give an account that's true,
I must resort to tricks at last,
For I must really find out fast."

Chapter Fifty-two

Liz got a letter which was long,
And written in the English tongue,
She went and sat down in the wood,
Just hoping that it would be good.

She opened it, prepared to read,
This letter that was long indeed.

"Your letter came, it has been read,
So now I know what you have said,
I plan now to spend half the day,
   Replying to what you did say.

I am surprised, I must say, though,
That of this matter you don't know,
And uncle, too, concurs with me,
That you should know much more than he;
No matter, though, to ease your pain,
I will with pen and ink explain.

The day last week when I got back,
By coach – there is no railway track –
One Mr Darcy – you know he –
Had called quite unexpectedly.

EBENEZER BEAN

He said that he had found the pair,
That they were living round somewhere,
And he said, although not on oath,
He had been and talked to them both.

George Wickham he'd seen several times,
They had talked over gin and limes,
But Lydia he'd seen just one time –
She wasn't one for gin and lime.

Back when we were on holiday,
He'd left for London but one day,
After we had ourselves all quit,
And that's about the shape of it.

The reason he took on this task,
If you should venture now to ask,
Is 'cos he had kept quiet 'bout,
The fact that Wickham was a lout,
And consequently, you might say,
Girls might be taken in one day.

He therefore thinks he is to blame,
For all the dreadful, awful shame,
That's visited upon you all,
By actions of your sister small,
So now he wants to make amends,
Which is indeed what he intends.

He also has advantage too,
For Mrs Younge, unknown to you,
Had been dismissed – well, more or less –
As Georgiana's governess;
He said not why she had to go,
But maybe that bit you might know.

She took a large house after that,
Letting it out in rooms and flats,
And she knew Wickham, Mrs Younge,
So if Darcy gave her a bung,
He might get her to spill the beans,
By which phrase one generally means,
That she would tell him where to go,
In exchange for a pile of dough.

Address in hand, he then went round,
To where they had both gone to ground;
He talked to Wickham then the girl,
Whose head seemed to be in a whirl,
For his entreaties, based on fears,
Were simply falling on deaf ears.

He told her that she should return,
To family, now taciturn,
And he would help, she ought to know,
If back to them she would now go.

EBENEZER BEAN

But Lydia would have none of this,
She did entreaties all dismiss,
And though she would not him deceive,
She neither would George Wickham leave.

So Darcy now had to change tack,
He'd have liked to her bottom smack,
But smacking bottoms as you know,
Is not somewhere you want to go,
For everything is now PC,
So if you do this as might he,
You'll probably end up in court,
For now engaging in this sport.

But back then it was not the same,
Darcy's type would not take the blame,
So they would get away with it,
Including groping round the . . . leg.

Enough of this, let us resume,
The plan to end the Bennets' doom,
So Darcy now began Plan B,
Which was for them to marry, see.

This phrase sounds Welsh, I hope you know,
For sometimes I just have to go,
To the land of the pointed hat,
And use a phrase about like that.

RHYME AND PREJUDICE

It is a useful stock in phrase,
Designed my readers to amaze,
I have used it a lot of times,
Because it is a cinch to rhyme.

Despite emergence of Plan B,
Darcy could see quite clearly,
That Wickham's plan, it must be said,
Did not include that they be wed.

Darcy sought to investigate,
What was back then the going rate,
For Wickham to get out the red,
And get young Bennet into bed.

Wickham knew Bennet was not rich,
And he'd hoped for a better pitch,
With some far richer girl than this,
More easily to debts dismiss.

But here we have the bird in hand,
Who might come with about a grand,
Or possibly, if in no rush,
Proverbial two in the bush.

In time Darcy's approach prevailed,
Which meant of cash he was availed,
And such was how the thing was fixed,
An outcome, though, with blessings mixed.

EBENEZER BEAN

When all had been agreed at last,
Darcy went round to Gardiner fast,
But he discovered Bennet was,
Still there in Gracechurch Street because,
However much the man might moan,
He still had not set off back home.

He didn't want Bennet to see,
For he thought easier than he,
Would be the uncle who had sense,
In present, past and future tense.

So he did not then leave his name,
Went back the next day just the same,
And then he told him man to man,
About the meeting and his plan.

They met again over three days,
Debating who the money pays,
And in the end your uncle lost,
Which was not really to his cost,
For Darcy then paid all the cash,
To Wickham and his wife so brash.

But since this must quite secret be,
As then insisted on by he,
Your uncle would the credit gain,
Which doth upset him in the main.

RHYME AND PREJUDICE

So now you know the tale in full,
Though you may think it rather dull,
My husband now it will relieve,
For he does not like to deceive.

But from now on you must take care,
This information not to air,
I hope I do myself make plain,
But you can tell your sister Jane.

Elizabeth, I do suppose,
You know what he has done for those,
Delinquent people, both now wed,
And possibly right now in bed.

He cleared their debts and then some more,
With cash they didn't have before,
The reason I've already told,
Is Darcy wasn't very bold,
And he should Wickham have revealed,
Whereas instead he was concealed.

To think that he should take the blame,
Is probably a crying shame,
Because the couple's blatant gall,
Is really not his fault at all.

EBENEZER BEAN

Uncle would not have let him pay,
On this or any other day,
If he'd not thought that you and he,
Perhaps one day would married be.

And finally, I have to say,
He came back on their wedding day,
To check that they had tied the knot,
And see that his cheque did not blot.

Before they wed the two lived here,
Wickham polite but, Lizzie Dear,
Your sister was so bad and rude,
And has a dreadful attitude.

I lectured her both night and day,
But I could tell that by the way
She acted all the time I spoke,
She thought it was a great big joke.

Most times she ignored what I said,
Which really did make me see red,
I could have clipped her round the ear,
But then I thought of you, My Dear,
And since you are so kind and gentle,
I just pretended she was mental.

RHYME AND PREJUDICE

Darcy returned as you now know,
So to the wedding he could go,
And I will say if you don't mind,
That, really, he is rather kind.

I like him I just have to say,
He dined with us the next Wednesday,
He's quite all right I clearly see,
But could more animated be.

So sort this out he needs a wife,
To share the last half of his life,
And if he chuses well with care,
He'll have a much more lively air.

I'd like to visit Pemberley,
And hope that neither you nor he,
Will stop me going round the hall,
So that I might just see it all.

Oh damn and drat! The kids now cry,
Did I say Darcy did seem sly?
Perhaps today that is the mode,
Oh hell! The boy's now caught a toad!"

Liz really knew not what to make,
Of all this that her aunty spake,
She wondered why Darcy had paid,
And for himself such trouble made.

He'd had to meet folk very low,
And in the final bit to go,
And bribe a man he couldn't stand,
To take her flighty sister's hand.

It was clear that he must despise,
The girl for whom Wickham had eyes,
And from all this Liz did infer,
Perhaps he'd done it all for her.

But as she thought now more and more,
He would be Wickham's brother-in-law,
And though he was of great renown,
She recalled she had turned him down.

Oh how much she to Darcy owed!
As can now be expressed in ode,
And she regretted nasty rhymes,
That she had uttered several times.

Of his behaviour she was proud,
Would like to sing his praises loud,
For all these noble things he'd done,
Not for himself but everyone.

RHYME AND PREJUDICE

At this point Wickham came in view,
Said, "Hello, Sister, how are you?
I do not wish to be abrupt,
But think that I might interrupt,
Your loneliness and solitude,
Please do forgive if I am rude."

"Of course," Elizabeth replied,
"Tell, are the others still inside?"

"My wife has gone out with her mum,
To Meryton, that's going some;
I don't know why they've gone today,
Perhaps they have some bills to pay.

Your uncle and your aunt tell me,
That you have been to Pemberley,
I could go back myself you see,
But it might be too much for me.

And did you the housekeeper see?
I don't expect she mentioned me,
Although she was on me quite keen,
When I was small and also teen."

"I can assure you that she did,
Said you had in the army hid,
And though she really would not tell,
Thought it had not worked out too well."

Liz thought he might shut up at last,
For dragging up George Wickham's past,
Would not be what he'd want to do,
Well, you would not like it would you?

But then George Wickham with a frown,
Said, "I saw Darcy when in town;
Although I really couldn't care,
I wonder what he wanted there."

"Perhaps," said Liz, "he might prepare,
For marriage to the Rosings' heir;
Did you not him at Lambton see?
That's what the Gardiners told me."

"Why, yes he did, he introduced,
His sister whom I once seduced;
I have heard she is much improved,
Compared to when I last her viewed;
That I like her there is no doubt,
And hope that well she will turn out.

Tell me did you to Kympton go?
For I'll tell you if you don't know,
That there should I a parson be,
Complete with first-class rectory."

RHYME AND PREJUDICE

"If you had but a parson been,
You'd always on Sundays be seen,
Preaching a sermon to your sheep,
Except for those who've gone to sleep;
I wonder if you'd like to do,
Things like that expected of you?"

"Fantastic! I would do it well,
With lots of brimstone down in hell;
Just frighten them, that's what I say,
So they'll be in church every day;
But, as you know, 'twas not to be,
Because of our rich friend Darcy."

"I heard on authority good,
The living was bequeathed with 'would',
So someone still had to agree,
The living should still go to thee."

"That's sort of true, this fact I cursed,
I think I told you from the first."

"And, too, I heard another thing,
That when you heard the church bells ring,
You vowed that you would never take,
The orders of which you just spake."

"I also told you that before,"
Said Wickham as they reached the door.

"Come, come Sir, we are siblings now,
We shouldn't quarrel anyhow,
For I hope that we will now find,
The two of us are of one mind."

Chapter Fifty-three

Well, in a few days it was time,
As I shall tell you now in rhyme,
That Wickham with his wife in tow,
   To Newcastle was due to go.

And Mr Bennet had been pressed,
By Mrs B, by now distressed,
To follow thither so they could,
Spend time with them which would be good.

But Bennet would hear none of this,
His wife's entreaties did dismiss,
   So Mrs Bennet was resigned,
   To separation so she pined.

"Oh Lydia," she said in pain,
"Just when might we two meet again?"

"Oh Mother, I don't really know,
When I to Newcastle must go."

"Do write to me, express your views,
For I'd so like to hear your news."

"I'll write as often as I can,
But now that I have got a man,
I really won't have time to do,
The writing that I now ought to.

But tell those lazy siblings that,
They should write words on paper flat,
And they can write oft it is true,
For they have nothing else to do."

If you think these last lines are bad,
You're likely right because I had,
No inspiration at this time,
Owing to lack of beer and wine.

But now the drink doth flow again,
To lubricate my mind and brain;
I'm sure the next bit you will clap,
'Cos it will not be total crap.

The two set off, Wickham contrite,
And as always very polite.
"He is," said Bennet, "so polite,
And always tries to say things right.
I am so proud, of him in awe,
For he's a right good son-in-law."

RHYME AND PREJUDICE

Bennet, it seems, had changed his tune,
About his youngest daughter's groom,
But maybe he'd been taken in,
By Wickham's silver tongue and spin.

For several days her mum was glum,
Which really made her pretty schtum,
This was almost beyond belief,
And was something of a relief.

"I often think," said she, "to part,
With friends or even one's own tart,
Is very bad, I have to say,
I wish it wasn't just this way."

"This is a consequence," said Liz,
"Of the fact that your daughter is,
Just wedded and has now jumped ship,
Or in a civil partnership.
You must be pretty pleased to see,
Your other girls still single be."

"It's no such thing," her mother cried,
"It's not because she's been a bride;
It is, as you know very well,
'Cos Wickham works in Newcassel*."
 * local dialect – or something

But very soon the news improved,
For word came, Bingley had removed,
From his expensive London pad,
Back to the local one he had,
When he'd lived there not long ago,
And sometimes there did parties throw.

This was good news for Mrs B,
Another match she'd like to see,
But she had really to pretend,
That she no longer did intend,
Pursuing him for daughter one,
Now that the little one was gone.

Ms Phillips first brought her the news,
While sharing some new facts and views,
And what with all she said that night,
You'd think her head might not be right.

"So much the better, I don't care,
He's not important, I won't stare;
I don't want to see him again,
But if he comes here in the rain,
He's very welcome in the main,
But no use to my daughter Jane.

It's possible they'll fall in love,
But I will not my daughter shove,
In his direction, we agreed,
We would not mention him indeed.
But are you certain, Sister Dear,
That he is coming back to here?"

Her sister said, "There is no doubt.
Last night at eight when I was out,
I met Ms Nicholls who told me,
That he was coming def'nitely.

The housekeeper's been buying meat,
So visitors can have a treat,
And she has got six ducks to kill,
So Bennet's guests can have their fill."

At this news Jane went white or pink,
Jane Austen doesn't say, I think,
And she said, "Liz, I need a rest,
For when I heard I was distressed;
But in fact I was just confused,
As all this through my mind diffused.

I can assure you, Dearest Liz,
That I do not care where he is,
If he goes then it is no loss,
Because I couldn't give a toss."

EBENEZER BEAN

Liz knew not what to make of this,
Her sister did Bingley dismiss,
For back at Pemberley 'twas plain,
He was quite fond of sister Jane.

While waiting for him to appear,
Liz thought Jane looked a trifle queer,
For her mind was so much distressed –
She was in love, you might have guessed.

"When Bingley comes," said Mrs B,
"You will go round, perhaps take tea."

"That I will not, I did before,"
Said Bennet, "I'll not do it more.
Last time I'm pretty sure you said,
If I saw him the man would wed
One of our daughters in a tick,
No matter two of them are thick.

So I will not do this again,
It would be foolish in the main,
If he wants to with us converse,
He'll have to come and find us first."

His wife replied, "That's very rude,
So I will offer him some food;
I am determined he will dine,
So make sure you have got some wine."

RHYME AND PREJUDICE

So Mrs B was all at sea,
Her husbands incivility,
Might mean others saw Bingley first,
Which made the woman fear the worst.

The day rolled on, the time drew near,
Jane said, "I am afraid, I fear,
I'll talk to him as Austen wrote,
But then what really gets my goat,
Is people talking endlessly,
Of my relationship with he.

And the worst culprit, I must say,
Who blethers each and every day,
Is mother who, though she means well,
Has made my life a living hell."

"I'd comfort you now at this hour,
But such is now without my power,
I could just say 'Keep calm today',
But that's what you do anyway."

Quite soon Charles Bingley did arrive,
And Mrs B did so contrive,
To learn of this without delay,
So she could plan respects to pay.

She counted, therefore, up the days,
Which must elapse before her gaze,
Could settle on the Bingley man,
For secretly she was a fan.

And with her husband, Idle Jim,
There was no chance of seeing him
Sooner than this, I have to say,
There wasn't any other way.

In spite of this, three days went by,
Then from the corner of her eye,
She saw said gent upon a horse,
And riding up to have discourse.

Apart from Jane who stayed sat down,
Which made her mother curse and frown,
The other girls the glass looked through,
And Kitty said, "A-ha, look you!
There is a man with him, Mama,
I can't quite see him from this far;
We may perhaps need some more tea,
Do you know who this man could be?"

"A friend of Bingley's I dare say,
But I'm sure that he will not stay,
And as to who it is, it's true,
I really do not have a clue.

Well, at this point, Kitty recalled,
She'd seen this man so dark and tall,
And she recalled he'd lots of pride,
And a great deal of cash beside.

"Well fancy that," mother replied,
Thinking perhaps she might have lied,
"'Tis Mr Darcy, it is he,
And as a friend of Charles Bingley,
He will be welcome to come in,
Though I can't stand the sight of him."

Now Jane was certain she could see,
Her sister might embarrassed be,
For all she knew, though never dim,
Was Lizzy had rejected him.

But Lizzy knew far more than her,
To him they all indebted were,
And also she was rather keen –
I'm sure you will know what I mean.

She hoped that Darcy wouldn't mind,
Her family had been a bind,
And surely this visit must mean,
That on her Darcy was still keen.

She thought this but could not be sure,
He might, like formerly, be dour,
So she said, "Let's see how it goes,
Though what he might say goodness knows."

She turned back to the task in hand,
Embroidery she could not stand,
And when the servant showed them in,
The conversation was quite thin.

But though words might be rather light,
All that was said was so polite,
Except, that is, for Mrs B,
Whose cold, polite civility,
To these, the latest of her guests,
Was hardly welcoming at best.

Liz was distressed by this approach,
But could not her mother reproach,
Knowing that Lydia's future was,
Secure now and only because,
Darcy had found her and had paid,
To have her reputation made*.
* Re-made actually

Darcy enquired after her aunt,
But after that his words were scant;
He sat there looking at the floor,
As if he'd not seen one before.

RHYME AND PREJUDICE

Liz wanted speech with him today,
But couldn't think quite what to say;
She asked about his sister but,
Thereafter kept her gob tight shut.

So now it fell to Mrs B,
To keep the talking going, see,
And both the sisters cringed as they,
Wondered what the old bat might say.

"It seems a long time, Mr B,
Since you went – should I best say flee?"

"What you have said is quite correct,
Due doubtless to your intellect."

"I was afraid you'd gone for good,
Since you my daughter up have stood,
A lot has happened in that time,
So listen to my list in rhyme.

Miss Lucas, though she is quite plain,
Has married someone not quite sane,
And one of my girls has now wed –
The notice in the paper said.

EBENEZER BEAN

It was a notice rather terse,
Although I have seen even worse,
My brother Gardiner chose the words –
Sometimes he can be quite absurd."

Bingley said that he had it read,
One night when going off to bed,
And he spoke to congratulate,
The daughter Bennet and her mate.

Lizzy dared not lift up her eyes,
And so her brain could not devise,
How Darcy looked upon this news,
And what, perhaps, might be his views.

But still her mother carried on,
Lizzy now wishing she were gone,
"It is delightful, Mr B,
To have a daughter married, see,
But she has gone up north, that's far
From where at this point we all are.

He's joined the army, that's all new,
Has some friends but perhaps quite few,
He should have more, though mostly male,
But that is quite another tale."

RHYME AND PREJUDICE

This slight on Darcy made Liz mad,
For it was shameful and so bad,
So she asked Bingley if he would,
Stay here a short time or for good.

"I will stay for a few weeks more,
But who knows really what's in store?"

"I hope when you your birds have shot,
You'll come and start on Bennet's lot,
They squawk like mad, they make a mess,
And cause to me untold distress;
So come on round and shift a few,
That's what you really ought to do."

Liz thought this right over the top,
Was willing for her mum to stop,
"I wish," she thought, "I'll never see,
These two men whose names rhyme with lee.

It's so embarrassing to hear,
The crap my mother spouts round here,
And nothing really can atone,
For these words from her head of bone."

But very soon Lizzy observed,
How Bingley, seeming undeterred,
Was chatting to Jane more and more,
And certainly more than before.

The gentlemen then rose to leave,
And Mrs Bennet did perceive,
That she should invite them to dine,
A few days later, after nine.

She had thought to ask them to stay,
So that they could all eat today,
But if she put them off some days,
Her table really could amaze
The one who might still marry Jane,
The other with wealth to his name.

Chapter Fifty-four

Liz wondered why Darcy had come,
To sit around just looking glum,
He could still very pleasant be,
To her uncle if not to she.

I really don't know if he cares,
While mostly at the floor he stares,
His liking of me must be dim,
So I will think no more of him.

As she was thinking, Jane appeared,
And as she her young sister neared,
She said, "The meeting went quite well,
Bingley's polite as one can tell,
But we are just indifferent friends,
Discussing all the latest trends."

"Oh yes, Dear Jane, you should take care,
He's looking for a girl that's spare,
And it is clear to more than few,
The one he really wants is you."

Next Tuesday's dinner date arrived,
And Mrs Bennet had contrived,
That Bingley next to Jane should sit,
So that they could get on with it.

EBENEZER BEAN

Liz watched the two throughout the meal,
And by the end of it did feel,
That just as mother had procured,
Their life together was assured.

Darcy, however, far from she,
Was seated as far as could be
From her, but next to on one side,
Mother of the intended bride.

Liz could not hear what those two said,
But sat there thinking in great dread,
That though she owed the man a debt,
He mother was still scheming yet,
To make sure he did not enjoy,
Things as much as the other boy.

Liz hoped that they would get to speak,
That they'd not have to wait a week,
So when the men-folk all returned,
She hoped advantage could be turned,
And maybe he would sit with her,
No matter it might cause a stir.

But Lizzy had to pour the tea,
No chair next to her then for he,
So Darcy stood across the room,
Drinking his tea in silent gloom.

RHYME AND PREJUDICE

His cup now empty, he came back
To Liz, but ... Oh! alas alack,
She asked but one question that day,
Then could not think of more to say,
Knowing if she was so tongue-tied,
That she would never make a bride.

Darcy by her in silence stood,
He knew his small-talk was no good,
And after mins with nought to say,
He just turned round and walked away.

The servants came, the tea things went,
And folk knew how evenings were spent,
So card tables in there were placed,
For packs with queen and king and ace.

Liz hoped Darcy with her might sit,
But mother would not hear of it,
And she took Darcy right away,
So at whist he could with her play.

So Liz now had to give up hope,
Sit and stare at the cards and mope,
And she hoped, though she couldn't tell,
He wasn't playing whist too well.

Her final chance, when cards were o'er,
Was also a disaster for,
A late night over supper chat,
Was destined also to fall flat,
For Darcy's carriage came too soon,
At which the two gents left the room.

"Well now," said Mrs Bennet when
The gents had gone by half past ten,
"I think it went off to a T,
And you should all be proud of me.

The dinner was well-dressed by jove,
Far better than last Tuesday, Shrove,
The venison was pretty good,
And cooked just right as so it should.

Then there's the soup cooked in the pan,
Not like Lucas served from a can,
And Darcy did himself remark,
The partridge we got from the park,
Was well done and well-liked by he,
And he has French cooks – two or three.

And Jane, you looked so pretty for,
This I asked Mrs Long before;
She is a good sort, Mrs Long,
Has nieces who all mind their tongue,
And I like them, their chests are flat,
And none are quite worth looking at.

Over the moon was Mrs B,
A wedding coming she could see,
But sister Jane would not accept,
That Bingley an ambition kept,
To marry her, that's Jane, post-haste,
So that she would not go to waste.

Chapter Fifty-five

Some days went by, Bingley returned,
And consequently Lizzy learned,
That Darcy had to London gone,
Hence here was Bingley – just the one.

He sat and talked at least an hour,
His attitude was far from dour,
And Mrs B, not losing time,
Invited him that day to dine.

"I really would so like to come,
And I must now thank Jane's old mum,
But, sadly, I am due elsewhere,
Not good because Jane won't be there.

But if another day will do,
I will still come and dine with you,
Tomorrow might be a good date,
I've nothing on so won't be late."

Well, next day Bingley came too soon,
The girls were in their powder room,
And Mrs B who was half-dressed,
Was really getting pretty stressed.

RHYME AND PREJUDICE

"Jane, hurry up and get down there!
To keep him waiting isn't fair,
You met him first back at the dance,
So do not now throw up your chance.

Here, Sarah, where is Jane's new gown?
The one we bought last week in town;
Don't worry about Lizzy's hair,
It's Jane that we must get in there."

"We will come when we are both dressed,
In brand-new gown and Sunday best;
Although it might just be a hoot,
I'll not come in my birthday suit.

But Kitty's probably ahead,
Because, as I have not yet said,
At dressing she is still the queen,
And has upstairs for ages been."

"For Kitty I don't give a toss,
If you're not quick 'twill be your loss,
Downstairs you really must now dash,
And now where is your bloody sash!?"

But Jane now scuppered mother's plans,
To get towards the wedding banns,
No matter how much she might moan,
She wouldn't go down on her own.

So after tea mum tried again,
To get Bingley alone with Jane;
Bennet soon to his library went,
So easing his wife's good intent.

And Mary who was pretty dull,
Not interested in all this bull,
Went off to play her harpsichord –,
Her method of not getting bored.

Two obstacles now thus removed,
The other two much harder proved,
So mother winked at them enough,
To tell them both to bugger off.

Whether by ignorance or design,
The two refused to see the sign,
And in the end young Catherine spoke,
"Is this some oddball kind of joke?
You can't stop winking at we two,
What is it we're supposed to do?"

"Why nothing, Child, I didn't wink.
You're much mistaken so I think,"

RHYME AND PREJUDICE

Five minutes passed, mum said, "My Dear,
I really want you out of here."
Then when she went she called back in,
"Lizzy don't you dare stay within!
I want to speak with you somehow,
Get off your arse and come here now!"

Catherine and mother went upstairs,
Apparently quite unawares,
That after she had gone away,
Liz went back in with Jane to stay.

So mother's scheme did fail that night,
Bingley was charming and polite,
But, really, he had little hope,
Of any snog or maybe grope.

He was, however, very keen,
To be next day back on the scene,
With Mr B to shoot some birds,
As I can tell you in these words.

Liz now concluded Jane was keen
On Bingley, he'd stopped being mean,
And likely Darcy had agreed,
That these two should be wed indeed.

Next morning Bingley came on cue,
The partridges to scare and shoo,
Bennet thought he was rather nice,
And might go shooting with him twice.

The shooting done, 'twas time to eat,
And Charles again the five did meet,
And Mrs Bennet, as you know,
Wanted all but just one to go.

Liz went off to a letter write,
Thinking that the plan for the night,
Was cards, now starting after tea,
So as for Jane and Charles Bingley,
To get them on their own I guess,
Mother would not have much success.

Imagine, then, her sense of shock,
When she returned at six o'clock,
Of letter writing having tired,
And saw them standing by the fire.

The two stepped back, they went bright pink,
None of the three dared speak, I think;
Then Bingley to Jane whispered words,
Too quiet to be overheard,
And as if with no time to waste,
He turned round and rushed out in haste.

Jane ran to Lizzy and embraced,
As if her drink had just been laced,
"I am as happy as can be!
Why're others not as glad as me?"

"Bingley is seeing father now,
For him to bless our marriage vow,
So I must off and tell my mum,
No more again will she be glum."

Liz said that she was very pleased,
Her sister's worry had been eased,
And then Jane hastened up the stairs,
To wipe away her mother's cares,
By telling her her latest views,
Which she'd interpret as good news.

So Liz, alone, said, "This is good,
It's ended like a story should.
Despite his sister, Carol's, lies,
Bingley has, in the end, been wise."

At this point Bingley came back in,
Perhaps a bit the worse for gin,
"Where is your sister?" he enquired,
To marry her he now aspired.

"She is upstairs," Liz then replied,
"Telling her mum and more beside.
She is allaying mother's fears,
And likely she'll be down in tears."

While waiting, Bingley shut the door,
And said that he had done so for,
He'd like Liz to congratulate
Him on his new and happy state.

Liz said, "Well done," she happy was,
She knew this was good news because,
He and Jane were both pretty cool,
And that was helpful as a rule.

The meal that night was happy time,
Not beer to drink but lots of wine;
Catherine hoped that she might be next,
And Mrs B was far from vexed.

When Bingley had taken his leave,
Bennet wiped his nose on his sleeve,
And said, "Congratulations Dear,
I really, truly have no fear,
That you will very happy be,
For you have a good catch in he.

RHYME AND PREJUDICE

Your tempers are so much the same,
You won't decide things in the main,
You're easy-going, folk will cheat,
Including that man selling meat.
And though you have no streak of greed,
Your income you might well exceed."

"'Twill not be so, I hope to God,
Some folk think I am a tight wad."

His wife chirped up, "This cannot be.
He's on five thousand quid you see."
And then she carried on and on,
And on and on and on and on,
Extolling virtues of them both,
Now that they soon might plight their troth.

Jane's sisters were soon on the scrounge,
While seated with her in the lounge,
Mary would like to borrow books,
Because she hadn't much in looks,
While Catherine said that ball was nice,
She'd like to go another twice.

From now on Bingley came each day,
With more than just respects to pay,
They sat and talked without a break,
Until they both had earache.

EBENEZER BEAN

Jane said, "He really didn't know,
That I to London town did go."

"Then how could he this bit explain?
It seems unlikely in the main."

"It has to be, I would opine,
That sister of his, Caroline;
She really is a dreadful bitch,
Will all the time just moan and snitch,
But if she now good wishes sends,
That might just partly make amends."

"Well said," said Liz. "Just you beware,
Of Caroline Bitch Bingley there;
This wedding will her disappoint,
And put her nose right out of joint."

"Oh happy, happy, happy me!
Singled out from my family.
I hope quite soon that you will find,
A man who's just as good as mine."

"Even with forty men like yours,
I'd not be so happy because,
My disposition's not as good
As yours is, though I know it should.
But maybe my luck will turn yet,
And I'll a Mr Collins get!"

RHYME AND PREJUDICE

The news of this soon got around,
For folk had their ears to the ground;
With Wickham B's had come unstuck,
But now they just had all the luck.

Chapter Fifty-six

A week went by, Bingley was sat,
At Longbourn with four girls and cat,
When their attention was then drawn,
To a coach coming 'cross the lawn.

It was indeed a chaise and four,
No-one had seen the thing before,
And visitors should not arrive
So early – it was ten-o-five.

Bingley said, "Oh well, damn and drat!
I hadn't bargained quite for that.
If we're still here when they come in,
Our snogging will be rather thin.

So let us quickly up and go,
Down to the shrubbery and so,
We will there doubtless take our ease,
And do exactly as we please."

So off they went, the others stayed,
And of their guest conjecture made,
Until the door flew open and,
There in the doorway, very grand,
The person from the chaise and four,
Was Lady Catherine from before.

Her entrance did not show much tact,
The three girls were all so gobsmacked;
She swept right in, nobody spoke,
The floor on which she stood was oak,
She entered with ungracious air,
And quickly sat down in a chair.

She really didn't speak at first,
But one might expect an outburst,
And Mrs Bennet, though uptight,
To her was really quite polite.

She sat a moment then she said,
"Miss Bennet I hope you're not dead.
And that lady in skirts and hose,
Will be your mother, I suppose."

"She is indeed," then Liz replied,
"You'll often find her here inside."

"And that!" she said, "there by the door,
Must be your sister, one of four."

"Why, yes indeed," said Mrs B,
"She is next to the youngest, see.
My youngest recently got wed,
To someone not by name of Fred.

And Jane, whom you perhaps don't know,
Now has a lover on the go,
Who pretty soon I think will be,
A member of our family."

Then Lady Catherine looked around,
At first she didn't make a sound,
But then she made just one remark –
That Bennets had a smallish park.

"With Rosings it may not compare,
But one can sit and take the air;
The Lucases who are quite tall,
Have got one which is *very* small."

"This sitting room looks bad to me,
The windows all face westerly."

"They do but then it matters not,
For we don't sit here when it's hot;
But tell me, Lady Catherine, pray,
How are the Collinses today?"

"Yes, very well, I have to say,
I saw them just the other day."

RHYME AND PREJUDICE

"I beg of you," said Mrs B,
"To take some coffee, maybe tea
With us, for sleep you may have lacked,
And might now be completely whacked."

But her entreaties were in vain,
For Lady Catherine, such a pain,
Refused to take the drink or food,
And her refusal was quite rude.

The woman now turned round to Liz,
"I noticed, when I came, there is,
A wilderness beyond the ground,
Where we might take a turn around."

"Well, off you go," her mother said,
"And for the ducks here is some bread."

So Liz now ran upstairs and got,
Her parasol for it was hot,
And then guided her noble guest,
Outside and down towards the west.

They passed her carriage where there sat,
Her waiting woman who was fat,
And Liz decided that she would,
Not converse with her as she should,
For she seemed to be in a mood,
And had just been extremely rude.

So as they embarked on their walk,
The lady thus began to talk,
"Miss Bennet, you must surely know,
Why out of my way I did go,
To journey hither you to meet,
And come by carriage, not by feet."

Liz really could not so surmise,
And stared then in complete surprise,
"Indeed mistaken here are you,
Because I haven't got a clue."

"Miss Bennet," she then said forthwith,
"I am not to be trifled with.
And though you might take this approach,
My character's beyond reproach,
And you will find like others do,
That I'm frank when I talk to you.

It's been reported back to me,
Your sister'll soon marry Bingley;
An advantageous match, I think,
Not like Lydia who caused a stink.

And you, Miss Bennet, now I find,
As if you thought I wouldn't mind,
Might be betrothed, if this be true,
To Darcy – that is my nephew.

RHYME AND PREJUDICE

I know this cannot be the case,
But I have still come round this place,
And just declined your mother's brew,
To make my views now known to you."

"If so sure of this thing you are,
I wonder that you've come so far;
To travel here you were not bid,
And so I wonder why you did."

"You should see if you are not thick,
That I think this is just a trick;
And so I must right now insist,
That of this thing you will desist."

"Your coming here," said Liz, "by strewth,
Suggests the story has some truth;
The content seems to you appall,
That is if it exists at all."

"If," (continuing to rave and rant)
"Of this are you quite ignorant,
Why have you and your family,
Been giving copy out for free?"

"I never heard that this was so,
And don't think we would stoop so low."

"And can you then likewise declare,
That you and he won't make a pair?"

"These questions that you do now pose,
Are of a type including those,
Which you may for an answer try,
But, actually, I won't reply."

"I cannot bear this, it's too bad,
Tell me if you've an offer had,
Of marriage from nephew Darcy,
And if you have replied to he?"

"You have just said, you silly cow,
This is impossible right now."

"So should it be but with your wiles,
Your allure and those sultry smiles,
And with your lips which always pout,
You might have driven reason out,
And thus infected Darcy's brain,
When normally he is quite sane."

"Well, if I have, I will not say,
So you will not learn more today."

"Miss Bennet, do not take the piss,
I've never been addressed like this;
He's close to me, relation-wise,
So what goes on behind his eyes,
Is my concern as well as his,
Just heed me for that's how it is!"

"Thus you may think but I don't care,
My business I chuse not to air,
Is none of yours and since you're rude,
I will maintain my solitude."

The woman said, "Now get this right!
I am now spoiling for a fight!
No matter what is done or said,
My nephew never will you wed!

For to my daughter he's engaged,
Which is why I am so enraged,
So having now heard this today,
Go on, now, what have you to say?"

"Just this. If what you say is true,
Then it should be quite plain to you,
That since he'd be no longer free,
An offer he'd not make to me."

She paused now as a crack appeared,
Away from certainty she veered,
"The situation is," she said,
"That right from in the cradle bed,
His mother and I did agree,
The pair of them would married be.
And this plan should not scuppered be,
By his proposal now to thee."

"That's just tough sh*t," Eliza said,
"That to the altar you've them led.
You have been working to a score,
And really can now do no more.

For he his mind must up now make,
And figure out which bride to take,
And if he should decide on me,
Then I would be his bride-to-be;
I might be inclined to accept,
Although your plans might then be wrecked."

"If you act thus, among his friends,
You'll never, ever make amends,
And it is my avowed intent,
You will to Coventry be sent."

RHYME AND PREJUDICE

"This sounds quite bad," then Liz replied,
"Almost as if I had just died.
But as his wife let me observe,
I surely will not lose my nerve,
For I would very happy be,
With benefits attached to he."

"Let's just sit down, I came today,
Not to be talked to in this way.
When I profess something in prose,
Let me assure you that's what goes."

"As I said, your plans might be wrecked,
But on me it has no effect."

"Just shut your gob and don't be dense,
I will be heard here in silence.
The two of them are both first-grade,
And for the other have been made;
Their families are stinking rich,
So you must not dare queer the pitch.

For you've not status, neither cash,
And really are just so much trash;
You really ought to want to stay,
With people that you know today."

"My father is," the girl replied,
"A gentleman and more beside.
And Darcy similar must be,
So I am equal now to he."

"Your mother's line, though, is just pants,
And what about uncles and aunts?"

"If Darcy doesn't mind its true,
It surely matters not to you."

"Just tell me now," she said enraged,
"Are you and he right now engaged?"

"No we are not," Lizzy replied,
"And on this point I have not lied."

"And promise if you're asked by he,
That you will not with him so be."

"I will not," Lizzy said out loud,
No longer by this lady cowed.

"Miss Bennet, I am shocked indeed,
On this point I will not concede;
Until you speak and answer 'No',
I'll stay right here and will not go."

RHYME AND PREJUDICE

"Then you'll be here a long long time,
For as I will now say in rhyme,
If I agreed, I don't think he,
Would want your girl in place of me.

Your arguments are all to pot,
What Darcy thinks I do know not,
But this is really my affair,
And I don't want you poking there."

"Now not so hasty, if you please,
I am, as you know, a big cheese,
And I must have a master stroke,
Allowing me to go for broke.

I know about your sister who,
Has just eloped like harlots do,
And you must know as well as me,
She cannot be sister of he."

"You can now have no more to say,
You have insulted me today,
And surely have ended your grouse,
So we must go back to the house."

They set off back towards the place,
She said, "It really will disgrace,
The name of Pemberley if he,
Associates himself with thee."

EBENEZER BEAN

"I really have no more to say,
I've finished talking for today."

"You are resolved, then, to have him,
And so to act against my whim?"

"I have, in fact, said no such thing,
But if he should give me a ring,
I will decide just what to do,
Without again recourse to you."

You might think all this pretty dull,
Catherine's entreaties very full,
In fact she still went on some more,
And I fear that they might you bore.

So as now on and on she whines,
I think I'll miss out a few lines,
It might put noses out of joint,
But one should just get to the point.

"Miss B, you do not as you ought,
So your plans I will surely thwart,
Of you I will now take my leave,
For I am seriously displeased."
So saying, she got in the door
Of her fine carriage from before.

RHYME AND PREJUDICE

As Catherine's carriage disappeared,
Liz turned and the house entrance neared,
To be accosted by her mum,
Who was indeed exceeding glum,
And wanted to know why her guest,
Would not now come back in and rest.

"She chose to go," then Liz replied,
"And so did not come back inside."

"She's a fine lady," said her mum,
"Has lots of money and then some;
She came, I suppose, for to tell
Us that the Collinses were well,
And probably while here today,
She didn't have much more to say?"

Liz mumbled something, sort of 'aye',
Revealing not it was a lie,
For she could never really say,
What Lady C had said today.

Chapter Fifty-seven

Liz now found this a real bind,
Could not get it out of her mind,
And Lady Catherine, it seemed had,
Made a long journey, sometimes bad,
For the sole purpose to break off,
Her s'posed engagement to a toff.

She could not work out how she knew,
Of what they only *might* still do,
But then she recollected he,
Was the best friend of Charles Bingley.

And she the sister of his tart,
So people who were very smart,
Knowing of one wedding to come,
Perhaps would wish another one.

The Lucases were suspects prime,
Because in speaking out of rhyme,
They were inclined to be quite bold,
And likely they had Collins told.

And you can bet that in a flash,
To Rosings this rector would dash,
And to his patron spill the beans,
Most likely using verbal means.

RHYME AND PREJUDICE

This Chinese whisper likely was,
Exaggerated then because,
Most folk like weddings as you do,
So if one then why not have two?

But Lizzy now had got an itch,
That Catherine might just queer the pitch,
By entreaty to her nephew,
That wedding her he should not do.

She didn't know what he would say,
If accosted by her this way,
But likely he'd have sympathy,
For arguments proposed by she,
That she to him was far beneath,
By distance quite beyond belief.

And if Darcy was none too sure,
His resolution might he fewer,
And if so, then she'd lost the plot,
And probably would see him not.

(If you think 'fewer' seems not right,
And I'm in error here tonight,
I've put the word in, you might guess,
'Cos 'sure' doesn't rhyme with 'less'.

And I feel in the English tongue,
When people speak in words or song,
They get their diction in a mess,
And meaning 'fewer', they say 'less'.

But now that you this guff have read,
It's back to what Jane Austen said.)

"So if," said Liz, "he makes excuse,
To help avoid him turning puce,
I'll understand his reasons and,
Know he no longer wants my hand.

He could have had me in true love,
Symbolised by the turtle dove,
But if he gives me up like this,
All thoughts of him I will dismiss."

Next morning, as she went downstairs,
Her father caught her unawares,
And bid her come into his room,
And shift her arse and do it soon.

He had a letter in his hand,
Sent from some place within the land,
And she thought that, with sinking heart,
It must have come from that old fart,
Who lives at Rosings, one of two,
And was the sort of thing she'd do.

RHYME AND PREJUDICE

They went inside, they both sat down,
She knew not whether she should frown,
And then he said, "This letter came,
And though addressed to me by name,
Of pages it comprises two,
And most of it doth concern you.

That I've a daughter soon to wed,
I know because it has been said,
But I knew not there might be two –
It seems the second must be you."

Liz thought now that this letter must,
Be treated by her with disgust,
For he should really ask her first,
About 'for better or for worse'.

Her father now read with his eyes,
Something which gave her great surprise,
And told her the letter was writ,
By Mr Collins, stupid twit.

"From Mr Collins?" tell me pray,
"Whatever can he have to say?"

EBENEZER BEAN

"He starts off to congratulate
Me on your sister, Jane's, new state,
And then he rambles on a bit,
Through which you do not have to sit;
I do not want to disappoint,
So now I'll get right to the point."

"Your second daughter, Bennet, may,
Perhaps be single still today,
But very soon it's rumoured that,
She'll be wed in a few weeks flat.

This man whose hand she may desire,
Is rich and could not be much higher,
But let me warn my cousin Liz,
That although he attractive is,
There are evils she may incur,
If she does not this match defer."

"So Lizzy, tell me if you know,
Who this is – is he friend or foe?
He clearly is not a lout,
But ... A-ha! now see, his name comes out."

"For we're given to understand,
That his aunt, lady of this land,
Looks on the knot that she may tie,
With a not very friendly eye."

RHYME AND PREJUDICE

At this point dad said "It's absurd,
That he should write like this these words;
Darcy would not behave like this,
So he, I think, doth take the piss."

Her father now continued on,
Until all Collins' words were gone,

"I told her ladyship last night,
At which she nearly had a fright,
And said she never would agree,
To this match between she and he.

I therefore thought I had to write,
About all this to you tonight,
So my cousin can think again,
And avoid lots of dreadful pain.

And finally, another point,
Which has put my nose out of joint,
I'm pleased that for your daughter five,
You have been able to contrive,
To hush up what she's doubtless done,
While out with Wickham on the run.

Nevertheless I have concern,
That people generally could learn,
That ere the marriage banns were read,
They likely were shacked up in bed.

Imagine, then, when I did hear,
That you let them back into here,
It wasn't really very nice,
And just goes to encourage vice.

If I had been the rector here,
I'd have objected never fear;
You should forgive them as one should,
For being naughty, that's not good,
But banish them you surely should,
Because they're bad which means not good."

"So much," said Bennet, "for his view,
On Christian forgiveness too.
Oh this is really so absurd,
We must just laugh at every word.

The silliness is plain to see,
I'm sure, Lizzy, you will agree."

"It seems so strange, I do concur,
No sense from it can I infer."

"To Collins I may write again,
And hope to enjoy in the main,
The comedies that he retails,
Will make me laugh from here to Wales.

RHYME AND PREJUDICE

Thing is, had it not Darcy been,
Supposed the one within the scene,
There would be nothing much to tell,
And might have been correct as well.

And finally, Eliza, pray,
When that old woman came today,
Did she arrive with the intent,
Of him refusing her consent?"

Liz now knew not how to reply,
And had to be a little sly,
By laughing when she should have cried,
For she was quite upset inside,
That father had this quite mistook,
He *would* give her a second look.

Chapter Fifty-eight

A few days later, a surprise,
And Liz could not believe her eyes,
When Bingley came and Darcy too,
Quite true as I am telling you.

Their mother had not time to tell,
About their former guest from hell,
Before Charles said, "It's rather droll,
Perhaps we could all take a stroll."

Now Mr Bennet walked nowhere,
And Mary had not time to spare,
But all the others thought it good,
And so they mostly said they would.

As they walked Jane and Charles fell back,
So they could take another track,
And Kitty soon went off alone,
To visit the Lucases home,
So Lizzy now prepared a plan,
For what to say to her young man.

"Kind Sir, I must now thank you well,
For all the things I have heard tell,
Of all your kindness to my sis,
Because a stupid fart she is.
And if my family all knew,
I'd be speaking for all them too."

"I'm very sorry you know this,
So anxious thoughts you can't dismiss,
I'd thought Ms Gardiner to be,
Trustworthy, perhaps more like me."

"You mustn't blame her, Lydia said,
About the starring role you led,
And when I heard you were involved,
I very instantly resolved,
To find exactly what you did,
And on this mystery lift the lid.

I thank you more than I can say,
For all you did before today;
You must have delved down in the grime,
And had a really rotten time."

"I have to tell you this – it's true,
I did the whole thing just for you."

EBENEZER BEAN

Liz really knew not what to say,
As she stood next to him that day,
There was a frog there in her throat,
And while she waited Darcy spoke.

"I know you will not lead me on,
If your feelings for me are gone.
I really do love you to bits,
But simply tell me now if it's
Reciprocated you to me,
And if it isn't I will flee."

"Well actually," she said, "it's true,
That I am now in love with you.
I think it's true that you will find,
I have now deigned to change my mind;
It is a woman's right, it's true,
So I can do it but not you."

Well, Darcy was so very chuffed,
That Rosings girl could now get stuffed,
And as for aunt who was a pain,
He might never see her again.

RHYME AND PREJUDICE

The two walked on, now hand in hand,
The ground was grass this time, not sand,
And Liz soon learnt his aunty had,
Been telling him of things so bad,
Intended to persuade him that,
He should now just turn her down flat,
But happily, you might suspect,
It had the contrary effect.

"When you refused," he said, "to tell,
You would decline the wedding bell,
It gave me hope because I knew,
You'd otherwise have told her too."

"I criticized you pretty bad,
Because I thought you were a cad,
And I was rude both to your face,
And also in some other place."

"What did you say of me so ill?
You were mistaken, maybe still;
But I was rude to you as well,
And am now this ashamed to tell."

"Let's not compete to see who was,
The worse in manners then because,
We've both improved, I have to say,
Which is why we're polite today."

"But I was really much the worse,
With words which were so very terse,
And you reproofed me, you recall,
With words that now do me appall.

You said, to my eternal shame,
I did not live up to my name,
And should perhaps get on my bike,
I was so ungentlemanlike."

"I did not think," said Liz, "my jibe,
Would have the effect you describe."

"I'm sure that what you say is right,
You thought me rude and rather tight;
And then you said whatever I,
Might do or say or even try,
No matter whether charged or free,
You still would never accept me."

"Let us not dwell on times now past,
Because we have both been so crass."

"My letter, Darcy said, "did it,
On reading give me some credit?"

RHYME AND PREJUDICE

"When I had read it through and through,
I gave some credit back to you;
It did your character improve,
And my prejudices remove."

"I knew my words would give you pain,
But necessary in the main,
I hope you'll not again it read,
And will now burn the thing indeed,
For if you read it one time more,
You'll possibly show me the door."

"Opinions change from time to time,
Sometimes assisted by red wine,
But reading that would not make me,
Have changed opinion of thee."

"When I wrote it with pen and rule,
I thought that I was calm and cool,
But now I think that was absurd,
And it was full of bitter words."

"Perhaps it did begin that way,
But now I really have to say,
That by the end it was quite nice,
I even thought to read it twice."

EBENEZER BEAN

"But let us no more speak of this,
Events of history now dismiss,
For we have changed beyond belief,
And so should turn another leaf.

That one of us is good is true,
But that's not me, I think it's you,
And, really, I have selfish been,
And on occasions pretty mean.

When young I learnt both wrong and right,
To say my prayers most every night,
But I was taught, nay was allowed,
To see that other folk were cowed,
And no-one could important be,
Except for family and me.

So Lizzie, you've shown up my pride,
My many faults and more beside,
And so I owe to you a debt,
Which I have not repaid you yet."

"My manners," Lizzy said, "were poor,
You surely hated me some more,
When we first met there are the ball,
And didn't like my words at all."

RHYME AND PREJUDICE

"I was quite angry there at first,
But that bit really was the worst,
And that anger of which I spake,
A proper direction did take."

"One more thing I'm afraid to ask,
In case you should take me to task,
Is what you thought when you saw me,
There in your house at Pemberley."

"It simply was one of surprise,
For I could scarce believe my eyes."

"I, too, was much surprised like you,
For you gave me more than my due,
While I was really quite uptight,
You were exceedingly polite."

"My object," Darcy said "was to,
Show I'd improved and did like you;
I don't know when this took effect,
In half an hour I now suspect.

Georgiana likes you you should know,
Was upset when you had to go,
And when in the inn I was cross,
It was 'cos I was at a loss,
And knew finding Lydia and he,
A difficult struggle would be."

EBENEZER BEAN

"Thank you again," to him she said,
"Now let us put that thing to bed."

They walked on for a few miles more,
A bit past ten but not a score,
They were still on the same old track,
And it was time now to turn back.

The two talked then of Charles and Jane,
They were both happy once again,
And Liz said that he had agreed,
Which really was the truth indeed.

Darcy continued, "I told him,
When I had spoken on a whim,
And told him all was off because,
Your sister so indifferent was,
I had been wrong to tell his self,
To leave your sister on the shelf.

I changed my own mind later on,
And from my own observation,
And so he now thinks she is great,
Or pretty good at any rate.

I'd not told him she was in town,
Which made him really curse and frown,
But now that he has got a date,
He's pardoned me, albeit late."

Chapter Fifty-nine

Back in the dining room that e'en,
They all enquired where she had been,
But Lizzy really didn't know,
Except they'd walked about quite slow,
So she said they had wandered and,
Not that it had been hand in hand.

And though, while speaking, she turned pink,
Her listeners didn't stop to think,
So none of them suspected they,
Might have done more than she would say.

The evening, I think, went OK,
The lovers had a lot to say,
But Liz and Darcy, still secret,
Did not want to advise folk yet.

Liz didn't know how it would go,
Because they all disliked him so,
And maybe all his wealth and might,
Might not suffice to make things right.

At bedtime she announced to Jane,
That Darcy wasn't such a pain,
And that the two were now engaged,
So she should not be so enraged.

Jane said, "This surely cannot be!
You cannot stand the sight of he!
To think that he would marry you?
I know it just cannot be true."

Liz wiped a tear, she said, "My Friend,
I hoped support you would me lend;
But if you won't believe it's true,
Then I am in really in a stew.

For what I say is true enough,
It isn't just a load of guff,
He still loves me I can attest,
And also I love him the best."

"But Lizzy, Lizzy, it can't be,
You're surely still deceiving me!"

"You do not know and so can't judge,
My feelings for him will not budge,
I liked him less back in the past,
But luckily no die was cast."

"I s'pose I must then believe you,
Congratulations may be due,
But are you sure – now look at me –
That with him you can happy be?"

RHYME AND PREJUDICE

"Most certainly, there is no doubt,
Our differences we've sorted out,
And you shall have a brother who,
    Is also fond of Bingley too."

"That's very good but are you sure,
    You've never had a lover truer?"

"I really do love him to bits,
Compared to him Charles is the pits;
I hope you don't mind what I say,
    I can't explain another way."

"How long have you been in this state,
When feelings turned to love from hate?"

"It happened slowly, I don't know,
    But probably when I did go,
    To Pemberley with aunt in tow,
    And also uncle as you know.

And now, so you'll know what it means,
Perhaps I'll have to spill the beans,
About the cash that he did bung,
Direction of our sister young."

"Good gracious," Mrs Bennet cried,
"Looks like Darcy will come inside,
With our dear Bingley whom I like,
So Lizzy, take him on a hike,
So Jane and Bingley can be free,
To do what they chuse without he."

Liz laughed, it suited her that she,
Could be again alone with he,
And Kitty said she'd rather stay,
At home this particular day.

Liz went upstairs to get her hat,
Mum followed, said, "I'm sorry that,
I have dumped Darcy on you so
That Jane can off with Bingley go."

So off they went, both then resolved,
To try to get the problem solved,
To which end, Darcy after tea,
Would plan there in the library,
To ask her father for her hand,
No matter would he sit or stand.

And Liz decided she would break,
The news to mum but how she'd take
It, really she just could not say,
But might just try it anyway.

RHYME AND PREJUDICE

No matter she thought bad or good,
It was quite certain that she would,
Make inappropriate response,
Because she didn't use her bonce.

So evening came, the moment there,
Liz on the point of going spare,
With Darcy talking to her dad,
Who she assumed would go quite mad,
By being asked that very day,
To give his favourite girl away,
To Darcy whom he thought not great,
And like the others did just hate.

Darcy returned, he smiled at Liz,
Said "Darling, now your father is,
Waiting to see you in his room,
But don't think it's completely gloom."

Liz went right in, he said, "My God!
You want to marry that old sod?
You've hated him since you first met,
About as bad as it could get."

At this point Liz wished that she'd been,
In former views not so extreme,
But maybe she'd been off her guard,
And hoist now by her own petard.

"So you are sure you will him wed?
For that is what you have just said.
He's stinking rich so you will get,
Much more than any of us yet;
But still an answer you must tell,
That's will you happy be as well?"

"Apart from thinking that it's me,
Who of him can indifferent be?
Tell me if there are other grounds,
To put this marriage out of bounds."

"No, none at all, I do attest,
His character is not the best;
He is unpleasant, proud though fit,
And some think he's a real sh*t;
But if you like the man today,
These other points will fade away."

"I really do like him, I do,
He really is my lover true;
He is not proud, he's really nice,
So pray do not now say it twice."

"Lizzy," said Bennet, "I have said,
To Darcy that he can you wed,
It matters not what are your views,
He's not a man I could refuse.

RHYME AND PREJUDICE

So now it's really up to you,
To make your mind up what to do,
I know that you could not accept,
A husband of low intellect,
So do take care what you decide,
And if you want to be his bride."

Liz then explained to him in rhyme,
How her views had changed over time,
And as she spoke, after a while,
His views dad did now reconcile.

"Well, My Dear," father said at last,
"It seems to me the die is cast;
If all of this is largely true,
He'll be a good husband to you."

Liz then went on to tell her dad,
Of all the expense Darcy had,
Incurred to sort out Lydia's mess,
And so avoid fam'ly distress.

"Well goodness me, I have to say,
I'd really like to Darcy pay.
But I know that he will refuse,
And thus the matter will diffuse.

Now off you go and if you find,
There are suitors of any kind,
That might do for Kate and Mary,
Just send them in – I will agree."

The evening passed, not much was said,
And then when it was time for bed,
Liz followed her mum up the stair,
And said, for she was unaware,
That Darcy would her husband be –
The one she'd just had round to tea.

When mother up to this had wised,
She seemed completely paralysed;
She didn't move, she didn't speak,
She could have sat there for a week,
And it was quite some little time,
Before she spoke in prose or rhyme.

"Good gracious, Lizzy! Bless my soul!
It's hard to take in what you've told.
This Darcy man was such a pain,
But now that he's got you in train,
He is so charming and so tall,
With money to eclipse us all.
And if you wed, you will, it seems,
Be rich beyond our wildest dreams."

RHYME AND PREJUDICE

Liz knew now that the wealth had spoke,
And all that mattered with this bloke,
As far as mother was concerned,
Was how much money he now earned.

For Lizzy, luckily, her mum,
By his status was overcome,
And so she controlled what she said,
From daybreak until time for bed.

And she was quite pleased to observe,
Her father had not lost his nerve,
And trying hard to get to know,
The man who had her now in tow.

Chapter Sixty

Liz thought Darcy she'd take to task,
For she was wanting now to ask,
Just what had caused his change of heart,
And when did this new thinking start.

"I can't say justly when or what,
Because I think I have forgot;
It was some time I have surmised,
And also, when I realised,
I'd passed the starting point and so,
I really, truly do not know."

"You didn't think much of my looks,
Which often is one of the hooks,
That females use to catch a mate,
Or try to do at any rate.

And mostly, when I spoke to you,
My manners really wouldn't do,
For I was often rather rude,
And had a right bad attitude."

"Your lively mind I did admire,
What more could any man desire?"

RHYME AND PREJUDICE

"My view," said Liz, "is that you were,
Sick of those people who defer,
Just to impress you, nothing more,
Because you are so rich, not poor.

And if you'd not been well disposed,
You would have liked me less than those,
And though your feelings were well hid,
You likely liked the things I did.

But tell me, when you came to dine,
Why to me you then took no shine?
And it seemed plain for all to see,
That you just did not care for me."

"You did not show me your intent,
And gave me no encouragement,
And I was quite embarrassed too –
Perhaps the same applied to you?"

"I was embarrassed once or twice,
But luckily I broke the ice,
By thanking you for what you did,
For my errant sister called Lyd.

This was a breach of promise and,
It led to you to take my hand;
Although on this we should not dwell –
It did the trick so what the hell!"

EBENEZER BEAN

"But what then really did the trick,
Was my aunt who made me quite sick,
By trying to us separate,
So I'd take her girl as my mate.

And as she tried to tell the tale,
I saw this was to no avail,
And so I might give you a ring,
I wanted to know everything.

'Twas thus that I to Longbourn came,
The purpose of which, in the main,
Was to make judgment if I could,
About whether you ever would,
Love me and maybe be my wife,
Not only now but all my life."

"I wonder if you'll ever tell,
Your aunt back there to go to hell?"

"I'm not afraid but need some time,
To write it and to make it rhyme,
If you've some paper I will sit
Down now and just get on with it."

"If I had not myself to write,
I might sit by your hand tonight,
So to admire how well you write,
Just as another lady might."

RHYME AND PREJUDICE

Then Lizzy got the paper out,
And wrote to tell her aunt about,
The good news that she had to bear,
And that she was so keen to share.

"I would have thanked you, Dearest Aunt,
For your news which was far from scant,
But in fact I was rather cross,
And, too, at something of a loss,
Because some facts were less than those,
You evidently had supposed.

But right now everything is changed,
I'm happy, possibly deranged,
For as for my betrothed and me,
Life could not any better be.

I am so happy, more than Jane,
Although she's smiling once again,
With Darcy, who is not a toff,
It's difficult now not to laugh.

He sends his love unto you both,
This is before we plight our troth,
And when Christmas comes round we'll see,
The two of you at Pemberley."

While she was writing, Darcy wrote,
To his aunt quite a terse, short note,
And later on old Bennet penned,
A letter to Collins, Reverend.
Some niceties he likely missed,
Of what he wrote here is the gist.

"Dear Sir, I must now trouble you,
Congratulations once more due,
For cousin Liz quite soon will be,
Herself renamed Mrs Darcy.

I would invite you to console,
Your patroness who is quite droll,
But as you will have to take sides,
To go with Darcy I'd advise."

Miss Bingley now sent her congrats,
To her brother although in fact,
She likely had to shed a tear,
And what she said was insincere.

She also wrote a note to Jane,
Again insincere in the main,
But although Jane was not deceived,
She really said she felt the need,
To reply to that load of sh*te,
With a note that was more polite.

Georgiana, though, was really chuffed,
That her aunt had now been rebuffed,
And, really, she just could not wait,
For Liz to live on the estate.

Before Collins could make reply,
Some people who all played I-Spy,
Reported that they had been seen,
At Lucas Lodge across the green.

The reason was quite soon explained,
That back home things were rather strained,
'Cos Lady Catherine was so cross,
That Darcy didn't give a toss,
And he would not her daughter wed,
But went for Miss Bennet instead.

Charlotte was really very pleased,
And so that tension might be eased,
She decided to take a break,
And so avoid the earache.

A problem now for Liz arose,
To shield her man from most of those,
Friends and relations who were rude,
And on occasions rather crude.

The worst of these was on his side,
Mrs Phillips, a former bride,
For she was vulgar to a T,
And really was quite rude to he.

But Darcy, always so polite,
Just ignored all this verbal sh*te,
And until it was time to go,
He didn't let his feelings show.

Liz tried to see that he conversed,
With acquaintances, not the worst,
And she looked forward to the day,
When all this would be swept away,
When she quite soon would married be,
And bugger off to Pemberley.

RHYME AND PREJUDICE

Chapter Sixty-one – and last. Phew!

The wedding day arrived at last,
And Mrs Bennet's joy was vast,
As her two girls were married to,
Darcy and Bingley as you knew.

It did indeed seem she had won,
Her life's work pretty well now done,
But she was still foolish by heck,
And sometimes still a nervous wreck.

Bennet missed Lizzy constantly,
Quite often went to Pemberley;
We do not know what there he did,
But likely of his wife was rid.

The Bingleys, by now Charles and Jane,
At Netherfield would there remain,
For twelve months only, I heard say,
And then they moved to get away,
From Mrs Bennet and her friends,
Whose tittle-tattle never ends.

They bought an estate in the north,
Moved in not on July the fourth,
And Liz and Jane thought it was smart –
They lived but thirty miles apart.

Kitty, meanwhile, now left her home,
But didn't just go off to roam,
She stayed with her two sisters where,
Society was better there.

She learnt a lot and did improve,
A consequence of having moved,
And though her sister Lydia might,
Have asked her down to stay the night,
With promise of balls and young men,
Her father always vetoed them.

Mary, alone, stayed back at home.
Since her mum would not sit alone,
She had to spend less time with books,
But one advantage was her looks,
Which had with sisters been compared,
Mattered less now for no-one stared.

And that leaves Wickham, man and wife,
Source of much of the Bennets' strife;
Wickham resigned himself that Liz,
Would find how bad he was and is.

And he lived in hope that one day,
Darcy might feel inclined to pay,
More money to the pair of them,
For they could not their spending stem.

RHYME AND PREJUDICE

Lydia wrote then to Liz one day,
Congratulations for to pay,
But she, too, had another plan,
Which you should read here if you can.

"My Lizzy Dear, I wish you joy,
If you do love that Darcy boy,
Just half as much as I love mine,
Then you will have a happy time.

I am so pleased you're stinking rich,
Please think of us and do not snitch;
We'll find it hard to make ends meet –
Handouts would be right up our street.

A few hundred would do the trick –
That is per year, I am not thick –
But don't pester Darcy a lot,
Because, maybe, you'd rather not.

I do not have much more to say,
It's been nice writing you today,
So I think I've now said it all,
And now I've got another ball."

EBENEZER BEAN

Liz did prefer the 'rather not',
Lydia deserved what she had got,
And implied in replies she made,
There would be no financial aid.

Liz knew the way she lived her life,
Would always mean financial strife,
And she would to her sisters write,
That things were just a little tight,
And could they help her pay the bills,
'Cos her cash had gone in the tills.

But Wickham soon went off his wife,
Began to live a separate life,
Lydia her reputation kept,
Because of he with whom she slept.

When Wickham was out on the town,
Lyd was sometimes invited down,
To Pemberley, but not with him,
Even when Darcy was not in.

They visited the Bingleys too,
And though occasions were quite few,
A nuisance of themselves they made,
And often their welcome outstayed.

RHYME AND PREJUDICE

Miss Bingley, you recall quite well,
Who looked as if there was a smell,
Was mortified you might infer,
That Darcy hadn't married her.

She was so devastated but,
Decided to her losses cut,
And did in truth or in pretence,
Pay necessary deference,
To Darcy and his ladies fair,
So she might still call on them there.

Georgiana, Darcy's sister young,
Had always Lizzie's praises sung,
And now they lived in the same place,
Georgiana thought that this was ace.

She learnt from Lizzy women could,
Have conversation fair and good,
With men now on more equal terms,
Which folk back then still had to learn.

And that leaves Lady Catherine who,
Replied to Darcy like you do,
But in language that was so rude,
And about Lizzy rather crude,
That for some time, perhaps a year,
Darcy would never speak to her.

Eventually, 'cos Lizzy smiled,
The two would both be reconciled,
And Lady Catherine came to see,
The two of them at Pemberley.

And finally, my parting verse,
Which I will keep both short and terse,
The Gardiners, I have to say,
Would often go up north to stay,
With Lizzy and her husband who,
Were always pleased to see these two.

It was 'cos of their holiday,
That Lizzy had gone up to stay,
And if the two had not there met,
We wouldn't have an ending yet!

Finis

Epilogue

So there we are, I've done my bit,
For twelve months just got on with it;
Jane Austen's masterpiece on speed,
Now writ in verse for all to read.

It's mostly accurate, I think,
A few lines might just make you blink,
And sometimes words just will not scan,
So I must do the best I can.

So where my script is just plain wrong,
Please do not dwell on it too long,
And to Jane Austen please refer,
In her book's centenary year.
* bi- actually

I hope I will not on this point,
Put anyone's nose out of joint,
'Cos what I want you all to do,
Is go out now and buy a few.

And when you've read it give a cheer,
Jane Austen will soon reappear,
Her prize for all the books she wrote? –
Her picture on the ten pound note.

EBENEZER BEAN

BOOKS BY EBENEZER BEAN

REBEL RHYMES
Twenty famous fairy stories told in hilarious verse. Much funnier than the originals.

CRUNCH!
Over thirty sketches of political foolery and other important matters of the day for politicians and other nuisances. Witty and amusing although some of the politicians may not agree.

OUCH!
Lessons from history for politicians who think they know best.

HILARIOUS HISTORY
Two thousand years of English history from the Romans to the Victorians told in verse in five volumes. Comprehensive, accurate and hilariously funny – but not necessarily in that order.

FIRST SEPTEMBER
A gripping terrorist novel set in the aftermath of the bombing of PanAm Flight 103 over Lockerbie.

THE LONG SPOON
A fictional political thriller telling the 'inside story' of the Irish Peace Process.

RANDOM WRITINGS
Witty commentary on the important matters of the day including the Credit Crunch. Plus a collection of general ramblings about all sorts of things including some jokes and a puzzle.

RANDOM WRITINGS
(Second Edition)
More witty commentary on important matters of the day. Includes all the content of the first edition.

RANDOM WRITINGS
(Third Edition)
Yet more witty commentary on important matters of the day. Includes all the content of the first and second editions.

RANDOM WRITINGS
(ZigZag SpeeedRead Edition)
The witty commentary of *Random Writings* (Second Edition) set in ZigZag SpeeedRead for extra value. The world's first ZigZag SpeeedRead paperback.

RHYME AND PREJUDICE
Jane Austen's famous classic novel re-written in verse. Accurate and faithful to the original but absolutely hilarious. Written and published during the novel's bicentenary year for added authenticity. Expect to see it mentioned on the next ten pound note!

Made in the USA
Charleston, SC
14 August 2013